DIAMONDS ARE NOT ALWAYS A GIRL'S BEST FRIEND

DIAMONDS ARE NOT ALWAYS A GIRL'S BEST FRIEND

by Lena Long

Library of Congress Control Number:		2012907888
ISBN:	Hardcover	978-1-4771-0656-3
	Softcover	978-1-4771-0655-6
	Ebook	978-1-4771-0657-0

This book was printed in the United States of America.

To order additional copies of this book, contact:
Xlibris Corporation
1-888-795-4274
www.Xlibris.com
Orders@Xlibris.com
116152

Acknowledgements

I would like to thank my family & friends for supporting me throughout my journey. I love you guys very much.

I would like to give a special thanks to my parents Elizabeth & Bobby Long.

Chapter 1

KENNEDY
NO WORK TODAY

The girls are over at my place today. We're having brunch on the rooftop deck of my condo. It's Diamond's last day in Florida. Diamond lives in New York and has been here visiting for a week, but this is her first time at my home. She will be spending her last night with me.

"I love the way you've coordinated the picture frames on the walls to match your hardwood floors," Diamond says. "I always imagined your place would look this elegant."

"Let me show you to the two guest rooms," I say, motioning for her to follow me. "They're right across from mine. You're welcome to choose whichever one you like. I had them decorated especially with my guests' comfort in mind." Diamond's sweet-smelling perfume follows her as she steps ahead of me and into the first room. Her long hair is perfectly managed—as usual—and is stunningly complemented by her flawless dark skin.

"I like the pink color you chose for the walls," Diamond says.

"Yes, this is my room when I sleep over, Diamond, so you'll have to choose the other room," Portia jokes.

"Well, Portia, I'm the overnight guest tonight," Diamond replies with attitude, "and I will sleep in whichever room I choose. You can go home to your perfect house and your perfect family."

I quickly step in between them and pause for a moment, hoping to defuse the intensity. Satisfied that I've succeeded, I walk back into the hallway and on into the next room. I'm relieved when only Diamond follows me, while Portia rejoins the rest of our friends in the living room. I'm proud of Portia for not taking the bait. She shouldn't have to justify her "perfect life," as Diamond calls it.

"Take a look at this room, Diamond," I suggest. "I think you might like it."

"You're right, Kennedy," Diamond says, stepping into the room and dropping her luggage. "This room has my name written all over it." I guessed she would prefer this room, with its summer-yellow walls and white furniture. Diamond loves bright colors.

"Okay, now that that's taken care of," I say, "it's up to the rooftop, ladies. Follow me through the kitchen."

Diamond is walking ahead of the group as we make our way from one room to the next. "There's no dividing wall between your living room and kitchen, Kennedy," she says in her usual arrogant tone. The open floor plan of my condo is clearly not to her liking.

"It looks breezy outside, ladies," I warn, noticing the waving palm trees from the kitchen window.

"I don't think it's too cold," Lola says.

"Nah, I don't even think we'll need sweaters," Tasha agrees.

"The door next to the refrigerator leads to the rooftop," I say as we walk into the kitchen.

Diamond is the first to reach the door. As she opens it, she screams excitedly, "I love the rooftop deck, Kennedy! Too bad you have to share it with other tenants." She says this loud enough so that the two women who are already enjoying the deck can hear. Then she heads for the table that has the most seating, nearest the railing and overlooking the parking lot. The midday sun is shining down hard, and I'm grateful for the breeze, which is keeping the climate perfectly comfortable up here.

"The scenery isn't all that great," Diamond says, "but I guess it will do."

"Jealousy will get you nowhere, Diamond," Payton chides.

"Me? Jealous? Of who?" Diamond scoffs. Payton rolls her eyes and decides to let it go.

Seemingly satisfied that she's deterred any further comments from Payton, Diamond turns to Portia and resumes their earlier exchange. "Portia, I am very proud of your accomplishments. I may seem hard on you, but it's only because you didn't get where you are because of what you've accomplished, or even on your own. Dylan gave you a free ride. So, Portia...do you know how lucky you are?"

"Yes, Diamond, I do," Portia answers. She appears to be fighting hard to keep her composure.

I worry about the antagonizing nature of Diamond's behavior toward Portia. I can feel the tension escalating. "Here we go again," I sigh.

Diamond continues torturing Portia. "Do you think you would have accomplished any of your goals if you'd had to do it on your own—you know, without Dylan's money and all?"

"Diamond, why does it matter to you so much that my husband is rich?" says Portia.

"Yeah, why is that such problem for you, Diamond?" Lola cuts in. Tasha, Sky, and Payton all look at me as if to say, *Here we go.*

"It doesn't bother me," Diamond says defensively. "I'm just saying that Portia got where she is through no hard work of her own. I mean, take a person like me. Dealing with the daily struggle of raising three kids on a tight budget is extremely hard work. I deserve a rich man."

"I'm not following you," Portia replies. "Why is it that you deserve a rich man, and I don't?"

"Because I'm less fortunate than you."

"Ladies," I chime in gently, "let's remember that we're here to enjoy Diamond's last day with us. So why don't we take advantage of this beautiful, sunny afternoon and get some burgers going on the grill?"

"No, Kennedy, I would really love to hear this," Portia says. "Diamond, you have the floor. Please elaborate."

"Okay, I will," Diamond says. "Portia, you completed your education. You have degrees and graduated with honors. Therefore, you stand a much better chance at having a successful career than I do."

"So now I'm responsible for your lack of education?"

"No, you're not responsible. That's not what I'm saying at all."

"I'm sorry, but it sounds like you're blaming me, and your're projecting your insecurities onto me." Portia says.

"So why didn't you go to school for your degree?" Portia asks.

"Where exactly would I find the time?" Diamond spits back. "I had to raise three kids."

"Come on, girls," Sky interrupts. "Please stop this before it gets out of control."

Lola stands up from her chair. "Can I talk to you for a minute, Kennedy?" she asks quietly. "Over there." She gestures to the area by the door that leads back into the condo. I get up from my chair, and my earring falls out of my ear and onto the deck top. As I reach down to pick it up, I notice that the sun has disappeared behind a mass of clouds that have formed right above the building—just like in a scary movie. I rise slowly, staring at the sky.

Lola shouts, "Kennedy!" It's enough to snap me out of my trance. "Would you come on?" I follow her away from the table and the rest of our friends.

"Why do you always stick up for Diamond when she attacks Portia, or any of the rest of us, for that matter?" Lola asks when we reach the doorway.

"I do not stick up for her," I answer. "I just feel sorry for her sometimes."

"Sorry for her? Why do you feel sorry for her?"

"Because she's less fortunate than the rest of us. And I don't think she's coming from a bad place when she runs her mouth off. She's just jealous, that's all. We've been friends with her since childhood. I'm not going to let her leave and go back home thinking she no longer has friends here."

"What about how we feel when she attacks us?" Lola asks. "You never step up to rescue us from her."

"Lola, you know I love you guys. We're like family. But we all have so much; we're strong. Diamond is vulnerable. Try not to say anything you'll regret, and please just try to understand where Diamond is coming from, okay? Can you do that for me?"

"Yeah, okay. I don't have to like it, but I'll stay on my best behavior...for you."

"Thank you, Lola," I say as I pinch both her cheeks.

As we walk back over to the girls, I hear Portia saying to Diamond, "You can't blame me because a man who happens to be rich fell in love with me. Maybe you should blame your man for not being rich," Portia suggests sarcastically.

"Anyway, let us please exit this conversation before its natural end. I'm not going to tolerate being dominated by you. Just shut up and enjoy your last day here."

Why did Portia have to say that?

Diamond gets up out of her chair and yells, "Why don't you come over here and shut me up, Portia?"

Portia stands up, but before she can make a move, I grab her shoulders and force her to sit back down. Soon after, I'm startled by a loud, piercing sound. As I remove my hands from Portia's shoulders, I see the frightful expressions of the two women sitting across the rooftop deck. One of the women has her hand frantically moving across her mouth.

I turn back to the table and immediately zero in on a red stain seeping through the chest area of Portia's white blouse. The red spot is growing fast, and I start to scream. Portia looks down at her blouse and realizes why I'm screaming. She starts to panic when she sees the blood. The girls do not respond to my screams because they are shocked when they see what Diamond is holding in her right hand. I try to say something, but I can't. I continue screaming, but my friends remain transfixed, as if they can't hear me.

In a last-ditch effort to get their attention and break the spell, I flip over the table. I try to grab the gun out of Diamond's hand, but a high-pitched sound comes out of nowhere and distracts me. The sound is relentless and is coming from my left side, where Portia is now attempting to stand. The irritating beep-beep-beep continues to get louder. I try to turn to my left to learn the source of the sound, but I'm finding it difficult to turn in any direction. My head feel like it's being forced down, and try as I might, I can't seem to lift it...

~~~

My eyes pop open. My alarm is beeping. The oversized numbers on my clock look like a doctor's eye chart and read *8:30 a.m.* I switch the alarm over to the radio and hear Jennifer Hudson singing "Spotlight."

Relieved that it was just a dream, I sit up in bed and brush the mussed curls from my forehead, still damp from sweat. "What a nightmare," I say out loud as I kick off my Downy-smelling sheets in an attempt to cool myself.

Diamond has envy and jealousy issues with all of us, but she's especially jealous when it comes to Portia. Lord knows they've had their arguments; Diamond has spoiled more than a few outings and parties with her negative attitude. The rest of the girls are becoming weary of her dark energy.

The dream—it stands to reason. I can almost sense that something is going to go very wrong one of these days. Diamond will take it too far, and Portia will finally lose it. I just hope I'm there to intervene. I don't want our longstanding friendship to fail. It's up to me to keep us all together. We've been friends far too long to allow differing points of view to divide us.

I have to get myself together to go into the office. I raise the wood blinds in my bedroom and survey the current weather. *Damn, it's raining.* In fact, it's a particularly gloomy Monday morning. I listen to the rain patter against the window, and it makes me feel like calling in sick. And I can, because I am the boss.
~~~

My name is Kennedy Owens. I'm single, thirty-five, no kids. I drive a beautiful 2009 Infinity Coupe and run my own interior decorating company that I built from the ground up.

My company is still relatively small, but it's growing more successful every day. I am relentlessly ambitious, and I'm not planning to slow down anytime soon. I have every confidence that I will reach all of my goals of success.

I have been blessed with my very own three-bedroom/three-bath condo here in Orlando, Florida, where all the rich white folks and rich black athletes live. What I love most about my condo is the kitchen. It has huge mahogany cabinets that perfectly complement the earth-toned countertops, and a wraparound breakfast counter with tall leather bar stools.

I am so proud of myself. I am a fine-ass Black-Asian woman who has accomplished most of my goals in life without a sorry-ass man to help me. It wasn't easy getting here, but I made it. Only thing I need a man for is to get laid from time to time when I grow bored of the boxes of toys that I have stored in their very own closet for those times when I need to gang-rape myself. My success has been a long and challenging journey, but here I am. I'm an unstoppable juggernaut who possesses the tools to dominate and make it to the top.

I describe my life as nothing other than perfect. I'm five foot seven, 130 pounds, light-skinned, with long, thick brown hair. I have a beauty mark above my lip and a dimple on my cheek. To top it all off, I've got tons of money in the bank. I have a right to brag about all of this because I did it all myself—with no one else's help. If you don't like it, or feel a little envious, that's *your* problem.

My parents have five children—four girls and one boy. I fall somewhere in the middle. I'm unquestionably one of the most intelligent of my siblings. I'm closer to my brother than to my sisters because when we were children, my sisters and I were fiercely competitive with each other. I love them all equally, and as adults, we all get along great. Ours is a close-knit, working-class family. And while there was little money when we were growing up, my parents always did their best to provide for us.

Believe it or not, after forty years, my parents are still together—that's unusual in the year 2009. I don't know if I could ever be with just one man for that long. I love men too much; I need more than one. Call me a whore, I don't care. The way I see it? Once you've reached a certain age, you're free to have sex with whomever, whenever you choose, so long as you don't go messing around with married types.

My friend, Lola, always says to me, "Girl, there is a big-ass world out there for us to go fuck up in." Lola is one of my closest friends. When I moved here, she followed me. In fact, I have six best friends that moved here along with me.

It all started one night during our annual slumber party at my house in Brooklyn—a longstanding tradition when us girls get together for a night just to sit around, talk mess, and enjoy each other's company.

By this time, we all had one thing in common: we were all ready to leave New York. I grabbed the globe from the corner of my dining area, and we all vowed that wherever my finger was placed after spinning the globe, that would be the place we would all pick up and move to before the year was out. And that is the story of how we all made our way down to Orlando, Florida—our new home.

It rains more than I expected here in Florida, but thankfully not for an entire day. Sometimes it's just too damn hot. But I love living here, just the same. I loved living in New York, too. Well, mostly. I loved the city, and the summers, but I hated the criminals and those cold New York winters.

My best girlfriends' names are Portia Waters, Lola Santiago, Sky Smith, Payton Glover, Brooke Ariello, and Tasha Green.

Portia is thirty-seven and the only one of us who is happily married. Her husband's name is Dylan. They have a son, Dante, eighteen, who is in his first year of college at Howard University in Washington, D.C.

Dylan fell in love with Portia's sandy brown hair, which is similar to the color of her hazel eyes. (Most men are attracted to Portia's large breasts and her small waist.) Portia fell in love with Dylan's long, slender, muscular legs and his thick, dark, distinguished eyebrows. He has a dimple in his strong chin that, in my opinion, is his best feature. Dylan insisted that his wife stay home and raise their son in a positive, nurturing environment while he provided for their family. He has a very successful dental practice, so he can afford to take care of his family without the need for an additional income. He's made enough money for the both of them.

Portia met Dylan twenty years ago in the neighborhood where we're all from. They eloped seven and a half years ago—a fact they kept from us for a full three years into their marriage! One day, Brooke happened to notice a wedding ring on Portia's finger. Portia confessed that she and Dylan had been married for three years, but to this day has failed to give us a satisfying reason for why she kept it a secret.

Sky works for a large law firm in Fort Lauderdale. She commutes two hours both ways, five days a week. She's beautiful. Most people mistake her for Spanish because of her fine hair texture, but she's black. Her hair is long, brown, and curly, and it's almost always pulled back into a ponytail. She has a bump on her nose that was a source of constant childhood teasing, but it's now one of her best features—her signature look, as we call it.

Sky is thirty-four and married to Fuji, a street hustler. He has sandy-brown, short-cropped hair and a freckled nose. He walks around town like he's God's gift to women. No one knows exactly what it is that Fuji does for a living, but we're all reasonably sure that it is *not* legal.

They had a huge wedding in June 2008. It was romantic, classy, and expensive—the best that fifty thousand dollars could buy. I was her maid of honor, the rest of the girls her bridesmaids.

Sky and Fuji's relationship is strange in the sense that they both cheat on each other regularly, but somehow this arrangement seems to work for them. I suppose that's just the price you pay when you fall for a guy from the streets. She's managed to catch him with other women on occasion, but Fuji has never caught Sky with another man. At least, not yet. I still don't understand why she married him. I mean, if you're not going to be faithful, what's the point? When and if—and that's a big "if"—I ever get married, it will be for keeps. I will love my husband, and he will love me even more. He won't need other women. As to Sky and Fuji? Who knows? They really do seem to love each other, but trying to understand their relationship gives me a headache. Oh, and by the way, Fuji's real name is Jerome. If you ever happen to hear Sky calling Fuji by his real name, you can bet that our boy Jerome is in some serious trouble.

Lola is a straightforward person. She tells it like it is—her mouth has no filter. She can be wild, but also has a conservative side. She works at an art gallery that she dreams of owning someday. She's thirty-five and hopes to realize that dream by her next birthday. I believe she will.

I suppose you'd describe Lola as a bit on the "thick" side. Big boobs, big ass, big hips, and big lips—full and always glossy. She absolutely refuses to leave the house without a generous coat of her favorite shiny-clear lip gloss. She isn't fat, but she has it all. When she was in her early twenties, she gained the nickname "The Body" because of all those voluptuous curves. She also has beautiful, shoulder-length black hair.

Intimately speaking, Lola lives a somewhat carefree lifestyle. She takes full advantage of her single status. And she's honest with everyone she's sleeps with—sometimes all little too honest, in my opinion. One thing Lola doesn't care about is what other people say about her. Trust me when I tell you, she doesn't lose sleep over what others think. It's one of the reasons I love her so much.

Of all my friends, I've known Payton the longest. She's attractive, and what I'd call a young thirty-three. She has the gift of gab and a talent for getting whatever she wants. She's petite: five foot one, 110 pounds. She has smooth, dark skin, and her hair is cut short and sporty, which is a great complement to her face. She has a defining feature above her right eyebrow: a single, perfectly round mole.

Payton is a high school substitute teacher here in Orlando. She mostly keeps to herself because she fears being judged. She confides in me more so than the others. Every time she has a one-night stand, she cries. She acts as if she feels guilty about engaging in casual sex, but I'm beginning to wonder just *how* guilty, because she keeps letting it happen.

Brooke is thirty-five and a single mom. She's a natural redhead—fiery red. She changes her eye color—via colored contacts—depending on her mood, but her natural eye color is brown. She has a flawlessly shaped, round bottom and could probably pose in a designer jean commercial. She also has amazingly long eyelashes that accentuate her beauty.

Brooke's parents are rich. She claims she doesn't go to them for money, but from the outside looking in, she appears to be living a little too comfortably for that to be true. She *claims* to be living off of the nine-hundred-dollar child support check that she receives each month from her daughter's father, but if you saw how she lived, you'd see that that just isn't possible. Personally, I don't think there's anything wrong with taking money from your parents if they want you to have it, but Brooke seems to feel there's some sort of shame in it.

I met Brooke my first year at college. We shared the same dorm room and hit it off immediately. We've been close ever since. We have a lot in common, other than she happens to be Italian, and I'm Black-Asian.

Brooke's daughter, Bailey, is twelve. She's getting to *that age* and starting to cause Brooke nothing but stress. Bailey is a pretty girl; I've always said that black and white parents make beautiful babies together. Her long, straight, reddish-brown hair reaches the middle of her back. We sometimes call her "Skinny Minnie" because she's so thin.

Bailey's father, Randy, is Brooke's former college boyfriend. He sells life insurance—runs his own agency. They didn't work out as a couple, but Brooke is still giving it up to Randy practically every time she sees him, because, as she says, "the sex is bangin'." Randy has a thick, coal-black mustache, and it drives Brooke crazy. She can't resist it, or him. Poor girl doesn't realize that there are much better men out there waiting for her.

Last but not least is Tasha. She works for a company called All Star Realty. She helps people buy and sell homes here in Orlando. She's done well at it, and has even made a good bit of money—enough to purchase three houses back home in Queens, which she rents for extra income.

Tasha is thirty-three. She has a golden complexion, and straight hair that falls just below her ears. Her eyebrows almost connect, but not quite. She regrets the fact that when she was younger she had a permanent gold tooth put in on the right side of her mouth—the style in the eighties. My girl is *still* looking for a dentist to remove that thing. Dylan said he would try, but he's reasonably sure he'd have to remove the entire tooth. Tasha isn't willing to go quite the far.

Tasha hasn't had sex in eight years. She's saving herself for the right man. She believes in God, but she's not all that religious. I think she just got tired of having sex with men that weren't satisfying her. Foreplay is very important to Tasha. She got bored with men wanting to jump into the pudding just to get their shit off, so she closed up shop. I applaud her because that's something I could never do. I'm a horny bitch.

Speaking of horny, I'm not going into the office today. I'm going to make me a booty call instead. It's cloudy and raining—perfect weather to get my groove on. I'm going to give Myles a call. I met Myles on my first night partying here in Orlando. I spotted him almost immediately, just as I was sitting down at the bar. He's gorgeous. He reminds me of Shamar Moore. The only thing I don't like about Myles is that he thinks he's better looking than me. I do my best to shut down his ego every once in a while.

Myles is six feet tall and 220 pounds—all muscle. He has a light complexion, and his eyes look almost Asian. His nose is perfect. And he *always* wears a three-karat diamond earring. He reminds me of Tommy from the television show *Martin*, starring Martin Lawrence. He claims he has a job and is "always" working, but no one ever sees him *actually* working. He has yet to provide me with a work phone number, so what does that tell you? Of course, I don't need an office number because I can reach him on his cell. And, well, it's not like I really need any additional contact information for Myles, because I'm not looking for any sort of commitment from him. Myles serves one purpose and one purpose only.

I pick up the phone and call him. "Hi, Myles."

"Kennedy. To what do I owe the pleasure?" His masculine voice is smooth as silk.

"I'm playing hooky from work today. Are you free?"

"Why, yes I am, as a matter of fact. I'm not working today." *Surprise, surprise.*

"So…come over."

"Okay. I have a few short errands to run first. But I could be there in about an hour."

"Then I'll see you in an hour. Bye, Myles."

"Bye, baby."

Perfect. An hour gives me just enough time to shower, choose a sex toy from my collection, and put on some sexy lingerie. I choose a lacy red teddy because Myles loves me in red. My fingers and toes are already painted with red nail polish. Convenient that I just had my nails done on Saturday—it will save me time. I love looking perfect for this good-looking, perfect man.

Myles loves to sex me while I'm wearing lingerie because it turns him on. It's a refreshing change. I'm used to guys wanting me to get completely naked so they can judge my body, then talk about it later with their buddies. Myles also loves to watch me masturbate—and I love to watch him watching me. Damn, that turns me on just thinking about it.

First things first: change the sheets, make sure they match the comforter. I pull a clean set of sheets from the linen closet and hurry off to my bedroom.

The master bedroom shares a wall with the living room, and there is access to the gas fireplace from both rooms—very romantic. Whoever thought up this brilliant idea can join my decorating team any day. Aside from the fireplace, the main attraction of this room is the television that hangs above it—a plasma that appears to be a framed picture. My oak bedroom set is fit for a queen, and complements the space very well. The tan paint that covers my bedroom walls completes the beauty of the room.

I don't have to do much cleaning in my condo because I tend to keep it pretty much spotless on a day-to-day basis. That's a good thing, because now I can spend these remaining forty-five minutes getting *me* together.

I glance at the television. My current screen saver is a picture of a woman from the 1920s draped across a grand piano. She's holding a cigarette in one of those old-fashioned long-stemmed holders. The dazzling diamonds in the necklace dangling from her neck dance across her cleavage. She's wearing long, red satin gloves that reach nearly to her elbows, and they perfectly match her red satin dress that falls in loose folds over her ankles.

I decide to wear my hair like the woman in the picture. Myles likes my hair straight, in the wrap hairstyle, and his wish is my command. I don't need to put on any makeup; I'm fine as hell, naturally. "Makeup is for the birds," I always say.

Time to set the stage: I place the perfect CD—a mix of all my favorite slow jams—into my Bose system, which sits on my nightstand next to my king-sized bed. Myles and I will be serenaded by the likes of Toni Braxton, R. Kelly, George Michael, Maroon 5, and more. Oh, and I can't forget to light the candles. I want the scent of strawberries in the air by the time he knocks on the door.

I've been seeing Myles off and on for years, but the sight of him still gives me butterflies in my stomach. I think that might mean something, but I would never dare wear my heart on my sleeve because I don't trust him. If I allowed myself to, I could fall for him in one day, because he's the whole package. But that will never happen.

I pour myself a glass of my favorite Merlot. It's called Sweet Bitch. Who cares if it's only 9:43 in the morning? The wine helps to bring out my alter ego—Jade. Jade is a wild-ass whore in the bedroom. Myles loves her. I'm only going to have one drink, though, because whenever I have more than one, I can't have an orgasm, and I'm forced to fake it—and that just won't do today. This man refuses to release unless I cum at least three or more times. He's all about pleasing his woman in bed, and that's why I love sexing him.

The music is blasting, and I'm starting to feel excited for what's about to go down, when I think I hear a knock at the door. I turn the music down and listen more carefully—another knock. My stomach does a little flip. I'm actually nervous. "Okay, bitch, get yourself together," I say to myself.

I take one last look in the mirror and walk to the door. When I open it, I look my lover straight in the eye using my best seductive expression. That clues him in…Jade is in the house.

"Boom! Look who's here," he says as he walks inside. The outline of his body is intoxicating. I tell him to watch his step. I don't want him to trip on the steps leading down into my large sunken living room.

"I love coming to your place, it's so cozy and peaceful," he says. He always compliments the furniture in this room; he likes the white-on-white theme I have going in here. He especially likes the bar.

The self-playing, black-lacquered piano that sits in my living room is now playing my CD. Immediately, Myles begins taking off his shirt, then points to my bedroom and begins directing me toward it. By the time we reach the bedroom, his shirt is completely off. He begins kissing my neck and whispers into my ear, "Take off your teddy and go stand in the corner and masturbate for me."

As directed, I remove my lingerie, but before I can break away to do as he asks, he places a diamond necklace around my neck. Within moments, I'm completely naked save for the dazzling jewels. *Damn, this man turns me on.*

I turn and begin walking toward the corner of my bedroom while Myles slowly removes the rest of his clothing, then stretches back on the bed. His body screams loud and clear: *perfection*. He's a straight-up piece of art. I'm talking six-pack abs, definition like crazy, golden skin tone, and coolie hair—that's what we call brothers who look like they have Indian in their family.

He stares at me with that seductive look of his, then says, "Play with yourself for me." My wild ass doesn't hesitate. I take the dildo and thrust it up into my vagina, the whole time never taking my eyes off of him. Looking at Myles makes me so hot.

After about five minutes of watching me play, he can't take it anymore. He climbs off the bed, grabs his penis in his hand, and begins stroking it while walking toward me. When he reaches me, he grabs me by my hair and swings me around so that my back is to him. I can hear Toni Braxton's voice in the background. Myles slowly starts rubbing himself against my buttocks and grows even harder. Once the size of his penis meets with his approval, he parks his car in my garage and begins to moan in my ear. "You got some good stuff. I love sexing you because your love box is always so wet and perfect. When I masturbate, I think about sexing you till I explode. We make a perfect match." He sexes me with such finesse that I wonder, *Is he just naturally skilled, or did he take a class?*

He tackles me from the back for a good ten minutes until I'm practically climbing the walls. My screams and moans are making him squeeze tighter. He turns me back around so I'm facing him again. He looks into my eyes, practically glaring. He's enjoying the sensation a little too much. He slips his penis out of my love canal, then starts caressing and sucking my breasts. He doesn't want to burst too soon. He knows how much I like having my breasts sucked, especially the right one because it's the more sensitive of the two. Now I'm moving my body like a snake. I can barely control this buildup of sensation. I beg him, "Put it back in."

"No," he's whispers softly. "You aren't ready for it yet."

"Please baby, put it back in," I plead. At this point, my bottom lip begins to tremble.

He whispers back, "Yeah, I think you're ready for it now."

He picks me up and carries me to the bed. His broad shoulders are hovering above me. I'm staring at his chest, which looks as if it was cut with a chisel. He climbs on top of me; my body is shaking out of control. I can't wait to feel his rock-hard penis inside of me. He enters me in one thrust. I can feel his monster pulsating, eager to release. He's humping me now, violent and sexy. Just the way I like it.

"You're hurting me," I say to him in a sexy voice, just to excite him even more. He keeps humping as he places my legs over his shoulders. I look him straight in the eye and say, "You're about to cum, baby." He nods his head. I tell him, "You'd better tell me when you're coming, you bastard." He loves it when I talk dirty.

His eyes start to roll back and the whites begin to show. "Damn, girl, you got me about to cum," he says. "I don't want to cum yet, but I can't control it." He looks straight ahead with a blind expression and shouts, "I'm cummin', baby! I'm cummin'!"

His shouts excite me so much that I can't hold myself back any longer, and we climax together. I look up at the ceiling and mouth the words, *Thank you, God.*

He looks at me, kisses me on the forehead, and says, "I want to thank your mother and father for having you."

Chapter 2

DIAMOND

BACK IN NEW YORK CITY

I am about to cheat on my husband…again. I love him. He's the father of my three children. But he takes for granted that my father owns the house we live in.

There's a bucket sitting in the middle of the kitchen floor. I leave it there to collect the water that drips from the ceiling when it rains. Far be it from Victor to get up off his lazy ass and fix the hole in the roof. He thinks because it's not our house he shouldn't have to fix anything in it.

Well, what about the paint peeling from the walls? What about this old, tired furniture my mom passed down to us years ago after she bought all new? We need a pair of pliers to change the channel on the television, and we use a hanger for an antenna.

Victor needs to make himself more useful around this house. Ours is not a glamorous home, but I take pride in keeping it clean and livable. I want guests to feel comfortable visiting or eating a meal here.

My name is Diamond. I am forty years old. My father says he named me Diamond because I was as precious as jewelry worth a million dollars.

Victor and I have been together for nearly twenty-three years. We started dating our senior year of high school. Our two oldest children are now officially grown, but still live at home. We would like to be able to send our kids to college, but unfortunately, we just can't afford to.

Lillian, our oldest, is twenty. She works in a neighborhood shopping center, about a twenty-five-minute walk from our Brooklyn home. She has a full-time position in a clothing store where she was recently promoted to a manager position. She's making enough money to contribute to the household now, so maybe I can persuade her to replace my bedroom door. Her boyfriend punched a hole in it a few months ago. He was angry with Lillian—who knows why. She's saving most of her money and hoping to move out on her own in another year or so. Sweet girl—she promised to buy me a new stove and refrigerator before she moves out. Lillian is a go-getter, a good child. I am so proud of her. She's a motivated and responsible young adult.

Tillie, nineteen, is the opposite of her older sister. Her main occupation, it seems, is looking for a job. She occasionally accepts a position, and will even work at it...but only for a little while. She always ends up quitting for one childish reason or another.

Eventually, she'll find her way. Tillie still has some maturing to do, but I have faith in her. I know she'll grow up—hopefully sooner rather than later.

Our son, Blade, seventeen, is in his last year of high school. He is a true Mama's boy. I admit he's my favorite. I've never actually said this out loud, of course, but the girls have witnessed enough of my favoritism toward him to know how I feel. Strangely, they've never said a word about it. Maybe because they adore him, too. Anyway, in my eyes, Blade can do no wrong. He can live here with us for as long as he likes.

Quincy is a man who lives in our neighborhood. We've known each other since we were kids. He's also a friend of my husband, Victor. I wasn't attracted to Quincy back in our younger days, but I'm very attracted to him now. You know how sometimes ugly ducklings grow up to be so damned fine? Well, that's Quincy. People call him "Q" for short. In fact, almost everyone has a nickname here in the neighborhood.

I've been going over to Q's house for a good while now, but so far, I can't get him to sleep with me. He's trying to be loyal to his friend and my husband, Victor. But Q won't be able to resist me forever. Before too long, he'll break down and give me some.

Quincy is six foot two, and thick with muscle. He's chocolaty-brown, and keeps his goatee well groomed. He wears a size twelve shoe, and you know what that means, ladies.

The crazy thing about it is that Q lives only about three blocks from me. I definitely have to watch my back when I'm walking down to his place. He lives in a house with his parents. His room is in the basement, so I don't usually see his folks. They don't tend to know what goes on down there because their bedroom is on the third floor, and that's where they spend most of their time—thank God.

I'm close with Kennedy and the rest of the girls. Kennedy is the natural leader of the pack; everyone follows her like she's God's gift to the world. I love her, but I won't be one of her groupies, which is more than I can say for some of the other girls. I think she sleeps around to get what she has. I mean, let's be realistic. She has her own business, a brand new car, and a condo... all from one little interior decorating business? *Please.*

Last I checked, before she became an owner, she had a boss just like everybody else. She was a secretary living on a secretary's salary. I'm not exactly sure how much that is, but I doubt it was all that much. Certainly not enough to save the kind of money it takes to open your own business.

Kennedy is also a slut. She's seeing two different men, and neither of them knows about the other. I can't wait till that one blows up in her face. She has these two idiots wrapped around her little finger. And for the time being, it appears she has the best of both worlds: a sophisticated, suit-and-tie, business-minded, family-oriented gentleman, and a rough, good-looking, street-smart thug who appears to be a player.

Their names are Murphy and Myles, respectively. Murphy works for the city or the state, I can't remember which. And Myles...who knows what Myles does for a living? My guess is that he's a hustler, because I've never heard Kennedy talk about him working for any sort of real company. That, and he is *always* available.

Both of these men wine and dine Kennedy in those fancy, upscale restaurants. And they seem always to be showering her with expensive gifts. Sometimes they even give her cash! She has enjoyed many shopping sprees at their expense. I've let her continue to believe that I think she's just been very fortunate. It's hard to make it out here, but she makes it seem so easy. I mean, what do she and the girls have that I don't?

All that aside—I can honestly say, and everyone else would agree, that when we hang out with Kennedy, she *always* shows us a good time. Yes, Kennedy has a lot of money, but she's very generous with it. She usually insists on paying for everything when we go out. She also donates to several charity foundations. And during times when I've found myself backed up against the wall, financially speaking, Kennedy has always been there for me and my kids. But that's just what friends do for each other. If I had it like she has it, I would do the same for her.

My kids love her. A little too much, I think. I admit I sometimes feel jealous of their close relationship. When I feel threatened by it, I have a tendency to sabotage it—on purpose. My kids are all that I have in this world. It's difficult for me to see them enjoying a close relationship with another person, even a friend. The kids have told me that they sometimes feel more comfortable talking to Kennedy about their personal problems. That pisses me off. Kennedy has enough fans; my kids will *not* be jumping on *that* bandwagon. Not if I can help it, that is.

The other girls aren't all that different from their ringleader. For example, whenever I'm out with Portia, she goes on and on about how wonderful life is with her husband and son. I know she's just trying to rub it in, my marriage not being all that satisfying. You should hear how she rambles on.

In my opinion, Portia is living in a fantasy world. It will never last. It's up to me to show her that her life isn't real. She needs to face reality, and the only way that's going to happen is if she's forced to deal with some real hardships. She needs to be brought down from her pedestal—the sooner the better.

Sky is married to Fuji. Fuji has a swagger that's hard to ignore. He's incredibly attractive. Sky hasn't been shy about telling us how amazing their sex life is, and I wanted to see just exactly what I was missing. I was determined to have sex with Fuji. At first, I didn't think he would give me a chance, being that I'm Sky's friend and all, but it turns out that Fuji wasn't all that concerned about it. So we did it. It was exactly the way Sky described it to us: *good.* Of course, it's our secret—Fuji's and mine.

Sky is my girl and I love her, but no one told her to brag about her sex life. She talks too much. Some things you're better off keeping to yourself.

I remember the third time Fuji and I had sex. It was getting close to the holidays, and Sky was away for the day, shopping with the girls. I was at Renee's house, playing cards. Renee is another girl in the neighborhood. Her house is a popular place to hang out on weekends and play cards for cash.

Fuji and the rest of the guys happened to come by Renee's looking for a place to hang out. We're all cool like that, us girls. At least, I have them thinking we're cool like that. This particular day, it was cold and snowing, and we were getting ready to leave Renee's house. We wanted to get home before the weather got any worse. But the weather was so bad we were having trouble getting a cab. Finally, Fuji was able to flag one down, and we shared it. I knew this was another opportunity for me to get him in bed, so I went for it.

While we were in the cab, I started to feel on his leg, just to see how far he'd let me go. To my surprise, he didn't stop me. So, instead of making two stops, we only made one—his house. When we got inside, I went crazy on him. I couldn't wait to put his penis in my mouth. I think I have an oral fetish or something, because I live, breathe, and think oral sex. All day. Every day.

The first ten minutes were hot, and to my eyes, Fuji was clearly enjoying himself. But then something—I don't know what—came over him. Maybe the guilt sunk in. He commanded me to stop and ordered me to get out.

What could I do? I picked my jaw up off the floor, gathered my pride (and my clothes) and walked out of the house, totally embarrassed. I've seen him since then but we never talk about it. We've carried on with life as if it never happened. I figure if he ever gets out of hand, I can use our secret sex to my advantage.

All of the girls *seem* to have their lives pretty much together. I wonder how long that's going to last, though. I admit, I pray every night to be able to switch my life with theirs for just one month. Maybe that way they'd understand what life is like in *my* shoes—a person who's barely making ends meet. I had a plan and a dream once, but then I had three kids. Portia lucked up and married someone with loads of money. Why can't I meet someone that rich?

Currently, I'm not working. Our family is on public assistance. It's important for me to be a stay-at-home mom. I'm from the old school. I can cook my ass off, clean, take care of my husband, and look after my children. I help them with schoolwork and truly enjoy my family time. Sometimes, I think the girls look down on me because of my choices. There are people who may not agree with my lifestyle, but I don't think there's anything wrong with the way I live. I love to stay home, as do most people. Most people work because they have to, not because they want to. I can be home and let the taxpayers pay me, and it doesn't weigh on my conscience. I just think of it as free money. I'm not doing anything that the governor, mayor, and president haven't been doing to the taxpayers every chance they get—so screw 'em.

I tried looking for a job once, but because I had no experience, no one would give me a chance. There was an ad in the newspaper for a maid position at a popular downtown Manhattan hotel. I went in for an interview and they asked me, "Do you have any experience in the field?"

I answered, "I don't like dirt. Shouldn't that be enough?"

The woman interviewing me chuckled and said, "Thank you for coming in, Ms. Robinson, but I don't think there's a place for you here."

My family lives in the same house as my parents. It's a three-family residence, and we have one entire floor to ourselves. My parents rent the second floor to another family, and they lucked up because they're good tenants, always pay their rent on time. My parents live on the first floor with my nephew because my sister told him it was time for him to leave her nest.

We live on the third floor. It's comfortable enough and has three bedrooms. We're supposed to pay rent, but my father doesn't really need the money. Our rent, or lack thereof, won't make or break him. Dad's got a full-time job and a side gig selling illegal liquor to those who go looking to buy after the liquor stores close. My mom also works full time. So the way I see it, between their two jobs, Dad's side business, and the rent from the second-floor tenants, that's four incomes—more than enough.

I'm forty, but I don't look a day over thirty. My physical attributes are to die for. They say black people age gracefully, and I can vouch for that. I need whatever money I can spare so I can have a personal life and keep up my beauty. I like to go out on the weekends, but if I can't, I'm fine staying home with my music, my bottle of Alizé, and my Virginia Slims.

Back to Q. I'm walking to his house. I'm on the lookout to make sure I'm not spotted by any of Victor's or my friends, because people in this neighborhood are nosy. I make it through one block without anyone noticing me. Only two blocks left to go.

Oh shit! There's Snake on the other side of the street. Snake knows my man's entire family. I hope he doesn't see me. We call him Snake because he's tall and slim, and when he dances to reggae music, he moves his body like a snake. The girls in the club go crazy over him because he's such a good dancer. It's almost like a sexual experience watching that man move his body. Thankfully, Snake doesn't notice me.

I make it to Q's house without getting caught, but unfortunately have to make my way around a sea of empty soda cans and potato chip bags that people so carelessly throw onto the streets of New York.

I head down the three steps leading to Q's basement entrance. I put my hands up to knock on the door, but before my knuckles hit, the door opens. He explains that he saw me coming down the stairs through the basement window. A car drives past the house, blasting music that fades as I step into Q's room and close the door behind me.

Q doesn't have a complete apartment, just a bedroom with a twin-sized bed and a dresser. But that's okay. I don't think any less of him. He's my boo.

I walk in and take a good look at him. His eyes look like they're about to pop out of his head, like he's got a thyroid problem or something. I notice a thick cloud of smoke in the air, and his apartment smells like his clothes and sheets haven't been washed in weeks. I can tell he's been smoking something other than cigarettes because of the funny smell.

I sit on his twin bed, and he offers me some of what he's been smoking. At first I decline, but then he pretty much forces it into my mouth. "Let me show you how to inhale it," he coaches me. I do as he directs. "Now, just lay back and enjoy the ride," he says.

It feels like I'm floating way up into the sky. The clouds are white, fluffy pillows floating all around me. "What is this stuff, Q?" Before he can answer, I say, "I like the feeling this stuff is giving me." I ask him again, "What *is* this stuff?"

"Cocaine," he says. "A lot of people call it crack, but I don't like that word." Five minutes later, we've smoked the rest of his stash. He climbs on top of me—takes the sex without me having to initiate. I like an aggressive man who knows what he wants and takes it. I guess he knows he can get it, so why ask?

I've waited all this time to sex him, and now seconds later, I can't remember how good it was because I'm so high. A few moments after that, I feel myself coming down. "This high don't last long, Q," I complain.

"I know. You have to keep taking hit after hit to keep it going," he explains.

I doze off, wondering to myself, *How much have we smoked during our time together?*

I wake with a start and shake Q awake. "What is today?"

He looks at me with droopy eyes and mumbles, "Monday." He turns over and falls back asleep.

I'm panicked. I jump out of bed and start collecting my clothes, which are scattered all around the room. Dust from the leftover crack sits on the nightstand. The rest of the dim room is filled with Q's dirty clothing and a litter of beer cans and liquor bottles. *How am I going to explain my whereabouts to my family?*

I stop and look at Q, so handsome lying on the bed. His tight body is folded among the sheets. I want this man. Why do I care what my family thinks of me? This is where I want to be. Besides, my children are in good hands.

I continue collecting my clothes and go into the bathroom to change. So what if I have to go home and take a shower and change my clothes? I'm coming back, and I don't care who knows. As I leave Q's bedroom, I take one last look at him and reassure myself that I'm willing to give up everything to be with him. Then I walk back home.

Walking through the front door of my parents' house, I immediately smell the aroma of barbeque-something. *Mom must be cooking dinner.* When I enter our third-floor apartment, I find my mom and dad sitting on that raggedy-ass brown pleather couch they passed down to us. The kids are sitting on the creaky, worn-out floors, watching that old-ass floor-model television. Victor is leaning against the bookshelf in the corner of the room. He looks like he's about to lose his mind.

"Where the hell have you been?" he barks.

"None of your business," I spit back. I notice his salt-and-pepper hair and mustache, and think to myself, *He's starting to look old as hell.* He's forty-two, but like his father, he's turning gray early.

My parents take Victor's side and join the argument. It goes on for about an hour until finally I've had enough. I walk to our bed, reach under the mattress, and pull out my Friday money. I walk back through the apartment, turn the knob on the front door, and begin to leave. Before I close the door behind me, I look back at my husband with disgust because I know what's waiting for me. Q's house is where I want to be, and that's where I'm going to stay.

I get back to Q's house and find him sober and aware. I don't hesitate. I assault him right away. I'm sober enough now to realize that this size-twelve-feet man is *not* packing. He's barely making average, but he surely knows how to use his instrument.

"Well, there you go, ladies—the size twelve thing is just a myth," I say when we finish. Then I remember the cash I brought with me. "Oh, I have money to get more stuff."

"I'll be right back," he says as he eagerly snatches the money out of my hand and leaves.

While I wait for Q to return, I begin to think about what took place earlier between Victor and me. For a second, I get caught up. Then my thoughts turn back to the feeling I got after I took my first pull off Q's pipe. I hope I don't get addicted to crack, because it's been on my mind since I first left Q's house. The way I hear it, the first high is the big high that crackheads always be chasing to get back. I hope I can get it back. *Please God, let me get that high back just one more time. Then I'll stop smoking and go home to my kids, I swear.*

There's a knock on the window. I walk to the door and open it, expecting to find Q. To my surprise, it's Victor. "What are you doing here?" I ask.

"Why are *you* here, Diamond?" he demands.

"None of your business."

"What the hell do you mean, none of my business?" he yells. "I'm your husband! You're my wife! And Q is supposed to be my friend!"

"I don't want to be with you anymore, Victor. I want to be with Quincy." Without warning, he smacks me across the face—and then again. I smack his ass back, and we start fighting. He pushes me onto the floor, and my legs go flying up into the air. He punches me repeatedly in the face. I want to kick him where it would hurt, but I can't reach his groin.

I hear Q's mother yell from an upstairs window, "Who's that fighting in my house? Get out before I call the cops!" I guess she was alerted to the noise by the crowd of teenagers starting to form in front of her home.

Quincy yells back, "Mom, get back inside the window! I'll take care of this. These are my friends!"

"Well, you'd better get those people out of my yard before I call the police!"

Q waves his mother off, then reaches down and pulls Victor off of me. Victor stares at Quincy and opens fire. "Yo, how could you sleep with my lady that I've been with all these years? We have children together! You've been over to my house on a regular basis. You've had dinner with us! You're like a part of my family!"

"She came on to me every time I was at your house, man," Q explains. "Then she starts showing up here all the time without an invitation. I know it sounds like I'm trying to justify what I did, but I'm not. I guess what I'm trying to say is, I'm sorry, man."

Victor gives Q a look of disgust and starts to walk away, but then turns back around swiftly and catches Q with a closed fist in his left eye. Quincy falls back into some garbage cans that are sitting in the yard, then Victor sidles over to him, straddles him, and spits in his face.

I step down into the stairs in front of Quincy's basement door and shout at Victor, "You punk! You feel like a man now? Now that you've been pounding on a woman?"

Victor turns around and stares me down. "Since you like staying here so much," he says, "I'm taking my kids, and we're out of here!"

Finally, the perfect opportunity to tell Victor what I've wanted to tell him for years: "Take your kids then, but leave Lillian, because she's not yours!"

Victor's mouth drops open, and for a moment he's stunned. When he gathers himself, he says, "What, bitch? You telling me one of my kids is his?" Victor gives Quincy another look of disgust and turns back to me.

I look at him with a vengeful smirk. "No, I just started sleeping with Q. But I've been sleeping with your brother for as long as I've been sleeping with you."

"My brother?" he says, obviously trying to wrap his mind around this new and disturbing information. "So you're sleeping with my brother, too?"

"Yeah, I've been sleeping with him. And it's good—a helluva lot better than your corny sex. In fact, that's exactly why I keep cheating on your sorry ass, Victor. You don't know how to satisfy me in bed."

Victor's face contorts with anger and he starts to walk away. As he heads from Q's yard, he yells over his shoulder, "No, you're cheating on me because you're a slut."

I take a step toward Quincy, who is still on the ground. He turns his head to me and says, "Get off my doorstep and get the hell out of my life, bitch."

I leave…in total confusion.

~~~

I'm at home, standing at the sink, washing dishes and looking out the kitchen window, daydreaming. The phone rings. It's Portia. "Hi, Portia. Girl, I have so much to tell you."

"I have a lot to tell you, too," she says, "but you first."

"Well, Victor and I broke up, girlfriend."

"What do you mean, 'broke up'?" she says disbelievingly. I turn off the water so I can tell her the whole story. Her response? "Girl, Dylan surprised me with a brand new car!"

She claims to be my friend. She *claims* to care about what's going on with me. But as usual, Portia manages to turn the conversation around and make it all about her.

I'm so angry with her—not only for having a better life, but for rubbing it in my face at a time when *my* life is falling apart. I stare up at the blinds that cover the kitchen window—broken. I have a burning desire to destroy Portia's life and everything in it. I want to scream into the phone, *Hello! My husband just left me and took our kids with him! This is not an appropriate time for you to tell me how perfect your life is, you selfish bitch!*

Home doesn't feel like home anymore. Not without Victor and the kids. I don't like being here. I miss Victor, especially at bedtime, when he would
~~~

hold me with his arms around my stomach. I thought I'd fallen out of love with him. Isn't that why I've been longing for someone new? But to think of Victor with another woman hurts.

I know what people think about me and Victor. They view him as the pretty boy, and me the ugly duckling. He tells me that girls walk up to him all the time and ask, "How is it that a fine man like you got yourself hooked up with an ugly girl like that?"

People view me as ugly because I'm dark skinned. Society just isn't ready for my kind of beauty. I have a bangin' body, a nice shape. I'm five foot seven. I'm a B-cup. "B" being short for *big enough*. My waist is tiny, and I have a perfectly round, plump butt. My hair is long—and natural. Men go crazy for it. I inherited long, thick eyelashes that other girls would kill for.

I don't think people *really* believe I'm ugly. They're just plain jealous of what I've got going on. People *have* put me down, made fun of my dark color. I admit I do feel insecure about my complexion, but I try not to let it get the best of me.

I sigh to myself. I know I have a lot of sucking up to do in order to get Victor back before somebody else scoops him up, but I can't bring myself to think about that right now. I pick up the phone and call Renee, hoping to gossip with her about something or somebody—anything to take my mind of my current circumstances.

I met Renee through Kennedy. Since Kennedy moved to Florida, Renee and I have been hanging tough. Funny, I've only known Renee for four years, but we've lived in the same neighborhood our whole lives. I'd seen her around before, but never knew her personally. Renee and Kennedy met through Renee's ex-boyfriend, Simon, who Kennedy has known for years.

Renee is considered tall for a girl, five foot eleven. The girl is thick—wide butt, large hips. But she also has these dainty feet, and rosy cheeks. She's very pretty, actually. Guys go crazy for her when she walks down the street.

Renee and I share a similar view when it comes to Kennedy and the other bitches. She understands me. She appreciates me more than the other girls. She and I connect on the same level, so we can relate—despite the fact that I found out it was Renee who stole my phone at the bar.

I went to jail, because in order to cast blame away from her herself, Renee blamed another woman at the bar for stealing my phone. I believed her, because this woman happened to have the same kind of phone as I did. I ended up getting into a fight with this woman right there inside the club. Things got pretty rough. Then the club owner called the cops, had me arrested.

Renee paid dearly for it, though—quite literally, in fact. She had just bought a brand new Jeep, had only had it for a month. Late one night, I saw her Jeep parked out on the street outside her place. I decided to scratch up the paint on the driver's side door. The next day, Renee called me in tears. "I went out to my car this morning," she said, "and someone dumped tar on top of my jeep! It's going to cost me a pretty penny to repair it."

"I know it's not repairable." I thought to myself.

She broke down, sobbing. "Why would someone do this to me?"

Trying to hide my pleasure at hearing her pain, I spoke calmly and quietly in a confidential tone. "I know who did it."

"Who?" she blurted. I could just imagine her big brown eyes bulging out of her head.

"I'll tell you, but you can't repeat it, because I was with her when she did it."

"What are you talking about?"

"I'm saying I know who did it." It wasn't exactly a lie. "But if you say anything to her about it, she'll know it was me who told you. And you have to believe me when I tell you I didn't know what she was going to do till she did it."

Renee's tone grew impatient. "Tell me who!"

"Promise me you won't say anything, Renee."

Renee sighed. "I promise, Diamond," she snapped. "Now, who are you talking about?"

"It was Kennedy." I blamed it on Kennedy because I hated how Renee looked up to her.

Renee's voice cracked with confusion as she asked, "Why would she do that to me? She and I are cool."

"Renee, she don't like your ass."

"What do you mean she don't like me?" she asked, disbelievingly. "We've never had a problem with each other before."

"Trust me, she don't like you," I lied. "She's been jealous since you bought that car."

"I never knew that, Diamond. She always treated me like we were friends."

"Don't worry—payback is a bitch," I told her, adding more fuel to the fire.

"Renee, please don't say anything to her. We can get her back." I didn't want her to ask Kennedy about what happened, then find out I made the whole thing up.

"How?" Renee asked.

"We can damage *her* car," I said. "We'll do it tonight."

At approximately two o' clock the next morning, we slashed all four tires and busted out all the windows on Kennedy's car. Kennedy never did find out who did it. And we, of course, never told her.

Renee is so gullible. She completely believed my lies. If she knew Kennedy at all, she'd know Kennedy would never do something like that. Damaging someone's car just isn't Kennedy's style. To this day, Renee has never found out I lied to her. Damn, I'm good.

Kennedy doesn't even know Renee and I are close now. And she don't need to know. She only knows that we hang out sometimes. Kennedy is in Florida, and I'm back here in New York.

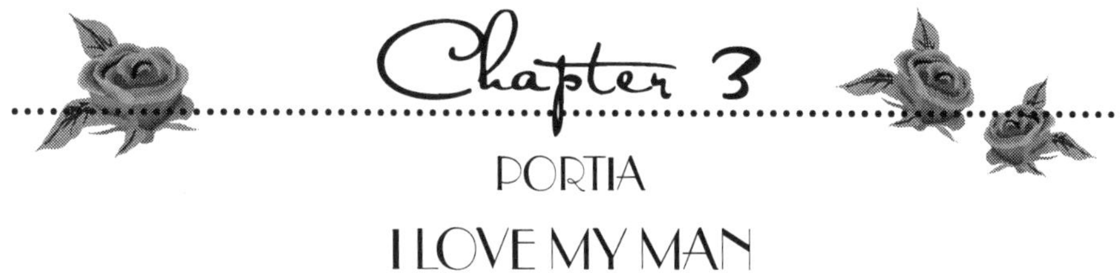

Chapter 3

PORTIA

I LOVE MY MAN

I just got off the phone with Diamond. She told me that she and Victor broke up. What a shame. Victor's a good man. I know he loves her. Maybe they'll find their way back to each other.

"Portia, honey, our college student son is on the phone. He wants to speak to his mommy," Dylan yelled from the other room.

"Okay, honey, I'll pick it up in the living room." I walk quickly into the front room and pick up the phone. "Hi, baby, how are you?" I ask him. "How's it going at school?"

"Hi, Mom," Dante says. "I love it. The girls here are slammin'."

"I mean, how is your *schoolwork* coming along?" I chide.

He replies, "It's going good—hard work, though."

"Well, you'd better get used to it. You have another seven years before you get that degree so you can become the best lawyer ever." We continue our small talk for another twenty minutes. "Okay, son—I love you. And *behave* yourself."

"I love you too, Mom. Tell Dad goodbye for me."

My husband, Dylan, comes into the room just as I'm setting the phone down. The sun streaming in through the window outlines his tall, lithe figure, bathing him in a halo of light. His ebony eyes sparkle with delight as though he has good news for me. "What's the good news, baby?" I ask, standing up from the couch.

A broad smile forms on his face. "Baby, you know I love you," he begins.

"You made me the happiest man in the world the day you agreed to marry me. I always told you I would take care of my family, and my word is my bond." He pauses. "Last week I purchased us a five-bedroom house in Winter Gardens, about twenty minutes from downtown Orlando." He pulls a set of keys out of his pocket and dangles them in front of me. "Here are the keys to your new home."

I run across the living room floor and jump into his arms. I wrap my legs around his waist and kiss him all over his head and his face. "When can I go see it, baby?" I ask, staring into his mysterious eyes.

"We can go right now," he tells me. "It's ours."

"Just let me grab my pocketbook!"

I'm impressed with the surrounding neighborhood and fall in love instantly with the whole area during our short drive to the new house. We pull up into the driveway, and I see a beautiful brick home and a three-car garage. Dylan and I get out of the car, walk up to the house, and open the glass front door. Dylan has already been here today. I can tell this by the trail of rose petals that are sprinkled in the foyer and up the staircase. I notice something shining underneath some of the petals on the second stair. I walk toward it and see that it's a diamond bracelet. "I know how much you love diamonds," Dylan says. He's holding the video camera and is recording the moment. He can see I'm over the moon, and he looks pleased with himself. He stands in the doorway, still holding the camera. I start to tear up.

"How can I be so lucky?" I ask.

"The question is, how did *I* get so lucky?"

"Dylan, I so appreciate you."

"I know you do, baby," he says, reaching for my arm. He looks into my eyes and repeats, "I know."

I follow the trail of rose petals all the way up the double staircase. They continue on into the master bedroom, which has already been furnished with a four-poster, king-sized mahogany bed.

"Kennedy will love this bedroom set. It's so her." The walls—golden yellow—match the tablecloth on the table for two near the double-bay windows. The brown-and-white plush carpet almost looks like mink. A beautiful piece of artwork hangs on the wall. It's a picture of a little boy standing on a chair playing the saxophone. This whole room puts me in a peaceful place.

Another picture hangs over the headboard. It depicts a couple relaxing together in front of a cozy fireplace. *Very romantic.* A third picture, on the wall nearest the closet entrance, shows naked bodies wrapped around each other. I look at Dylan and wink.

A beautiful, lacy peignoir is draped on the bed, and matching, high-heeled, feathered slippers sit on the floor just below. There's a breakfast-in-bed tray with a vase of roses, Chinese food, and a bottle of chilled white wine.

A large window overlooks the family room, which is also furnished, and the indoor pool on the floor below. There is recessed lighting above the pool, and the light shines romantically on the water. Large rock walls surround the entire pool.

I walk through the bedroom-sized walk-in closet and into the bath. The five-inch copper-brown tiles run across the ceiling, down the walls, and cover the entire floor of the master bath. A bubble bath is waiting for me. There are more rose petals floating in the water, and the scent of lavender rises from the bubbles. The huge Jacuzzi tub has room enough for two.

My husband takes an artistic approach to everything he does. I'm overwhelmed. Everything is just beautiful. Dylan has, once again, allowed me to see just how thoughtful and warm-hearted he can be.

"Do you like it?" he asks me.

I'm so overwhelmed with appreciation for my dear husband, I practically whisper, "I love it. I wouldn't change a thing. And who decorated this place? Because I *know* you didn't do it all by yourself," I say playfully.

"I had a little help from Kennedy," he replies. "Who else?"

"Oh my gosh!" I exclaim. "She *knew* about this? And to think, I spoke with her for hours on the phone yesterday. Well, this surely explains the bedroom setup," I say, chuckling.

"They *all* knew about it, actually," he confesses. "And they kept my secret for weeks." Not a second after he tells me this, my cell phone rings.

"Surprise, girl!" My friends yell into the phone together.

"We hope you love it," Kennedy says. "If there's anything you want to change, feel free to do as you wish. We won't be offended. But we're pretty sure we nailed it, knowing you as well as we do."

"Ah, thanks, you guys," I say. "I won't be changing a thing." My voice is trembling with emotion now. We all sob happy tears together. I even notice Dylan wiping his eyes, even though he's trying to hide it from me. I walk over to him while still on the phone, and say, "Thank you, baby. I love you dearly."

Dylan snatches the phone from my ear and says, "Bye, girls. I love you all. Thanks for all of your help. But I have to say goodbye now, because I am about to make love to my wife."

"Too much information, Dylan," Sky chimes in.

"Goodbye!" The girls chorus together.

Dylan hangs up the phone, throws it onto the chair next to the balcony, undresses me slowly, and carries me to the tub. He places me into a lavender-scented bubble bath, lights all the candles, kneels down beside the tub, and begins bathing me with a soft sponge.

Did I mention my husband can sing? While he's washing me, he sings an R. Kelly song, "Your Body Is Calling for Me." When he finishes the song, he gently dips his hand under the water and slips two fingers into my vagina. He uses his thumb to play with my clit. My vagina is becoming engorged and slippery as Dylan continues to move his fingers gently in and out.

I can see that his penis is becoming hard, even though he is still wearing his pants. I lie back in the tub and bring my knees up to my chest so I can thoroughly enjoy the finger fucking. Dylan's hot breath is over my breasts now. It arouses my nipples, which are peeking out of the soapy water. I start to moan, completely caught up in the activity above and below the water.

He knows his touch turns me on. He picks me up out of the tub and doesn't bother to dry me off. Soapy water drips from my body and onto the bathroom floor. He places me on the bed and takes off his clothes, moving everything else—the tray, the peignoir—aside. He climbs on top of me, and with his hand, directs his penis toward my vagina, then slowly pushes it inside me until our hips meet. He pulls out and pushes back in—slowly at first, then increases his speed. He gyrates his hips and buries his head between my breasts. His breathing is becoming heavier. He cups my breast with his hand. He sucks one, then the other. My nipples are so hard they resemble baby bottles. His penis thrusts deep inside of me, and the combination of the sucking and the fucking bring me to a fast and intense orgasm. I cum so hard my pelvic area cramps. It feels like a headache in my vagina. We make love for hours. I never get the chance to wear the beautiful lingerie Dylan laid out for me.

When we are finally spent, we lie back on the bed, look at each other and sigh. Before we can say anything, my cell phone rings. I answer it and hear our son's voice, shaking with excitement. "Were you surprised, Mom? Do you like the house?"

"Slow down. One question at a time," I say, giggling. "Okay. To answer both of your questions—yes, and yes. And you knew too, ha!"

He laughs. "Yes. It was so hard for me not to clue you in—I talked to you practically every day this week." He ends the phone call by saying, "Well, I know you're probably excited and want to continue exploring your new home, so I'm going to let you go. I'll call you tomorrow. I love you, Mommy."

"Okay, son, I love you, too." I'm way too tired after all that love-making to go looking through the rest of the house. I decide to hold off until morning.

~~~

I awake to sun streaming in through the window, warming my face. I look around and realize this was no dream. The right side of the bed is empty. "Where's my man?" I say out loud. I get up, wrap my robe around me, and go in search of Dylan. As soon as I open the door of our bedroom, I smell the aroma of food cooking from somewhere downstairs. I walk down the stairs and wander from room to room in an attempt to find the kitchen. I'm pleased to discover that we have a home theatre room—fully equipped.

After peeking in and out of rooms for several minutes, I finally find my way to the kitchen. "What a big, beautiful kitchen we have, honey," I exclaim. "It's a wife's dream."

Dylan is at the stove in nothing but an apron and a chef's hat—he's making breakfast for us. I sneak up behind him, put my arms around his waist, and squeeze him tight to show my appreciation. He reaches down and gently grabs my hands, squeezing them to let me know *he* knows how much I appreciate what he has done for me. He turns to me and says, "The table is set up outside on the screened-in deck. Go and have a seat. Breakfast is coming right up." I blush, snatch a piece of strawberry off the counter, and skip out to the deck. I'm just a happy ass.

The table is beautifully made up, and there is a newspaper for us to share. A pot of hot coffee is waiting for me, and it smells good. I sit down, place a napkin in my lap, and pour myself a cup. Then I pick up the newspaper and start reading.

Dylan joins me a few minutes later. I notice that he has slipped upstairs and changed into pajamas. The smell of his cologne is potent, intoxicating. I want him all over again...right here, right now. But my erotic plans are thwarted by the sound of the doorbell.

"Who could that be?" I ask quizzically. Dylan just shrugs his shoulders. Curious, I leave our cozy breakfast table. When I get to within ten feet of the front doors, I can see that it's my girls. I run the rest of the way, open the door,
~~~

and fall into their open arms. We're screaming and jumping up and down in a circle.

"Oh, boy. There goes the neighborhood," Dylan says with amusement. He's followed me and is recording again with the video camera. "Come on inside, ladies."

"Are we making too much noise, honey?"

"Yes, baby," he says as he disappears up the stairs. "I'm going to leave you girls alone, so you can talk shit about us men."

"Honey, did you eat?" I ask him.

"No, but I'm fine. Did plenty of tasting while cooking and managed to fill up. You girls go ahead—have at it."

"I'm not eating *your* cooking," Brooke jokes.

We walk back through the kitchen and onto the deck. We crowd around the table, sit down, and begin to eat the food Dylan has so graciously prepared for the two of us. I guess it's breakfast for me and the girls now. "Mmm. Dylan put his heart and soul into this breakfast," Lola mumbles. "The steam is still coming off the scrambled eggs."

"So girls," I begin. "Just *how long* did you all know about this?"

"Oh, about three weeks," Tasha and Payton say in unison.

"Well, of course Dylan called *me* first," Kennedy explains. "I *am* a professional interior designer, after all. And then, naturally, I called the girls because I was so excited for you I couldn't keep myself from sharing the news. I was worried that if I didn't tell *them,* I'd ruin the surprise by telling you."

"I love you all so much," I say. "There are plenty of women who would have been jealous that my husband was buying me a house."

"Like perhaps, Diamond?" Brooke practically shouts, twirling a strand of her red hair around her finger.

I sigh. "You're absolutely right, Brooke...but not you guys. Has anyone told you guys today how much they love and care about you? Well, I do."

"We love you, too."

"I decorated and painted the brunch area," Payton gladly points out.

"You did a great job painting the other rooms as well," Tasha says to Payton.

"Thank you for saying so, Tasha," Payton says.

"I guess you've probably already figured out that the paintings are from the gallery," Lola offers.

"I knew I'd seen them before!" I exclaim. "Thank you, Lola."

Each of my friends takes a moment to share with me which part of the house they helped decorate.

"So, getting back to Diamond," Lola says, changing the subject. "When was the last time any of you guys heard from her?"

"I spoke to her yesterday," I say. "She and Vic broke up."

Kennedy chimes in, "I usually speak to her at least twice a week. I think it's been two or three days since we last spoke."

"Well, I've heard—from two different people now—that Diamond doesn't like us," Lola says. "Especially you, Portia." I don't want anything to ruin this wonderful morning, so I ignore Lola's last comment.

"Who told you that, Lola?" Brooke inquires.

"I'm not going to name names."

"Well, I don't believe it," Kennedy says. "We've all been friends since childhood."

"I'm just relaying to you all what I heard," Lola says. "You guys can take the information and do what you want with it. But the truth is, I walked in on Diamond and Renee one time, and they were talking about me like I was a dog."

Now that she has our attention, Lola takes a deep breath and continues her story. "You know how Diamond always leaves her front door open—you can just let yourself right in? Well, that's what I did. I planned on sneaking in and trying to scare her because I think it's crazy that she's always leaving that door open. I figured if I could give her a good *Scared Straight* scare, maybe she wouldn't be so careless as to leave the damned thing open all the time. It just isn't safe.

"Anyway, I didn't know that Renee was there. On my way up the stairs, I could hear Diamond talking to someone. And then I heard my name. I stopped in the hallway and tried to listen. It didn't occur to me that they would be talking shit about me. I can't even remember exactly what it was that they said. I just remember it wasn't good. I decided maybe they both needed a good scare, so I jumped into the room from the hallway and shouted, '*BOO!*' They looked like they'd seen a ghost, and I said to them, 'I just heard everything you bitches was talking about.' They were so embarrassed—at a total loss for words.

"Then she did it again when I invited her out after work with my co-workers—*after* I introduced her to them as one of my closest friends! Come Monday morning at the office, my co-workers filled me in on how Diamond had bad-mouthed me when I'd stepped away from the table to use the bathroom. I thought they were getting ready to fire me. They were all crowded around, waiting for me at my cubicle that morning." Lola pauses and shakes her head. "It was so embarrassing. I told them that Diamond and I had been close since we were kids. I couldn't believe the things Diamond told them about me. One of my co-workers said, 'With friends like her, you don't need no enemies.'"

Before she can go on talking, I hold up my hand and signal for Lola to stop. "I've had enough of the Diamond talk this morning," I say to her wearily. "I don't want to waste one more minute on negativity today. I have a beautiful new home, a husband I love, and all of you wonderful and caring friends." I lift my glass and say, "Let's drink to that."

"Yeah, and I want a *real* drink, Portia," Payton says.

"Well, if I know my husband," I say, "I'm guessing there are a few bottles of champagne stashed around here somewhere. And I know there's at least one unopened bottle of white wine. Didn't get a chance to taste it last night because my mouth was already full...if you get my drift."

"Listen to your little nasty happy ass," Lola says, and laughs.

I smile big and yell, "Let's get this party started!"

"Where are the champagne glasses, girl?" Tasha asks eagerly.

"Maybe I should be asking you guys, since you did the decorating," I joke.

"I know where they're at," says Kennedy.

I tune the stereo to a popular Orlando jazz station. Kennedy is the first of us to start dancing in the middle of the family room floor. Payton and Tasha are already moving the coffee table out of the way to make more room. I look around this beautiful room filled with my dearest friends and think, *I wouldn't change anything about this glorious day. Thank you, God.*

I notice Sky behaving strangely. She seems worried, a little uneasy. She keeps leaving the room and stepping into the corner of the foyer by the grandfather clock. She's trying to reach somebody on her cell. I'm concerned, so I walk over to her and ask, "Is everything okay, Sky?"

"Oh...yeah," she stammers. "I'm just trying to get in touch with Fuji so I can let him know where I am." I think to myself that she's *probably* worried that Fuji is off somewhere doing something he isn't supposed to be doing.

"Sky, are you happy?" I ask her.

"Of course I'm happy, Portia," Sky says. "I just don't want him to worry."

"Well, good then. I want you and Fuji to be just as happy as Dylan and I."

"I know you do, Portia, and I love you for that."

"I want all of my best friends to be happy," I say. We stroll back to the rest of the girls, who are still dancing around the family room.

"Are you girls ready for New York next month?" Kennedy shouts over the music.

"Hell yeah, I'm ready," Sky says, holding the phone away from her mouth—in case Fuji happens to answer.

Our friend Infinity is playing a show next month back home in Brooklyn. Infinity is a talented singer who's been trying to make it in the music industry damned near all her life. As long as we've known her, she's been singing every chance she gets—on the streets, on the stage, on the train, in the school halls (when we were in high school). She would even sing standing on my Brooklyn steps after ringing my bell while she waited for me to come downstairs and let her in. She'd sing so loud when she had her earphones on, you'd have thought she had an audience in front of her.

Infinity knows she's good, and everyone who hears her sing agrees. I'd put her right up there with Anita Baker and Mary J. Blige. Her voice is gorgeous, and she has the power to mesmerize everyone in the room with it. We love to watch her perform every chance we get. We're all one hundred percent behind her; she deserves the dream she's after.

Next month, Infinity will be opening for Ne-yo, 112, Floetry, and Avant. It's a huge deal. That's why we're all flying up there together—to support our friend. We'll be staying in New York for a week, so we'll also get to spend some quality time with all of the friends we left behind. We're hoping our friends will return the favor one of these days and come down here to Florida for a visit.

"Well, I've had my nap. Now I'm heading out—going to hang with the fellas," says Dylan, coming down the stairs. I jump up as soon as his feet hit the landing at the bottom of the staircase. I run across the room and give him a great big hug and a kiss. During our embrace, Dylan whispers to me seductively, his soft lips touching my earlobe: "I want you in my bed when I get back."

I salute him and say, "Yes, sir!"

The girls and I decide to make this beautiful Saturday a sleepover, for old time's sake. We continue to have a blast. Tasha is so twisted, she starts a strip tease dance, but it's all in fun. We're all thoroughly enjoying each other's company. Well, almost all.

Sky is back in the foyer, sitting on the bottom stair with her cell phone to her ear. She looks more agitated each time she comes back into the room. She's still trying to get in contact with that no-good-ass Fuji, and he's not picking up her calls. She loves that man so much. Maybe a little too much. "I can't put my finger on it, but something isn't right." Kennedy says to me, gesturing discreetly with her eyes in Sky's direction.

"If there's anything serious going on, she would tell us, girl," I say. "Kennedy, I think you worry too much about the rest of us."

"I can't help it, Portia. You and the girls are my family."

"Well, I'm going to linger in the moment for the rest of this glorious day. I am blessed. And damn, I love my man."

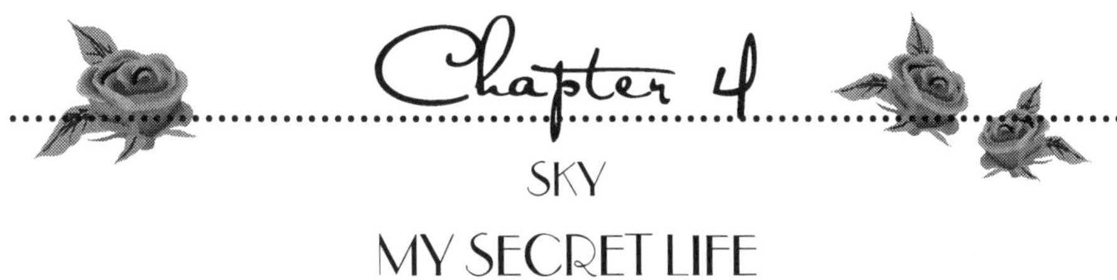

Chapter 4

SKY

MY SECRET LIFE

I awake to the sun beaming into my eyes. I've been sleeping on the couch in Portia's family room. It sits directly across from a huge east-facing window. In our celebratory state, no one bothered to close the shades before we all crashed out last night.

I wish I could sleep a little longer. I had way too much to drink last night—felt like there was more alcohol in my system than blood. As I scan the room, I see my friends scattered about, still sleeping. Too drunk to be bothered with finding the spare bedrooms, we settled for finding a decent-enough spot to crash, and called it a night. The couch, the love seat, the lounge chair, the floor—they're all in use.

I'm dehydrated. I stumble to the kitchen in search of something to drink. The stainless-steel refrigerator still has everything placed neatly inside, exactly the way we prepared it for Portia. I know I should drink the bottled water sitting in the fridge door, but I'm dying for some something scratchy like a soda.

Dylan must have come in late last night and covered us with blankets, because I know none of us bothered to cover ourselves before we passed out. Dylan is such a gentleman; Portia is lucky to have him. He is so good to her. I'm really happy for them. They are so lucky to have found each other in this big ol' world.

I admit, sometimes I feel a little jealous of Portia's marriage, but it's totally innocent. I only feel this way because I wish I had what they have. Of all of our friends, Portia and I are the only two who are married. Well, unless you count Diamond.

My marriage is good...when it's good. But when it's bad, it's *really* bad. There seems to be no in between for Fuji and me. It's black and white all the way, absolutely no gray. I'm not complaining. But I can't seem to help comparing my marriage to Portia's. The girls always tell me I can do better than Fuji, because he's such a player. But as the preacher man said, "For better or worse."

My friends and I are very close. It feels more like I have six sisters instead of six best friends. The relationship we share is filled with positive energy. I thank God we were chosen to be a part of each other's lives, because friendship isn't about whom you've known the longest. It's about who came and never left. Our families are just as close. I feel blessed to have this extended family. It doesn't matter that we're not related by blood.

If the girls knew how bad it gets between me and my husband, they would *really* hate him. My girls don't know it, but Fuji gets physical with me. And it's getting worse, becoming more frequent. Shit, who am I kidding? He beats the hell out of me on a regular basis. Sometimes it's my fault, though. I can't seem to keep from making him angry. I try to keep the peace by following the rules, but sometimes I forget the rules because there are just too many to follow.

I'm not ready to tell the girls the truth, and I'm not ready to leave Fuji. So I just carry on as if nothing is wrong. There are times when I know I should leave, but he always uses his charm to make things right again, always manages to talk me into staying. Then we're good...for a while. Until we're not again.

I know I'm going to be walking into something bad today. I tried to call him last night to ask if it would be okay for me to stay at Portia's, but he didn't answer his phone. I intended to leave Portia's at a certain hour because I wasn't able to get a hold of Fuji to ask permission. But I was so drunk I passed out on her couch. I know there will be hell to pay when I get home. He'll be there ready to start a fight. I'm going to try my hardest to avoid him, but it's usually not smart to ignore him because he becomes even more upset. I just have to put my big-girl shoes on and prepare for the worst.

I head to one of the bathrooms on the second floor of Portia's mansion. I rinse my mouth and splash some water on my face. I go back down the stairs, into the family room, and kiss each of the girls on the forehead. They're still asleep. I step out of Portia's house and head for home—to face the madness.

~~~

It's peaceful outside. Birds are singing in the trees. I reach into my pocketbook and take out my cell phone. Once I'm in my car, I look to see how many times the asshole called me. *Twenty-three missed calls. Ten messages.* I don't even care. This ass-beating will be worth it. Then my phone rings. I don't recognize the number.

"Hello."

"Hi, Sky," a familiar voice says. "It's Diamond."

"Hey, Diamond. What's up? What number are you calling from?" I ask.

"I'm using a friend's phone," she explains. "So, I just had the best sex. It was so good—I had to call somebody."

I start to laugh. "Oh, you're using one of my numbers."

"Yes, girl. You're always calling and telling me how good your husband is doing you. So, I called to let you know that the sex is good over here, too." We both start laughing.

"Diamond, can I call you back? I'm driving right now."

"No problem, girl. I just wanted to tell you about the sex I just had."

"Okay, Diamond, talk to you later. Love you, girl."

I really enjoyed myself with the girls last night. No regrets. I decide not to listen to Fuji's messages. I'll just go home and face him.

As I pull up into the driveway, my stomach lurches. His car is here. He's definitely home. I decide to enter the house through the back door, which opens up into the kitchen. From the doorway, I hear the television going in the living room. I assume Fuji is in there, waiting to pounce. But when I step into the kitchen, I'm startled to see him sitting on the kitchen counter, the back of his oil-sheened head pressed against my white cabinets. His face is screwed up. I know this look. He's totally pissed off.

"Sky, where the hell have you been?" he yells. "I've been calling your phone all night. I checked all your friend's houses, and you weren't with any of them either, so don't even try to lie to me."

"I was at Portia's house," I say.

"Didn't I just tell you I checked all of your friend's houses?" he barks back. "That bitch, Portia, and all the other whores you hang out with."

"Dylan bought Portia a new house," I explain. "That's where I was—where we *all* were. We were celebrating Portia's new place, and we started drinking. I ended up having one too many, and I passed out. But before that, I'd been trying to call you all evening. You didn't answer your phone. I—"
~~~

He cuts me off, "Why didn't you leave a message?"

"I left you tons of messages."

"Well, I sure didn't see any of them—liar!"

I'm still thirsty. I begin to open the cabinet where the drinking glasses are. I notice Fuji is holding an empty ceramic mug in his right hand. "And look at you. You got your hair done, and your nails. What the hell? You had a date or something?" Before I can answer, he smacks me across the face with the mug hand. I stand there, stunned, and start to sway, in excruciating pain. I fall forward onto the door of the open kitchen cabinet. For some reason, I didn't expect the blow at that moment. I have no time to react, because before I can even right myself, Fuji is in my face, smacking me repeatedly.

"I swear, Fuji!" I plead. "I was at Portia's new house with the girls!" But it's no use trying to explain. He punches me over and over. I curl up on the floor like a fetus and beg him to stop.

"You ugly, lying bitch," he says venomously. "I know you were with another man."

"Fuji, please!" I beg. "Just call the girls and ask them! Please, Jerome, please." Sometimes, if I use his government name, Fuji pays better attention. But it doesn't work this time. He just keeps yelling and hitting.

"You think I don't get that you already called those bitches and told them to lie for you? You think I'm stupid now?" He's sitting on top of me now. I can barely move, much less defend myself.

"All I want to know is why you didn't pick up your phone?" He gets up but remains standing over me, glaring down.

I plead with him, "I swear, baby. I didn't hear my phone ringing—the music was blasting, and we were drinking."

He grabs me by my hair and drags me from room to room over the carpeted floors. He's punching my back with his fist the whole time. I look up at him. He's biting his bottom lip, using all of his strength to give his punches more power. He pulls me into the unfurnished den. He grabs me by the shirt and pulls my face up to meet his. Our eyes lock. "Who were you with last night?" he screams, and spits in my face. He keeps repeating the question. My cries are out of control. I'm out of breath, and I'm trying hard to get the words out.

"Baby," I begin, "I swear I called you last night. Please go check your phone again. Or call Dylan."

"I know you were with a man last night. That's how you women do when you all have a date. You go get your hair and nails done, wax, make sure you smell all good. I'm not stupid. That's how you got me." I can smell stale liquor on his breath. "I know how you get prepared for a man, because I used to be that man. All you women are the same. The only thing you women is good for is to go down on me. I don't even know why I married your stupid ass. I knew you would do this to me. You're just like all the others." His voice is getting quieter. The punches are slowing. He seems to be calming down.

"Baby, I didn't cheat on you," I say. "Please, just take another look at your phone. I swear I called you. I even invited you over to celebrate with us. Please just listen to your messages."

"Sky, you stayed out the entire night. Are you crazy?" He's revving back up. "What the hell do you think I am, a punk? It's not okay for you to stay out the whole night! You must have fallen and bumped your head. Well, I'm gonna make damned sure this doesn't happen again." He's tired, out of breath. The pounding finally stops. He lets go of my shirt without warning, and my head hits the floor. Luckily, we're on carpet. Before he walks away, he gets in one last kick—into my ribs—and walks out of the room.

It's over, I think to myself. I let out a sigh, but stay on the floor and cover my face with my arms. My heart starts pounding when I hear Fuji's footsteps reentering the room. I peek through my arms and see him standing over me. My voice is weak, fragile. I'm still blocking my face with my hands. "No more," I plead. "Please, no more."

He stands over me, eyes like daggers. Then he proceeds to pour an entire container of milk over my head. "Oops," he says. "I guess I messed up your lovely new hairstyle." He's walks out of the room again, leaving me in my saturated state. I hear him say, "I bet you won't try that again," as he walks down the hall and up the stairs.

I break into sobs. I'm staring at the tall vase that sits on the floor in the corner of this otherwise empty room. At this moment, I would give anything to be that vase—to be not living, not hurting.

The blinds are closed, so I lie on the floor in the absence of light. My head feels like it's about to explode. I remove a hand from my head and see blood. My other hand is on my ribs where he just kicked me. I try to stop crying. My head hurts terribly. I wanted to call somebody, but I can't. Who would I call? No one knows about what's going on with Fuji and me. I don't want anyone to know I'm in love with a monster. I do understand his anger. I should have come right home when I realized I wasn't going to be able to get a hold of him. But no, I went ahead and got so drunk I couldn't drive. *Stupid!*

I can't tell him to leave. Beside the fact that he'd probably refuse to go, I'm not financially stable enough to take over all the household bills. He likes to remind me of this. I'm staring at the phone. I want so badly to speak to my girls. I need them—now more than ever. But I can't find the courage to pick it up. I don't want to involve them. And I especially don't want any of them to judge me. I don't need that right now. I have enough on my plate. I need someone who will listen without voicing an opinion. I just don't think my friends are capable of that—just listening.

Fuji hates them. He doesn't want me hanging out with them, or any of my family, for that matter. Why make a bad situation worse? He thinks the girls are a bad influence, that they will eventually corrupt me.

The girls think of me as a tough chick. I know it would be unbelievable to them that I could tolerate an abusive man. I could never face them about this situation; it's just too embarrassing.

I don't know what went wrong with Fuji and me. In the beginning, things were good. He could be verbally abusive sometimes. I knew it was dysfunctional. But it wasn't too bad. The words didn't really hurt me. Not much, anyway. The physical abuse started later. Now, fighting with Fuji just feels…natural. It's just the way we are.

I hear him coming back down the steps. I'm shivering and praying to God that Fuji's not coming back down here to resume the beating. He walks into the den and finds me exactly where he left me. His puppy-dog brown eyes look apologetic. He's checked his phone, and now knows that I *did* try to call him last night—numerous times. He knows I left messages asking him to join me.

He walks back out of the room and is back quickly with some paper towels from the kitchen. He helps me sop up the milk and holds a clean paper towel to the wound on my head, to help stop the bleeding. "Sky, I am so sorry," he apologizes. "I just get so upset when I imagine you with another man. It drives me crazy just thinking about it." He kneels next to me with tears in his eyes and says again, "I am so sorry." He draws me in with his dreamy eyes, freckled nose, and his cute, pointy ears.

"I believe you're sorry, baby," I say. Not for the first time, I convince myself that he's sincere, that his tears are real and full of regret. "And I'm sorry for getting you so upset," I say to him. "I promise to try harder next time."

"I love you, Sky."

"I love you, too." I'm sniffing and trying to hold back my tears. He pulls the paper towel away and kisses my head where it's bleeding. He kisses my nose, then my lips. He lays my head back down on the carpet and climbs on top of me. I start to moan in pain because my body is so sore from our battle.

"I'm sorry, Sky, for hurting you." He gently begins to remove my pants. My lips still sting from his punches, making his kisses feel like tiny daggers. He realizes he's hurting me and stops, then begins kissing my face, which is sticky from the milk. My pants are all the way off now. He gently and passionately makes sweet love to me. Our quarrel is a distant memory—vanished without a trace.

~~~

We must have fallen asleep after we made love. When I wake, I gingerly turn over onto my side and look at Fuji, who is sleeping next to me. We're still lying on the floor in our mostly empty den. I haven't had time to furnish this room. I want to take my time decorating this part of the house. I don't mind leaving things undone or empty. I'd rather wait for the proper inspiration and do it one time, right.

Until now, we've never actually made use of this room. The walls are a brick color. The brand new, plush carpet is beige. It has two bay windows on one wall. In between the windows hangs a picture that Fuji bought, which reads, "LOVE ME OR HATE ME, BOTH ARE IN MY FAVOR. IF YOU LOVE ME, I WILL ALWAYS BE IN YOUR HEART. IF YOU HATE ME, I WILL ALWAYS BE ON YOUR MIND."

I turn my eyes back to Fuji. I feel pain trickle down the left side of my neck. It works its way up to my face and over my head. Reality sets in. I think back to our fight, and I feel...tired. I struggle to get up without waking Fuji. I want to go to the bathroom and assess the damage.

When I reach the bathroom, I don't want to look in the mirror, but I know I have to. My reflection startles me, and I start to cry. I don't even know this person staring back at me. I begin talking out loud to my reflection. "This is the dark secret of Sky's life," I begin. "I know this is a dangerous situation, but I feel trapped. I love this violent man. I can't tell the girls that I'm married to such an abusive man. I have to keep this a secret. It's just too embarrassing. How could he beat me like this? Love is not supposed to be like this—yelling and punching, blood and bruises."

The bruises are beginning to swell. My eye is bulging and is already turning purple and black. I start to think about what my best friends would say if they saw me like this. I'm afraid if they find out, they'll see me as weak and desperate.

I thought things would be different between Fuji and me once we moved
~~~

to Florida. That's what he promised. I feel so alone. There is no one I can call. I feel as if I am the only person in the world going through this.

The bathroom door opens. It's Fuji. He must have heard my cries from the hallway. I'm startled—I didn't realize he'd be able to hear me through the bathroom door. I continue looking into the mirror instead of turning around to face him. My eyes rise to meet his.

"Why?" I uttered softly.

He steps up from behind and wraps me in his embrace. "I guess I love you too much," he says. He sounds like a coward. "When I so much as think of you with another man, it drives me crazy," he explains. "I'm *sorry*, baby. I thought I already apologized to you earlier," he says, sounding a bit less contrite.

"I'm not trying to upset you, Fuji," I say. "I just want to know *why*."

He ignores the question. He steps in front of me and turns on the hot water. Then he reaches over to the tub and begins to fill it. "I'm gonna steam up the bathroom—make you more comfortable." I know this routine. He follows it after every beating. He always regrets hitting me.

The blow to my ribs is making it difficult for me to bend over. My fingers ache from trying to fend off his repeated blows. I'm completely naked now. I'm standing in the middle of the bathroom floor, hunched, holding my side, and shivering, even though I'm not cold. Fuji picks me up. He's kissing my body, his way of continuing his apology. He places me into the tub. He picks up a sponge, dips it into the tub, and squeezes it over my head to help wash the dried blood away from my face and head. I sit still and sob quietly.

After washing me, Fuji pulls the drain plug and dries me off gently, being careful not to cause me any more pain. He picks me up out the tub and wraps a towel around me. He carries me into our bedroom, places me on the bed, and begins brushing my hair. I feel like I'm five years old.

After a few minutes, he stops brushing. He places his fingers gently under my chin and lifts my head. "Baby, I'm going to get help, I promise you," he says. "I know I've told you this before, but I really mean it this time. I'm going to do it for us. I know I have a bad temper, and I want to fix it. I don't like hitting you. It's just that sometimes you make me so angry, I can't help myself. When your bruises heal, we can make an appointment to get some help."

"Yeah, both of us need the help," I reply sarcastically. I snatch the brush from his hand and throw it onto the dresser. I'm pissed. There is a folded blanket across the end of the bed. I pull it up over me and lie back on top of the comforter. I close my eyes and try to block out Fuji, who is standing over me, confused.

"What are you saying, Sky?" he asks. "That I'm the only one with a problem?"

"Jerome, just leave," I say flatly. I'm relieved when he walks out of our bedroom and closes the door behind him.

Next up for Fuji's after-beating routine is to go down to the kitchen and heat up a can of chicken noodle soup, which he will feed to me in bed. I want to scream at him, *Stop it, you idiot! I don't need any soup. I'm not sick—you just beat me. What I need is a doctor, you psycho!* Instead, I just lie there and wait for him to bestow upon me his sweet and considerate gestures. And like some sort of fool, I enjoy it.

Right on schedule, Fuji backs through the bedroom door holding a tray with the soup he's prepared for me, because of course, I have been suddenly stricken with a severe illness—an illness for which I will not need medical attention.

"Hi, honey," he says sweetly. "Look what I made for you. This will make you feel better. You'll be good as new by morning."

What I want to say is, *You jackass! I don't have a cold—you bashed my head in. These bruises aren't going to heal by morning. They'll take weeks to heal, like they always do! What the hell are you gonna do, feed me soup for two damned weeks?* But I don't say it. These are the times when I wish I had a brother—someone who could come here and fuck him up. I bet he wouldn't try that shit with a man.

Fuji sets the tray on the night table and props up my pillows so I can sit up straight while he feeds me the soup. He places the tray over my lap and begins the feeding ritual. I try to eat fast because I just want him to leave. At one point, some soup spills on my chin.

"Slow down, baby," he says. "You're making a mess." He wipes my chin with a napkin. When the soup is gone, he removes the tray from my lap and kisses me on my cheek. "I'm going to take off for a few hours. I gotta take care of some business."

As he walks out the bedroom door, he says over his shoulder, "I'll call and check up on you." If my memory serves, he is now on his way to make a major purchase, a formal defense of sorts—diamonds. Diamonds because... he knows they're a girl's best friend.

~~~

Finally, I'm alone. When I'm stressed or depressed, I really cherish my
~~~

alone time. It helps me regroup, to think about my next move or cry without anybody hearing. I depend on my alone time because it's the only time I can collect my thoughts, get some sort of peace.

I open the drawer in the nightstand, pull out the TV remote, and turn on the Lifetime Channel. Low and behold, it's a movie about a battered wife. I hate when this happens. *I refuse to watch this right now.* But sometimes I do watch. And I even catch myself calling the abused spouse "stupid" or "desperate." And then I realize that she is me.

I don't have the stomach for it today, though. I turn to my favorite station—TMC, the classic movie channel. I love old movies. I find them comforting. One of my favorites Hitchcock films is on, *Rear Window.* And I've only missed the first fifteen minutes. Watching old movies is an escape for me, a couple of hours when I can forget about what is wrong in my life—forget about my secret.

Chapter 5

LOLA
WHEN I BECAME LOVE'S PRISONER

My name is Lola. I'm loud, obnoxious, and pleasantly plump. I also happen to be the only Puerto Rican among my group of friends.

I am too old and too mature to worry about how others perceive me, or to care about the negative things they might say about me because I happen to be outspoken. I can be flirtatious, and sometimes people misunderstand that—they assume it means I'm promiscuous. Being flirtatious is just a part of my personality. I like people and I like to have fun, but I'm no whore. I gave everyone I dated a chance at love…until I met my ex, Winston.

Winston was the best thing that ever happened to me. Or so I thought at the time. Things were going along wonderfully till his unfaithfulness showed up. It was then that I decided to forever avoid the commitment end of relationships. Yep, when it comes to love, I'm just a cold-hearted monster now.

I was working at my desk one day when a tall, dark-skinned man suddenly appeared in front of me. "Hi, I'm Winston," he said, with a charming Jamaican accent. "I work on the third floor." A broad smile broke across his dark-skinned face. "I've seen you around," he added. "Would you care to have lunch with me today?"

"Well, I would, but my boyfriend wouldn't really like it," I responded politely, intending to put him in his place right away. I didn't find him particularly attractive, but his attention bolstered my confidence. Then my phone rang. I looked up at Winston and said, "I've got to get back to work now."

"Well, another time, maybe," he offered as he walked away, not seeming the least bit disappointed.

After that, he started visiting my desk two or three times a day. Sometimes he would even bring me things—flowers, cookies, or a soda. I confess that liked the gifts and the feeling that this man thought I was important. But I also wondered if I should report him to my supervisor for harassment, since I really had no intention of getting involved with him.

I asked Kennedy for her opinion on this guy. She convinced me to take a chance on him because, as she said, "He appears to have it going on."

My relationship history was not stellar. By the time I met Winston, I'd been in numerous abusive and dysfunctional relationships. But Winston seemed sincere, and he was definitely different than the men I was normally attracted to. So, with Kennedy's encouragement, I decided to give Winston a chance.

I'd hoped that dating him would lead me in the direction of love, marriage, and everything that comes with it. I admit I had a longstanding Cinderella fantasy. But up until this point, I had been disappointed several times over. Maybe it would be different with Winston.

Winston came from Jamaica. He was the first man I'd dated who wasn't from here. In truth, I never thought our relationship would go very far. After all, I was living with another man when we met. Yes, I volunteered this information on our first lunch date—in the company cafeteria. I didn't feel like I should lie to him, and besides, I don't think he cared all that much, anyway.

"Well, that just makes my mission to get you all to myself a little more challenging. I like a good challenge," he said confidently. "And fortunately for us, I don't have a girlfriend, so I have plenty of time to dedicate to the cause."

For the next four months we dated, but no sex. During that time, we enjoyed each other's company and got to be good friends—no strings attached. I felt very comfortable with him. He wasn't persistent about sleeping with me, and as a matter of fact, it never even came up. One time, when money was short, he helped me pay my bills. I didn't even have to ask for his help. He was simply a gentleman who seemingly liked doing things for me out of the kindness of his heart. It didn't even seem to bother him that I was living with another man. I was convinced that Winston's kindness was genuine, that he had a heart of gold.

As I explained, I didn't sleep with Winston right away because I was still living and sleeping with Milton—an abusive, marijuana-smoking bum. But after spending those four months getting to know Winston and seeing his goodness, I was ready to kick Milton to the curb.

The day I told Winston I was ready to leave Milton, he was elated. He was so excited that he offered to help me look for an apartment. I wasn't sure what to do at first, but Winston offered to pay my first month's rent and security deposit. How could I say no? After I moved into my new apartment, he insisted on paying my rent and my bills. I told him I didn't need him to do that for me, but he wouldn't take no for an answer.

It was fairly clear that Winston loved for me to depend on him. Eventually, it became a problem because I am a very independent person. I don't like to feel that a man has control over me. But against my better judgment, I allowed him to control the situation; sometimes you have to let a man be a man. I felt otherwise secure in our relationship. I didn't think he was going anywhere anytime soon. I felt we would be together for a long time, if not forever.

Winston lived alone. He owned a single-family home in Flatbush, in Brooklyn. I liked that he had his own place because it meant that I didn't have to worry about him wanting moving in with me. Later in our relationship, before I moved there myself, Winston bought a condo in Florida. He traveled there frequently for work. In fact, he was in Florida more than he was in New York.

I didn't want to take advantage of his kindness, but I was more than ready to get out of the bad situation I was in with Milton. So why not take Winston up on his offer? I deserved that type of treatment. And it was about time two good people got to fall in love without any baggage weighing down the relationship. I just wanted to live happily ever after with the man I was hopelessly in love with.

The treatment I was receiving from this man was indescribable. It almost kind of scared me at first. I was used to being the "giver" in relationships, so it was all very new to me.

The day finally came for me leave Milton. I found a one-bedroom apartment in Canarsie, in Brooklyn, and was ready after six long years wasted with Milton to start anew. But...I realized I couldn't dare tell him that I was leaving him for another man. Milton could act crazy jealous sometimes, and

I didn't want any problems. I needed a clean break. So, I slowly moved all my belongings out of our apartment when Milton was out for the day.

I was thankful we didn't have any babies together. The mere thought of being stuck with Milton for the rest of my life made me cringe. I would have loved to have seen the look on his face when he returned home to find all of my belongings gone. For months, I heard he was trying to find me. But one day, he just stopped searching. Last I heard he had a set of twins from some new chick.

Leaving Milton was the best decision I'd made in a long time. Leaving him for Winston was a good decision, too. Or so I thought…

~~~

It was May twenty-first, my birthday. Winston called and told me to meet him at his house for a little surprise. I'd been living in my apartment for about two months by that time, and I still hadn't slept with him.

When I walked through the door of his house that night, Winston was standing in the middle of his living room dressed in a tuxedo. He was holding a beautiful, black cocktail dress, with a heart-shaped diamond brooch attached. To complete the outfit, there was a pair of gorgeous, black leather, four-inch stilettos. His smile was so big it looked like he was saying, "Cheese," and waiting for me to snap a photo.

I was pleasantly surprised. Things like this just don't happen to simple girls like me from Brooklyn. And might I add, the man was looking good.

"Hi, my chocolate star," I said. That was my nickname for him.

"Take this and go on into the bedroom and slip it on," he instructed. "We have a schedule to keep."

I reached for the dress, but he snatched it back quickly, then stuck out his face and puckered his lips, gesturing for me to kiss him. I gave him a kiss and dashed in the bedroom, excited to put on my gorgeous new dress. I slipped it over my head and looked in the full-length mirror in the corner of the room. This man had surely accomplished making me feel like Cinderella herself. *Tonight he is definitely going to get some,* I remember thinking, *as long as he keeps up the good work.* I opened his bedroom door and stepped out. When he looked at me, his mouth dropped open. I felt like a big celebrity superstar getting ready to walk the red carpet. I will never forget that feeling. Not only did we look like a high-class couple dressed up like a million bucks, but we
~~~

were driving to our destination in Winston's brand-new BMW. I felt like a princess.

As we were driving over the Brooklyn Bridge, I started to wonder whether or not we were going to Manhattan, or if we were going to leave the state. I didn't know what to expect, but once we crossed the bridge, I figured we'd be celebrating in Manhattan, because we didn't travel in the direction of the Holland Tunnel.

When we reached our destination, I looked straight ahead and saw a huge ship lit up with twinkly white Christmas lights. It was so beautiful, I screamed with joy. He sat there blushing and smiling from ear to ear. He really enjoyed seeing me happy. That impressed me.

As we approached the boat, we were joined by a mature, upper-class crowd of passengers. I could tell just by looking at them that I was surrounded by a lot of money. The ship itself was nothing less than pure elegance. The tables were covered with white linen cloths, and gracefully lined the outside of the dance floor. A pianist was playing a beautiful song I remembered from the seventies. I turned and faced Winston. "Did you do all this for little ol' me?"

"You deserve nothing but the best, Lola," he said. "I am here to satisfy your every need…and want."

We ate from the top-shelf menu—filet mignon and assorted seafood dishes—my favorite. There was a nice bottle of chilled white wine which I had all to myself because Winston doesn't drink. We danced all night until the ship sailed back to the dock four hours later. On the way back to the car, I was thinking about the rest of our night together and what it would be like.

"Would you like to stop back at the house to pick up your overnight bag?" he asked me. "I noticed you had one with you earlier. Oh, and the night isn't over yet. I have one more surprise for you."

Back at his place, I asked, "Do you mind if I change back into my regular clothes?"

"Go right ahead."

Without saying a word, I started to remove my dress right there in front of him. A little tease, a taste of what he'd be getting later. To my surprise, he was more than eager to help me. Before I was even all the way out of my dress, he was on his knees, eating me out. I decided to help him out by lying down on the bed. *Wow, this man sure knows how to chow down.* He started by gently blowing his warm breath over the entire area, then parted the lips of my vagina to focus on my clit. He stroked and sucked at my clit with his tongue. The fast motion of his tongue flicking over my clit made me climax very quickly.

Milton used to put his tongue into my love hole, where there was barely any sensation. I wanted to scream, *That's not my clit!* (For you guys who don't know how to chow down, let me do the honor of informing you that the sensation is in the clitoris, not the vagina.)

I was nervous as hell, but the wine from dinner had given me some courage. After my orgasm, Winston stood up to undress himself. When he took off his final piece of clothing, his boxers, I couldn't believe my eyes. I had never in my thirty-five years seen, or had the pleasure of being introduced to, a penis that big. He was huge. As he climbed on top of me, he stared at me intensely, strong and powerful. It was almost as if he was staring through me, not at me. It intimidated me at first. But I didn't really have time to think about it, because at the same time, he was inserting his penis into my vagina. It was pleasantly painful. His penis was so large, but he was very gentle, and obviously very experienced. He whispered into my ear, "I've waited for this moment for months, and it was worth it."

Aggressively, I flipped us both over so that I was now on top. I wanted to increase my sexual pleasure and let him know I was just as excited to finally be here with him in this way. Straddling him, I reached for his penis and began to direct it inside of me. I felt more pain in this position, but I didn't care. The pain was not like the kind that came from a strike against my head or a fist across my face, but was instead tied to my intense desire for him. I wanted to impress this man as much as he did me.

He placed his hands on my hips then directed my movement to increase his stimulation. Something came over me. I started to pull my hair and scream with excitement. He discovered a spot no one else had ever found. I felt like an instrument he was playing. Our bodies were functioning as one. We made sense. It was time to let go, no holding back. I set my soul free. I was rescued from the sorrows, the suffering, and all the troubles that now felt far behind me. My screams were a clear indication to him that he'd done his job well. Now it was time for him to take over.

Winston flipped me over with the same force I had used on him just moments earlier, only now, I was lying face down beneath him. He reached under my stomach and gently raised the lower half of my body, then entered me from behind. He moved his hand onto my back and began gently stroking me with it, while pulling my hair with his other hand. I could feel his penis throbbing inside of me, and I noticed that the headboard was slamming against wall, rhythmically. I clutched the sheets with my fists and gripped the corner of the pillowcase between my teeth.

It was amazing—a tingling sensation was starting to make its way up from my toes to my head. He had pleasured me so skillfully, and now it was his turn to let go. With one more thrust, he gave into his desire and collapsed on my back, which caused me to drop to my stomach. For a long moment, we said nothing. It was complete silence, save for the sound of our breathing.

After a few minutes of lying there together, enjoying the afterglow of our lovemaking, he spoke. "The last surprise I have for you this evening is a penthouse suite at the Marriott Hotel," he said. "We can finish where we left off." He smiled and winked, then carefully stood up to go to the bathroom. A moment later, I heard the shower. I decided to join him.

When I stepped into the shower, his back was to me. His hands were placed above his head on the shower wall. He was standing still and letting the water run down his back. He was surprised, but happy to see me. I imagined we were together for a purpose, that no one else in the world existed but the two of us. That night, without any doubt, I felt that I'd found a man who was capable of excellence. I felt I had wasted years of my life with Milton and the men who came before him. And all the time, Winston was so close—we worked in the same building!

I truly believed this man would be the beginning of my future. Without a doubt, I became love's prisoner that night.

~~~

KENNEDY

I remember that night. Lola couldn't wait to call me and tell me she was officially in love with Winston. As soon as she was alone, she dialed me up.

"Kennedy, I think I'm in love," she blurted out, without even saying hello. "I had such a blast with him." Then she told me all about the surprise evening… and the good lay at the end of the night. It certainly *sounded* promising.

I didn't actually meet Winston until after we'd moved to Orlando. One day, I decided to surprise Lola at work and bring her lunch, but I wasn't the only one there to surprise Lola that day. Winston was already at the gallery when I arrived, food in hand.

I'd brought Lola some of my shrimp pasta, one of her favorite dishes. Lola made me promise to bring her some whenever I make it, and I had cooked the
~~~

dish for Myles the night before. Thankfully, Lola doesn't mind that I bring leftovers. She surely understands that when Myles comes over, he gets my undivided attention. No one else is ever invited when Myles comes to my place. I know what you're thinking—that I'm a sellout when it comes to my bed-buddy versus my friends. But if you had a man that sexes you as good as Myles does me, you would understand.

On the other hand, when Murphy visits, I invite everyone over. I like Murphy, but he's a square, boring…and so is the sex. On the positive side, Murphy is extremely intelligent, and he's good looking, too. But lately, I'm finding myself more and more drawn to Myles. I'm still careful about letting my guard down with him, though. Especially because of what Winston did to Lola. Winston, unfortunately, confirmed my fears about most men.

For a while, I felt responsible for their break-up because I was the one who persuaded Lola to go for it, to give Winston a shot. I truly thought he was perfect for her. Turns out he was a perfect asshole. He went out of his way to get her to fall for him, knowing that she'd never been truly in love before. She put him on a pedestal, like a daddy's girl does with a father figure. Hell, I still can't believe how that break-up went down. I was so tired of seeing Lola involved in one dead-end, abusive relationship after another. It wasn't always physical abuse—some were verbal, others emotional. But Winston took it to a whole new level. He created a monster after he pulled the heart from Lola's chest. It broke my heart to see my friend in such a bad way. After that, it took me a mighty long time to get on speaking terms with Winston again.

Chapter 6

BROOKE

SHE IS ALMOST A TEENAGER

Bailey will be home from school any moment, and I just realized I forgot to take the chicken out of the freezer this morning. *Damn!* I trip over the belt of my robe and then rush down the spiral staircase to the kitchen to check the refrigerator. *Okay, is there anything, other than chicken, that I can make for dinner?* I always try to have dinner on the table by six o' clock, so Bailey and I can burn off the calories before bedtime. "Tuna—that'll work," I say aloud to myself. I have all the ingredients for tuna casserole. *Perfect.*

My name is Brooke. I'm white and have a daughter whose father is black. Unfortunately, my relationship with Bailey's Dad, Randy, didn't work out. But thankfully, Randy and I have maintained a friendly relationship while raising our daughter. Our pregnancy wasn't planned. It was a total shock to me when I found out. But Randy wasn't surprised. He knew he'd slipped up. He kept it a secret, though, thinking there was no cause for alarm. Think again.

Initially, I was undecided about whether I was ready to become a mom. But Randy insisted that I keep the baby because he doesn't believe in abortion. I didn't expect that to be his reaction. I expected him to be like most other men, who wouldn't give a single thought to actually keeping the baby.

I'm chopping onions at the kitchen counter and thinking about men and their lack of responsibility toward having and raising children. As my angry thoughts accumulate, I begin to chop more forcefully.

Some men expect women to use abortion as birth control. They never consider the seriousness of that procedure—or the emotional upheaval it brings about for most women. Men need to take more responsibility. Women can't control the release of sperm. I mean, we don't hold you down and make you ejaculate; you do so without consent. You may realize afterward that you slipped up, but then it's too late. The damage is done. Consequently, there are just way too many children growing up without fathers. It must be nice to have a choice of whether or not to take part in your kid's life. Mothers don't have that choice. I dare men to take responsibility for their actions. A little control can go a long way, fellas. Or better yet, use protection. Stop making it the woman's responsibility.

Then there are the men who complain about child support. Maybe you don't want to take the time to actually *be* a father, but you still have a responsibility to your child. The least you can do is help pay the bills. Raising a child isn't cheap. Children need clothes and food, and a home. They need healthcare—the good stuff, not the plan that costs a mint and covers next to nothing. Medicaid, for those who can get it, doesn't go very far. And later, what if they want to go to college? They're going to need tuition. The expenses involved in raising a child are endless. And single mothers have it tough. It's a daily struggle just to make ends meet. Is it too much to ask that absent fathers at least pay their fair share?

And what about these sorry-ass men who quit their jobs when they find out the government's going to garnish their wages to obtain child support? Don't even get me started on those good-for-nothing jerks.

Then there are the fathers who promise to personally pay for whatever it is their child needs, but don't actually do it, because they refuse to put *their* money into the hands of the child's mother. They don't trust that *their* money is being spent properly. They assume that the mother will spend the money on herself. Bottom line is, it's just another excuse for deadbeat dads to justify why they shouldn't have to take care of their children.

I can't imagine how cold you'd have to be to refuse to acknowledge your own child or children. It's inhumane and cruel. I truly believe these men will receive some kind of karmic retribution. They will never be right with the world until they've gotten right with God and their own children.

For all the men doing the right thing—keep up the good work. But remember, you don't get a trophy for doing the right thing. Women have been doing it since the beginning of time, and no one has ever decorated us for doing so. Supporting and raising your children is just something you do.

I have to give praise to those men who date single mothers and actually give a damn about her kids. And the ones who continue to support the kids and remain in their lives even after the relationship with the mother has ended? Well, they get a special mention in my book. And...

"Shit!" I yelp. I nearly cut my hand with the knife. I pause for a moment and reach for my phone. I press a button, and my screen lights up. I see my favorite picture of Randy. I want to stare at his beautiful face while I finish preparing the casserole.

Randy is one of the good ones. He's always been there for us, Bailey and me. He has absolutely made a positive impact on our daughter's life. Bailey is twelve and has always been Daddy's little girl. She's one of the few lucky ones. She has a father who genuinely wants to take care of her.

Bailey has been challenging to deal with lately. She's starting to talk back and is quite abrupt and self-centered most of the time. I suppose I'm getting a glimpse of what life is going to be like once she's officially a teenager. I know it's not all that unusual for girls her age to behave this way, but she'd better get a grip—her current behavior is just *not* acceptable.

Bailey is a pretty girl—unique. I suppose it has something to do with her parents being of two different races. If I may say, I have always maintained that black and white people make beautiful babies together.

I often wonder what Bailey's preference will be once she starts dating. Will she be attracted to white boys or black boys? Or both? I don't really care one way or the other, of course, just so long as she brings home somebody her dad and I approve of.

Randy was the first black man I ever dated. I met him at college.

The fried onions smell good. I hear two women passing under my kitchen window, talking about the weather. It's a beautiful, warm day. My phone rings. I can see on the screen that it's Kennedy, but I don't pick up right away because my hands are covered in onions. I try to wipe them off on my apron, but by the time my hands are clean enough to pick up, the phone has stopped ringing. *I'll have to call her back.*

My friends and I have a very strong and special friendship. I think a person is blessed if they happen to find one true friend in this lifetime. I've been lucky enough to find six.

We argue from time to time. But thankfully, healthy debates are the extent of our disagreements. We are seven very different people, with seven distinct personalities. Our circle is strong and positive, and we do not allow an outsider's negativity to influence our group. We just don't care for the drama. We all raise our children together, too—well, those of us with kids, anyway.

Bailey. The girl has been testing my patience lately. She has this whole new attitude—not necessarily a good one. She's become extremely defiant. Frankly, there are times when I am at a complete loss for how to deal with it. I'm trying to understand, trying to remember what it was like to be her age, but I'm worried if she doesn't change her sassy attitude, it will compromise our close relationship. She seems to save this behavior especially for me. She still behaves like a perfect daddy's girl when Randy is around. In his eyes, Bailey is sweet, innocent, and can do no wrong.

I slide the casserole into the oven. There's a knock on the door. I walk out of the kitchen to the front door and open it. It's my neighbor, Mrs. Phillips. "Hi, Brooke," she says as the door swings open.

"Hello, Mrs. Phillips," I say. "What can I do for you?"

"Well, I baked some cookies, and I thought I'd bring some over while they were still hot."

"Thank you," I say warily. "Why don't you come in?" It never fails. Whenever Mrs. Phillips has a juicy piece of gossip, she shows up on my doorstep with freshly baked cookies. Unfortunately, today's gossip is concerning none other than my own aforementioned daughter.

"Brooke, I don't mean to be nosy," Mrs. Phillips lies, "but I wanted to mention that I've seen Bailey going in and out of Cory's house more than a few times now." Mrs. Phillips has this ugly wide gap between her two front teeth. I can't help but stare at it today as she breaks her latest "news" to me. "You know, the young man who lives directly across me."

Oh boy. Here it comes.

"I think Bailey is dating that nineteen-year-old boy, Brooke. And he's bad news." Mrs. Phillips's concern seems genuine, but I can't help but feel she is enjoying this somehow. A gossip is a gossip, I suppose. "I hear he's in a gang," she goes on. "And I'm pretty sure he's selling drugs. In any case, he seems like a real bully."

"Drugs?" I echo. It was difficult to imagine this kind of thing going on in our quiet suburban neighborhood. But I guess it's everywhere; you can't avoid it these days.

"Are you absolutely *sure* it was Bailey?" I ask her.

"Absolutely sure, Brooke."

"I'm not saying I think what you're telling me is untrue," I say. "It just seems so out of character for Bailey."

"I promise you," she says with confidence. "It's Bailey."

"Would you do me a big favor, Mrs. Phillips?" I ask, and Mrs. Phillips nods. "The next time you think you see Bailey walking over to that boy's house, will you let her know you see her, and send her home?" I'm spooked. The idea of my baby spending time with a nineteen-year-old boy—a possible gang member—is frightening. She's only twelve years old, for God's sake. She's barely ready to date at all, much less ready to become entangled with a boy seven years her senior.

I wait—not very patiently—for Bailey to come home from school. I have to confront her with what Mrs. Phillips has brought to my attention. I camp out by the front door. When I hear keys jangling outside, I turn the knob and startle Bailey standing on the doorstep. I don't waste time with a greeting. "Are you dating that nineteen-year-old boy, Cory, from down the street?" I ask. I'm anxious to get to the bottom of this.

"No." She drops her book bag just inside the door.

I decide to believe her. I don't waste any more time on the matter.

We carry on with the rest of the day, following our normal routine, until I happen to notice, while we're sitting at the table together, the diamond toe ring on her foot.

"Bailey, where did you get that ring from?" I ask.

"It's not mine," she says. "I borrowed it from Liz."

"Honey, that diamond looks real."

"I think it *is* real, Mother."

"Let me see it." I reach for her leg and pull it into my lap. "Oh yeah, that's the real thing, all right." I sigh and look at her. "I want you to call Liz and tell her to come and take it back…*right now.*"

"Mom, why do you have to make such a big deal about everything?" Bailey whines, sucking her teeth as she walks away.

"If something were to happen to that ring, if you lost it, I couldn't afford to replace it," I explain. "After you call Liz, I want you to go upstairs and wash your hands for a snack."

After eating her snack of cut-up veggies and fruit and completing her homework, Bailey asks, "Mom, can I go outside till dinner?"

"Yes," I say. "But be back by six o'clock."

Five minutes later, my phone rings. It's my neighbor, Mrs. Phillips. "Brooke, I can see Bailey going into Cory's house again."

Damn! "Thanks, Mrs. Phillips." I leave the house without even bothering to grab my keys or lock the door. If it's her, I want to catch her in the act. I can see Mrs. Phillips standing in her front yard, nosy as usual. I knock on the door of Cory's house. An attractive woman answers the door, wearing a multicolored scarf tied around her head. She looks too young to have a nineteen-year-old son. Assuming she's not his mother, I ask, "Is Cory's mom here?"

"I'm Cory's mom," the woman says.

"Oh. I'm sorry to bother you, but I think my daughter might be here."

"Who is your daughter?"

"Bailey."

The woman jerks her head back as if she's having a spasm. It's the same reaction I get from a lot of people when I tell them that Bailey is my daughter, since our complexions are so different. It's hard to believe that in this day and age, there are still so many people who are startled by those of mixed race.

The woman says, "Yes, she's here."

"Do you have a daughter about her age?" I ask.

"No," she says, sounding confused, "she comes here to see my son."

"Really," I say. "And how old is your son?"

"He's nineteen. Why?"

"Well, my little girl is only twelve."

From the disturbed look on her face, I can tell she had no idea. "You've got to be kidding me. Bailey told me she was sixteen. I did think she looked a little young, so I asked her how old she was. I didn't want to think she was lying to me, but I went so far as to question my son about it, too. He told me Bailey was sixteen. So I dropped it. Damn! I should have known better."

Before I can reply, she stomps away from the doorway and returns moments later with Bailey in tow. I grab my daughter by the elbow. "Go home!" I command. "I'll deal with you in a minute."

"Get off me!" Bailey yells. "You're so embarrassing!" Then she storms off toward our house.

I turn to Cory's mom. "Can you please see to it that my daughter is no longer allowed in your home? And can you please talk to your son about not seeing Bailey again?" Before she can answer me, I'm distracted by the sound of the front blinds opening. I can see someone peeking through them. "Is that your son?"

"Yes," she confirms.

I gesture for him to come to the door. I want to speak with him. When he arrives, he looks sheepish. "Hi, I'm Bailey's mom," I say. He looks older than nineteen. He's cute. But he looks like a hoodlum with his jeans hanging off his butt. He's tall, slim, and black for sure. "I wanted to tell you myself that Bailey is only twelve," I explain. "Please stay away from my daughter." I say it as nicely as I can manage.

"She told me she was sixteen," he says, brushing his nose with the back of his hand.

"I believe you," I say. "That's something girls tend to lie about. But I'm letting you know the truth so there won't be any further confusion. Please do not pursue her. I wouldn't want to have to get her father involved."

"I promise I'll stop seeing her," he says, nervously stroking his shaved head.

"That won't be necessary," his mother chimes in. "I give you my word. Cory will stay away."

"Thank you," I say kindly. "Now, if you'll excuse me, I have to go home and deal with my daughter."

Mrs. Phillips is still standing outside when I pass by on the way back to my house. I mouth the words, *Thank you*, to her. She smiles back sympathetically.

When I walk into the house, Bailey is slumped at the kitchen table with tears in her eyes. "Mom, why did you embarrass me like that?" she asks with attitude.

"Who are you?" I ask. "Where is my little girl? Because this person sitting in front of me is a stranger. What the hell were you thinking? What would prompt you to visit a boy at his home? A nineteen-year-old boy, at that!"

"I'm sorry, Mom," she cries. "It's just that he shows me so much attention. He's always complimenting me. He makes me feel pretty."

"Are you having sex, Bailey?" I ask sternly.

"No, Mom!" she says, her eyes wide with surprise.

"You'd better promise me you won't see him again, young lady, or I'll be forced to tell your father." She has a defiant look on her face as she nods her head. I repeat, "Promise me. Promise me, and I will give you the benefit of the doubt till you make me believe otherwise. Do not disappoint me.

"And for your information, men will always make you feel good about yourself till they sense you're comfortable enough for them to make a move," I explain. "Don't be gullible and believe everything a man tells you." And so, Bailey and I begin a deep discussion about the birds and the bees.

In the middle of our conversation on life and love, I hear a key in the door. I'm not expecting Randy this evening, but he's the only one with keys to the house. He usually gives us a courtesy call before stopping by, so I'm a little surprised. We haven't been considered a couple for years, but he never returned the keys to the house after we broke up, and I never asked for them back. It hasn't been an issue up to this point because I'm not dating right now.

I make a mental note that if I should ever start seeing someone, I'll have to change the locks. I want to avoid having to ask Randy for the keys back—just too awkward.

Randy strides into the house, and right away, he notices I'm uneasy. "What's going on?" he asks.

"Nothing. We're just having a little girl talk," I say. "You startled us. I didn't know you were coming over. Is everything okay?"

"Yeah, everything's okay," he says. "I was just in the neighborhood, thought I'd stop in and see my family." My heart melts when I hear him include me in his family, and I feel a pang of regret. I wish things had worked out between us. "Do you ladies have any plans this evening?" he asks.

"Not really," I say. "Bailey and I were just about to eat. Care to join us?" Even if I did have plans tonight, I would have said I didn't.

"No thanks. I already ate. But I have some movies in the car. I was thinking I could run to the market and pick up some microwave popcorn. What do you two girls say to a little movie night?" Sunday movie nights were a tradition when we were still living together.

I want to tell him what happened today. It feels like lying if I don't let him in on it. But I don't want to make a bad situation worse. One thing I've noticed about black fathers is that they are extremely protective of their daughters. They don't deal very well with their little girls growing into young ladies. In my experience, I've found that white men have a somewhat different take. They can be just as protective of their "little girls," but by and large, they're more accepting of the changes that take place when those girls begin growing into women.

Randy and I are still sexually involved with each other. Somehow we never got around to eliminating that part of our relationship. I'm sure it's one of the reasons he feels he can just show up here unannounced. And I can't exactly say that I'm bothered by either of those things.

Randy is a loving and beautiful man. I feel lucky to have him in my life. He is a majestic person who is capable of heroic deeds. Even though we're not together anymore, Randy is still a part of my soul. The connection we share is what most marriages are lacking. Our desire for each other is hard to ignore. Something happens when Randy and I make love. Our bond is not just sexual, but spiritual.

Given all that, it's probably easy to understand why I'm not involved with any other men. When we were together, we were both extremely jealous. That definitely played a big part in our breakup. Randy and I just can't seem to pull off a committed romantic relationship, so we settle for being lovers—and friends. But truth be told, I would marry Randy in a New York minute if he asked.

Randy returns from the supermarket, throws a bag of popcorn into the microwave, and the three of us sit down on the leather couch in the family room. We certainly *act* like a family. We watch *Taken* with Liam Neeson, and it turns out to be a really good movie. I make a mental note to watch it with the girls sometime.

"Well, I'm tired," Bailey announces as the credits roll. She stands up from the couch and stretches. "I'm going to bed. Goodnight."

"Goodnight, sweetie," Randy says. "Hey, aren't you going to give me and your mom a kiss?"

Bailey smiles, leans over, and gives each of us a little peck on the cheek. Then she heads to her room for the night.

Randy and I decide to watch another movie, *A Family That Preys* with Tyler Perry. I like Tyler Perry, and can see from this film he's growing as an actor. Bailey and I went to see this movie when it first hit the theaters, but I don't mind watching it again.

I wonder how long it will take Randy to start putting his hands all over me. I'm not really in the mood right now, given all that took place earlier. But if he tries, I'll give in like I always do. I've tried saying no to him, but Randy has a spell on me. It doesn't hurt that he satisfies me in every sense of the word.

I'm content with what Randy and I have. The idea of starting a relationship with someone new feels like way too much work. New relationships are tiring, what with all the getting to know someone new, their habits, and their quirks. And it's daunting to think I can't really be myself around that person until the new becomes old. It seems like I've been with Randy forever, even though we're not really together anymore. But somehow, it's enough. I'm comfortable being single. I don't need a constant romantic partner to validate me.

It's been nearly an hour since Bailey went up to her room, and Randy has yet to make a move. I'm surprised...and suspicious. I don't feel like initiating myself, but I realize that his lack of initiation has me feeling insecure. When a man isn't following his usual routine, it's usually cause for concern. *He could at least make me feel wanted.* It would break my heart if Randy ever stopped loving me. I glance over at him. The movie is about to start. He notices that I'm checking him out, and he draws me in close to his chest and whispers, "Our little girl is growing up."

At some point, we drift off. We miss the end of the movie.

Chapter 7

KENNEDY

GOSSIP

I'm sitting on the toilet lid, waiting for the bath to fill, when my phone rings. It's Brooke. "Hey, Kennedy," she says. "Can I talk to you? I have some real concerns."

"Concerns?" I repeat. "About what?"

"Well, Randy didn't try to have sex with me last night," she explains.

"Brooke, your relationship with Randy is much deeper than sex. You guys just haven't figured that out yet."

"You don't think there might be someone else?"

"I seriously doubt this has anything to do with Randy seeing another woman," I assure her. "Has it occurred to you that maybe he just wanted to come over and enjoy a nice evening with his family?" I sigh. "I'd be willing to bet that last night was more important to him than you think. Your relationship with Randy is more than just skin deep, Brooke. Neither of you will admit it, but you have the makings of a family. Maybe it's time to stop over-thinking it and just let it happen."

"Oh, I hope you're right," she say, feeling somewhat relieved. "I would die without Randy."

"I assure you, I'm right," I say confidently.

"Has anyone told you they love and care about you today? Well, I do."

"I love you too, Brooke."

Just as I hang up the phone, Diamond calls. "Hey, girlfriend, I'm seeing this new guy, Rob." As usual, she doesn't bother with a proper greeting, just starts right in.

"Girl, have you ever been faithful to Victor?" I ask.

"Like you're one to talk, Kennedy," she snaps. "Besides, Victor left me."

"First of all, we ain't talking about me," I say. "We're talking about you. Second, I'm not married—and you are."

"Married, but separated."

We talk for a while. She tells me a disturbing tale of how, a few months back, Quincy tricked her into smoking crack. She said he put it into a cigarette and she didn't notice because she was already tipsy from having had drinks earlier that day. I don't know if I believe her, but I make her promise she won't try it again.

"I'm not going to lie to you, Kennedy," she confesses. "I smoked it again…a few times. The high was amazing. But after a few months, I quit—cold turkey."

"Good."

"I wish you were here with us, Diamond," I tell her.

"I wish I was there, too. I miss you all."

"Are you sure you miss *all* of us, Diamond?"

"Of course I miss *all* of you," she snaps, suddenly defensive. "Why would you ask that?"

"Oh, I don't know—maybe because you always go in on Portia and her marriage."

"I only do that because I love her."

"Whatever." Talking with Diamond can be so exhausting. "I'll talk to you later. I'm about to get into the bath."

"Okay, Kennedy, talk to you later."

Diamond is not exactly inside our friendship circle. One of the obvious reasons for that, of course, is we live in Florida, and she lives in New York. Diamond tells us all the time, "You guys think you're better than me." But we don't actually think that. If anything, it's Diamond who thinks *she's* better than *us*.

But thinking and being are two different things. The fact is, Diamond is not a leader—she's a follower. That's why she gets herself into one mess after another. We all love her dearly, but she has to learn how to love herself. Victor is a good guy, but Diamond doesn't appreciate him. I'm afraid she won't get that until it's too damned late. Isn't that the way it always works? We can't realize a good thing till it's gone.

After my bath, Tasha calls and says she's coming over. She wants to celebrate her new job as a corrections officer. A short while later, the doorbell rings. "Wow, you got here quick," I say, smiling. She looks so happy.

"You know it! I need a celebration drink, girl."

"So...when do you start?"

"Next week—Tuesday. I'm so excited. I tell you, it's not *what* you know, it's *who* you know. If it wasn't for my aunt being the warden and pushing along my paperwork, I'd still be selling homes."

"But you made good money selling homes."

"I did, but the market's taken a dive. There's just no way to make a living at it right now. Thank God I've got the rentals in New York. Without them, I wouldn't be able to pay my bills."

"Hey, I love the bronze color in your hair," I say. "It matches your complexion perfectly."

"Thanks, I was ready for a new look. Geez, it's hot in here. Is the air conditioner even on?"

"You don't hear the motor humming?"

Tasha pauses. "Oh, now I hear it. Well, turn that thing up!" she jokes. "So, I think I'm going to ask Dylan to extract my tooth," she announces. "I just can't stand having this gold in my mouth anymore. He says he can replace it with a permanent fake tooth and that it'll look real." She gives me a wicked grin. "And girl, I got to find me a man. I haven't had sex in *eight years*." Tasha is clearly on the upswing.

"You're good, girl," I tell her. "I could *never* go that long." We laugh.

"I'm not going to have sex with just anyone, though—I can't totally cave just because I'm having a horny spell. I think what I'm saying is that I want more. I'm ready to open my mind, body, and soul. I want a man who will make love to me while my favorite music is playing. That's the key to lovemaking for me. Music brings out my passion.

"And you know he'll have to embrace the foreplay, girl. No point in having sex without that—unless you're into forgettable sex. I want him to leave an impression on me. I want to go to work the day after having great sex with my good man, and walk around with a permanent smile all day long. I imagine myself sitting in a meeting and not paying attention because I can't stop thinking about the night before. And I don't want just good sex. I want a real and loving relationship—maybe even one that leads to marriage."

"Well, we'd better get on finding you that man, child," I say, "before you hit the nine year mark!" We laugh hysterically. "But seriously, I'm happy for you, girl."

"Hey, I'd better sit at the piano," she says. "I don't want the dye from my jeans to rub off on your white couch."

"Better yet, let's sit at the bar together. You did want a drink, right?"

"Hell, yeah!" she shouts. "That's what I came here for."

We sit down, and I pour us each a drink.

"So, I gotta tell you," Tasha begins, "when we were at Portia's house the other night, I was coming out of the upstairs bathroom when I overheard Dylan talking on the phone with one of his buddies. They were talking about women and cheating, and I admit, Kennedy, I stood there eavesdropping in the hall for a good ten minutes. I just couldn't help myself." She giggles.

"Well, what did they say?"

"Well, first of all, when it comes to gossip, men are just as bad as women!" Tasha says. "But mostly, Dylan was praising his relationship with Portia. He was very clear with them that he's never cheated on her."

"Yeah, Portia really lucked up with Dylan," I say.

"He made me so proud, Kennedy. I actually got teary listening to him confess his love to his friend without any shame whatsoever."

"You actually cried, Tasha? Why?"

"Tears of joy, Kennedy. I think I really needed to hear something like that from a man. And I must say, it's given me some real hope. Dylan is every woman's dream, for sure. I can't help but ask myself why I keep choosing men from my nightmares."

"Trust me, Tasha," I assure her. "You'll find the man of your dreams."

"Men and their cheating, Kennedy." Tasha sighs. "It's so hard to trust any of them."

"Yeah, and after what happened to Lola, it's really hard to have any faith in men anymore. I mean, I really liked Winston. We all thought he was great. None of us saw that coming. But Dylan? Dylan gives us all hope. The good ones are out there, Tasha. It's finding them that's the challenge."

"What is it with most men?" Tasha says. "Why are they so hell-bent on ruining perfectly good relationships?"

"Well, I've had conversations about that with men over the years, and I tell you, they were mighty enlightening—and not always in a good way. The excuses men use for cheating are endless. The one that really gets me is the whole competitive bullshit. Men sleeping with whomever, whenever, just so they can say they've sexed more women than their friends. Good fucking grief.

"Then there are the ones who say they're justified because their woman isn't giving it up at home. It doesn't even occur to them that if they were actually satisfying their women, maybe those women would actually want to have sex with them on a regular basis. It's never their fault. Oh, no!" I roll my eyes. "I say that sex takes *two* people. And if a man isn't getting any from his woman, there's probably a good reason. And when a guy says cheating is okay because sex with his girlfriend or wife is boring, do they ever stop to think that maybe they could do something about that…other than have sex with someone else?" I roll my eyes again. "Idiots."

"But then, sometimes women aren't totally blameless, you know. If you stay with a guy who repeatedly cheats on you, you're basically giving him the green light. You're not holding yourself to a higher standard, so why should he?

"And if we're being honest, women cheat, too. Not too many men can resist using *that* as an excuse to cheat right back. It's not very mature, but at least in that particular case, I can see the justification."

I'm out of breath when I finally take a break from my diatribe and take a sip from my glass. I realize that I have some mighty strong opinions about men who cheat. I can't help but wonder if it's the *real* reason I don't "need" men.

Tasha sighs and takes a big swig of her drink. "I'm starting to think the only men that don't cheat are the ones that can't."

"What do you mean, 'can't'?" I ask, intrigued.

"Because they too damn ugly to cheat!" Tasha and I bust up, and share a cleansing fit of laughter. "The problem with men," Tasha says, "is that men expect a perfect woman and a perfect relationship, but guess what? No one is perfect. Relationships are all about ups and downs. That's what helps them grow into something truly great. You have to take the good with the bad."

"Besides, perfect is boring," I add. "Sad part is, some women carry the pain of being cheated on through their whole life, and end up not being able to trust another man as long as they live. Then there are the ones who don't make it at all…end up offin' themselves to escape the pain permanently. And then…there's the women who decide maybe it's better—and safer—just to date other women. We just shouldn't have to deal with this kind of bullshit, Tasha."

"I hear you, girlfriend. I guess all this shit is exactly why Dylan talking about his love for Portia touched me so much. Speaking of committed men, what's up with Murphy, Kennedy?" Tasha asks.

"Girl, I'm bored with Murphy," I announce. "I'm about to kick him to the curb."

"You wasn't bored with him before you started spending time with Myles," she chides. "Myles is turning you out, girl."

"Yes, he put it on me," I confess. We talk, laugh, and enjoy our drinks until Tasha leaves around midnight.

~~~

I haven't seen Tasha in two weeks because of her new job. We had a short phone conversation a few days ago. She told me she already has her eye on one of the other officers, and that most of the women who work there have a crush on him, too. Seems to me Tasha's back in the game.

I'm standing in my closet looking into my mirrored wall. I'm trying to find an outfit to wear. I'm meeting Payton for dinner tonight because she's having an identity crisis.

I dropped my keys on the steps leading up to the front door on my way in last night. I was tired from a long day at work. I didn't even bother to turn on the lights when I walked in—just went straight to bed. I'm working with a difficult client right now. She's a spoiled rich bitch who likes to spend her husband's money. But what can I do? It's my job to please my clients and build my clientele—even when some of those clients become a huge pain in my ass.

I had my crew repaint and change out the flooring in this lady's kitchen and dining room three different times because she wasn't happy with her own choices.

"Dammit! I forgot my CDs," I say out loud. I'm on the way down to my car to go and meet Payton. I really want to listen to Mary J. Blige on the drive, so I run back up to the condo and grab my CDs.

I find street parking on the same block of the restaurant where I'm meeting Payton. It's hot as hell today, and I can see Payton sitting in the restaurant patio area at a table for two. "How are you, girl?" I ask as I approach her. Payton stands up and greets me with a hug. She looks so pretty wearing her short pink halter dress. Her hair is slicked back behind her ears, a perfect style for this damned humidity.

"Kennedy, you look beautiful," she says.
~~~

"Thanks, sweetie." I'm wearing my strapless blue denim dress and my red bottom pumps. "You're looking great yourself, girl. So what's going on?"

"Well, first I want you to know that I can only talk about this with you. I don't want the other girls getting weirded out."

"You know you can talk to me about anything," I assure her. "Your secrets are always safe with me, girl. Now tell me what's on your mind."

"Okay," Payton says. "Where to start?" She sighs. "Well, last week I went to visit Isabel in Dallas because her man got arrested. You know Isabel, my ex-roommate?"

"Yes, I remember."

"Well, we had sex," Payton announces.

I nearly fell off my chair. "*What?*"

"Kennedy, please hear me out," she says worriedly. "Don't judge me yet."

"I'm not judging you, I swear." I laugh nervously. "I just wasn't expecting you to say that."

"Okay, it started when I was comforting her," Payton begins. "She put her head in my lap as she wept. I started stroking her hair, just to comfort her, you know? Then she lifted her head up and started kissing me, and before I even realized what was happening, I was kissing her back. I don't know why...I guess I sort of liked it. Sort of *really* liked it." Payton pauses when the waitress comes over to take our order. "Can you just bring us an order of Buffalo wings and two glasses of Merlot?"

After the waitress leaves our table to put in our order, Payton continues her story. "There was just something about her touch. It was stimulating in a whole new way—so different from a man. Honestly, Kennedy, this is a feeling I'd like to experience again."

"I can imagine," I say, still a little stunned by Payton's revelation.

"The tension was unbelievable. But when she realized I was into it, the kiss became more passionate, and we both relaxed. It felt too good to be true. I feel like I've been missing out on a lot all these years. I've never felt this kind of a connection with a man. The way she touched me was...I can't even describe it. Do you think because she *is* a woman, she knows better how to *please* a woman?"

"I don't know." I shrug. "Finish the story." I'm extremely intrigued by Payton's sexy tale.

"She seemed to know exactly what I crave," Payton says. "With a man, I always have to direct. But Isabel climbed on top of me and knew exactly what to do. She kissed every inch of my upper body and sucked on my breasts so softly—the sensation was almost more than I could stand."

"Damn, Payton," I say. "Forgive me, but I'm sort of in shock here. This was the last thing I expected to hear. And I am *not* judging you, by the way."

"Kennedy, please don't make me regret telling you," she pleads. "It took a lot for me to confide in someone."

"No, no, no, no! Go on—I won't interrupt again. I promise."

"Okay, so every time she touched me with her lips, I got chills. My vagina was so engorged...*and hot!* Like it was on fire. I was tingling all over from beginning to end—almost like a stinging sensation.

"Even with all of that going on, I kept as quiet as I could. I thought by doing that, I could somehow deny what was happening. But the feeling was so perfect, it was driving me crazy. The girl turned me out. In my mind, this was morally wrong. It went against all my beliefs. But it didn't discourage me from enjoying it." Payton quiets again when the waitress brings us our food and drinks.

"You smell good," I say to the waitress. "What are you wearing?"

"Oh, thanks," she says and smiles. "It's called Cool Waters." But I'm really just being nice. I am so caught up in Payton's story I can't wait for the waitress to walk away again. When she's gone, I say excitedly, "Okay, go ahead."

"Well, here's the thing: Isabel reached a place inside of me that no man has ever been able to get to."

"Oh my God!" I exclaim. "Then what?"

"When she touched my clit with her tongue," Tasha whispers, "I was transported. It was a whole other world, girl!" Tasha's smile fades. "But when it came time for me to give back, I was really nervous. I kissed her mouth and worked my tongue down her entire body. But when I finally got to her pouring wet stream of love, something came over me."

"What...what came over you?" I'm literally sitting on the edge of my seat.

"Well, my face was right there. But I couldn't bring myself to return the favor. I was turned off instantly—like a switch had been flipped. When I looked up at her, her eyes were closed, her body yearning and waiting, ready for my touch. But I hesitated so long that she opened her eyes and looked down at me to see what the holdup was. I said, 'I can't do this.' She got upset, and I felt bad. But I just couldn't make myself do it."

"I would have been upset, too," I say. "I'm sure she was turned on by you responding to her, because you're damned well turning *me* on just by telling the story. And I'm not even into women!" I giggle.

"Do you think I'm gay?" Payton asks me. I can see the worry in her eyes.

"It's possible, I guess. But I don't think it's all that strange to be turned on by a woman's body—we *are* beautiful creatures."

"Maybe I'm bisexual," she wonders.

"Maybe, but I don't think so. I think you had a really powerful sexual experience with someone who happens to be a woman, but it doesn't necessarily mean that you're gay. Or bi."

"Can I confess something?" Payton doesn't wait for an answer. "When I watch porn, I'm more turned on by the girl-on-girl scenes."

"That's probably just because the men in porn movies are so careless! They're rough and self-centered—it's all about the man's cum shot. Where's the emotion? Ever notice that the woman's orgasm is either downplayed or totally ignored in the man-woman scenes? It's a total turn-off. On the other hand, the women are tender with each other. They actually spend time pleasuring each other and delight in each other's orgasms.

"Hallelujah, I'm not gay!" Payton exclaims. "I'm just human. My body's just craving the attention I can't get from a man." She seems relieved. "But it *was* an experience I will never forget." Payton smiles mischievously, then sighs. "I sure hope I can find a man who can give me that same experience."

The waitress approaches the table and asks if we need anything else.

"Actually, yes," I say. "Would it be possible for us to switch to a table inside, where it's cooler?"

"Sure, follow me," the waitress says, motioning with her hand. We collect our belongings and follow her through the door of the restaurant. On our way to our new table, Payton turns to me and says, "I'm glad we had this talk. I feel so much better."

I smile back at her and think, *She is so gay.*

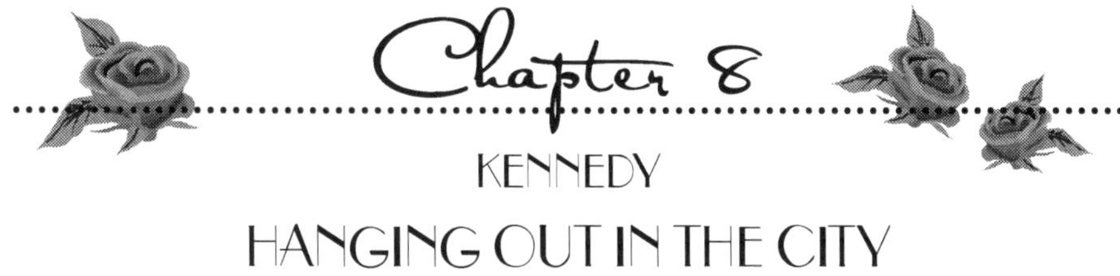

Chapter 8

KENNEDY

HANGING OUT IN THE CITY

My cell phone has been ringing off the hook all day. Today is the day we're all flying to New York to see Infinity open for Ne-yo, Avant, 112, and Floetry on Saturday night. My phone rings again. "Kennedy here," I answer.

A chorus of familiar voices screams into my ear, "Has anyone told you they love and care about you today? Well, we do!" This is something we say to each other a lot—our tag line, I guess you could say. The girls arranged for this little conference call so we can go over our schedule once we reach New York. Tonight and Friday, we're planning to meet up with Renee and Diamond. They're taking us to some lounge in Brooklyn they've been frequenting lately.

"Girls!" Tasha shouts over the rest. "We'll be staying in one of my houses in Queens." Tasha always arranges to use one of her rentals when we visit our old town.

One of her private homes has two separate apartments, one of which she always keeps vacant for just these kinds of occasions.

Lola pipes up and asks, "What's up with the rental cars?"

Portia chimes in: "I reserved three rentals for us just in case we have to go our separate ways for whatever reason." After a fifteen-minute conversation about our carefully planned schedule for our mini-vacation, we agree to meet at the airport at 2:30 this afternoon. Our flight is taking off at 3:35.

We land at JFK a little before seven o'clock that evening. We pick up our rental cars and head to Tasha's to prepare for our night out with the other girls. The rental cars turn out to be a smart decision, because there are ten more girls waiting for us at Diamond's house—a total of sixteen girls headed out for a night on the town.

The Chance 11 bar/lounge is on Fulton Avenue in Brooklyn. The ambiance is very elegant and classy. I'm very impressed with the introduction of the entrance. The beautiful bright colors on the walls compliments the white table booths against the walls. There is a comfortable number of people here; it's poppin', but not too crowded. Just the way I like it. We all love to dance, so the more room on the dance floor, the better. The bar looks like it can hold at least a hundred twenty people. I'd guess there are about seventy people here right now.

There are three women bouncers at the door which, in my opinion, is a little unusual. You don't see women working a job like that very often. It's nice to see, but I honestly don't feel all that secure. They're large women though, so maybe their size alone is intimidating enough to prevent anyone from getting out of hand. Security searches us on the way in, and once through that, we head to the bar and order drinks. I love the lighting included in the bar backround.

We drink, laugh, and have a great time with all our old friends whom we haven't seen in months. For a moment, it feels as if we've gone back in time, as if the six of us never moved to Florida. It felt just like old times.

"So, Diamond, don't go crazy on the drinking," Lola warns. "You always seem to be able to put away a lot more liquor than the rest of us."

"I'm gonna be cool," she responds. "I want to remember this night tomorrow."

"Yeah, let's keep that selective memory of yours in check, shall we?"

Lola adds, only half-joking.

"Yeah, and don't forget, she's also the *courage* drinker," Payton says, pushing a lock of hair away from her left eye. When Diamond drinks, she has a habit of doing things she wouldn't normally do when she's sober. "I don't feel like baby-sitting your ass tonight. And for God's sake, don't even think about getting in Portia's face just because you've had a few drinks."

"Oh please!" Portia rolls her eyes. "Diamond says what she wants to me when she's sober."

"Girl, just don't overwhelm us tonight," I say. "We want to have a good time." They say an intoxicated person speaks a sober mind. That's Diamond.

"Kennedy," Portia whispers into my ear, "if Diamond gets confrontational, or brings up something that may or may not have happened months ago—I'm leaving. I don't care how big or petty it is. I'm out of here."

"If she so much as tries that shit," I say, "I'm leaving, too." I decide that it might be a good idea to have a private chat with Diamond—tell her she has to chill out tonight. I slide off my stool and walk over to her. "Diamond, I'm serious," I say quietly into her ear, "don't start no shit tonight. We want to enjoy ourselves, okay?"

"What is this, mess with Diamond night?" she barks. "I said I'm *cool.*"

"Well, I know how you get," I remind her. "You're always bringing up shit that happened years ago. And most of it only happened in your mind." I'm still trying to keep our conversation discreet, but she isn't making it easy.

Diamond scoffs. "I can see the girls are sending you to rescue them again," she says with a devilish smirk on her face.

Brooke is staring at us—with blue eyes tonight. She can plainly see what's going on. "All Kennedy is saying is, just don't go blowing things outrageously out of proportion, Diamond—just because of your insecurities."

The relationship we share with Diamond is complex. She's very competitive with us at times, but other times, she can be the sweetest person in the world, which is why we remain friends with her. She makes it awfully difficult to be her friend, though. There is just no pleasing her. When we party, one of us always has hold onto her valuables. She loses or misplaces her things every single time we go out.

"Diamond, give me your pocketbook and your coat," I say. "There's no coat check." I sit down at the bar, pull up the empty seat next to me, and lay our coats over it. "Bartender, can we get a round of your best Merlot? You can just put it on my card." I hand him my Visa.

After a second round of drinks, we decide to hit the dance floor. They're playing a song we all like, "Love Is the Message."

"This record will never go out of style!" Lola shouts. "MFSB will be making money off this tune forever."

"We always end up in a huddle on the dance floor whenever we go out," Payton observes, and we all laugh.

The guys in the club are trying to move their way into our girl-crowd. One guy approaches me and says, "All eyes are on y'all this evening." He smiles. "Can I buy you a drink?" he asks, with his ugly, church-looking, big-lips.

"No, that's okay, but thanks anyway," I say. I rarely let guys buy me drinks. If I accept, they always feel like they own me for the night.

Myles always tells me he loves to watch me dance. It turns him on. Whenever we go out dancing together, he points out some guy in the club he thinks is a good dancer and then pushes me to go dance with him—tells me to go tear him up. Myles ain't crazy; he only does it during fast songs, never the slow ones. I wish he was here. There is not one man in this club tonight as fine as *my* man. "Where are all the good-looking men tonight?" I shout to my girls over the loud music.

"Yeah," Sky agrees, "what's up with that? Every man here is either old, fat, or dressed all corny."

"Normally, there are good looking guys here, this is just an off night," Diamond boast.

"Well, if this is all we have to choose from here, I'm gonna be picking my man up from the high school at three o'clock," Brooke jokes.

"It's times like this when I really appreciate Myles," I say.

"I like this little place," Payton offers, shrugging. "I'm really enjoying myself. The guys are looking at us like they just won the lotto."

"That's because we're hot, ladies!" Tasha proclaims, and then goes back to singing to the record, *"I wanna thank you, heavenly Father..."*

We do tend to draw attention to ourselves when we go out together. I'm sure people notice the different ethnic backgrounds of the girls in our group. I'm what they call a mutt. My mother is Asian—petite and delicate. My dad is black. I have a lot of my mom's features, but I'm darker skinned than most Asians. Speaking of Asians, I smell Chinese food.

"Diamond!" I yell across the dance floor. "They serve food here?"

"Yeah, girl!" she yells back. "You don't see that big-ass sign over there that reads, 'Kitchen?'" She gestures to a sign above the door to the right of the bar.

"Let's get a menu!" I say.

Sky interrupts, "I don't want to eat here!"

"The food here is really good," Diamond says.

"I want a White Castle burger. This is the only time we can get them—when we're here in New York," Sky says.

"Oh yeah," I agree, "that's right." We decide to wait and eat later.

An hour later, we're tired and getting ready to call it a night. We're all together, except one—Diamond. No one seems to know where she is. "Where the hell is Diamond?" Lola asks angrily, and then sighs. "Here we go..."

"Lola, don't get upset yet. Let's just wait till they clear everyone out," I suggest. We stand on the dance floor, looking around the club, waiting. "I know she has to be in here somewhere. I have her coat and her pocketbook." I open her pocketbook and see her money and belongings inside.

The club clears out, but no Diamond. We decide to go outside to see if she's out there waiting for us. We lean against a parked car in front of the entrance and watch the last of the crowd file out the door. I want to make sure I don't miss her. As the crowd clears away from the entrance, I notice a guy standing about twenty feet from us, and apparently he's been listening to our conversation. He comes over and asks, "Are you guys looking for the dark-skinned girl with the red shirt and the big butt?"

"Yes," Tasha and I chorus together.

"Well, last time I seen her, she was on the dance floor over by the kitchen suckin' somebody off."

I'm pissed by what he's insinuating. "Let me stop you dead in your tracks. You guys are always saying shit to belittle women. We don't get down like that."

"Okay, I didn't actually *see* his penis in her mouth. But she was on her knees, directly in front of the guy."

I blew him off with a wave of my hand—fuck his old ass and his nasty potbelly. I walk over to security and ask, "Can we check the restrooms to see if our friend is in there?

"Just you," one of them answers. I run back into the club and check both the men's and the women's restrooms, to no avail. She's not there.

"Did she leave?" Brooke asks.

I'm at a loss. "Where would she go? I have her coat, her pocketbook, her money. And it's freezing out here. It ain't summertime." Every time I let my guard down when hanging out with Diamond, something like this happens. I start dialing her cell phone but quickly realize it's with me, in her pocketbook. *Damn!* The girls are calling her home number. No answer. I look at my watch—almost five o'clock in the morning. We have no choice but to go to the police station and fill out a missing persons report.

We pile into the cars. I'm really worried. You just never know with Diamond. She could be anywhere, and more than likely, wherever she is, she's in some kind of trouble. "If anything happens to her, I will never forgive myself. What would I tell her kids?"

"Diamond is a grown-ass woman, Kennedy," Lola reminds me.

"I know, but I should have kept my eye on her. I know how she gets when she's under the influence."

"This is exactly why I don't like going out with her," Payton complains. "We always have to be on guard. We can never just relax and have a good time."

The other girls who joined us tonight decide to go home. They don't seem very concerned. "We're used to this shit when it comes to Diamond," one of them says. "See y'all later."

We drive away from the bar and reach the precinct a few minutes later. We walk directly to the front desk and I say to the officer on duty, "I'd like to fill out a missing persons report."

"When was the last time this person was seen?" he asks.

"A few hours ago," I answer.

"I'm assuming this person is female," he says. "How old is she?"

"She's forty."

The officer chuckles and I'm instantly annoyed. "What you will have to do first is check her residence, make sure she's not there."

"Is that all you can do for us?" Lola asks.

"Is she mentally disabled in some way? Does she have a physical illness?"

"No," Lola and I say together.

"Well then, technically, she's not considered a missing person. Emergency searches only apply to children and the mentally and physically disabled. Is it unusual for your friend to disappear like this?"

"Well, I guess it's not all that unusual," I concede, "but it is unusual that she would leave without her belongings, and without telling us. I can't just sit around and do nothing." I'm starting to feel desperate. "I can help with the search, anything but wait...I'm just so scared that something bad has happened to her. It's cold outside, and I have her coat," I say frantically. "And she has no money, because *I* have her pocketbook!"

"Here is what I can do…as a favor," he relents. "I'll alert one of the patrol cars in the area to be on the lookout. Can you give me a description of your friend? What did she have on?"

"A red, long-sleeved sweater," Portia offers.

"And blue jeans…with black boots," I add.

"Oh! I have a picture of her in my wallet," Portia says. She shows the officer the picture, the one we all had taken together the last time we were here in New York.

"Does she have a cell phone?"

"Yes, but I have it." I sigh.

He jots down all of Diamond's information on a piece of paper. I offer my card to the officer. "Here's my name and number. Will you call me if you see or hear anything?"

"Sure," the officer answers, and smiles sympathetically.

"Thank you so much. We really appreciate it." As we're leaving the station I say, "Okay girls, let's drop by Diamond's house and see if she's gone home." We pull up in front of Diamond's place about ten minutes later. I get out of the car and ring the bell for her third floor apartment. No answer.

"Check the door, see if it's open," Lola screams from the car. I try the door, but it's locked. Her parents live on the first floor, but they're probably asleep. I give up and head back to the car. The entire ride back to Tasha's house, we repeatedly call Diamond's home phone but she never picks up.

"You know, I'll bet Diamond is just fine," Sky says. "This is just another one of her drunken escapades."

I wake at eleven o'clock the next morning. I step away from where the girls are still sleeping and try Diamond's home number again. To my surprise, she answers. "Girl, where the hell have you been?" I scream into the phone, relieved. "Are you okay?"

"Yeah, girl, do you still have my pocketbook and my coat?" she asks groggily. She sounds like she has one hell of a hangover.

"Yes, of course I do. What in the hell happened to you? Why did you leave without telling us? And how in the hell did you get home without any money?"

"Girl, I don't know how I got here. Or why I left, for that matter," she explains. "All I know is I woke up in my own bed, and when I went to find my pocketbook to get a cigarette, I couldn't find it. I thought I'd lost it again. Thanks for holding onto it. You know I love you."

"I love you, too."

"Let me call you a little later, girl," she says. "I got a crazy bad hangover."

"Okay, bye." I run back to where the girls are just starting to wake up and tell them I spoke to Diamond. They're pissed—rightfully so.

Tasha rolls her eyes. "This is why I don't like going out with her—this kind of the shit. I mean, don't get me wrong, she's still my girl, but damn, she drives me crazy!" She sighs. "Okay, who of us is gonna give Officer Perts a courtesy call? 'Cause I personally refuse to embarrass myself."

"No problem, girl. I got it," I say. "I was the one who insisted we go to the precinct in the first place, so I should be the one to call."

"Hey, girls, Infinity left a message for us while we were sleeping," Brooke announces. "She wants to hang out tonight, wants us to be ready by eight. She's gonna meet us here, so we can all leave from here together."

"Where are we going?" Portia asks.

"How about the place we went last night?" Sky suggests. "I had fun."

"Yeah, it *was* fun," Portia agrees. "Let's go back."

"Well, I'm going back to sleep, you guys," Brooke announces. "I want to be refreshed for part two tonight." She does her little two-step dance, snapping her fingers, and disappears into one of the bedrooms.

Tasha's rental still has old-fashioned radiators and wood windows. You have to keep the heat cranked to keep it warm in here. Girl could really use some storm windows to keep the draft out. The apartment is otherwise cozy even though the walls are all plain white. Tasha uses colorful lamp shades to give the rooms a warmer feel. The house reminds me of my Grandma's house—everything antique.

"I need some coffee," Payton says. "I'm gonna put on a fresh pot. Anyone else wants coffee, it'll be ready in the kitchen in just a few." The kitchen is at the end of the apartment's single long hallway. In fact, you enter every room from the hallway in this place.

My cell phone is ringing from my coat pocket, which I can't see right away. "Anyone seen my coat?"

"On the rocking chair in the living room," Tasha answers.

When I reach my coat, I pull out my phone and sigh. "It's Murphy. I was hoping it was Myles," I say, disappointed. "I don't want to smell his stink breath through the phone...I'm not answering." I hear the girls laugh from the other room.

"We can hear you, Kennedy!" Payton shouts, and the rest of the girls giggle. I can't date a man with bad breath. Or any other kind of body odor, for that matter. I tried to tell Murphy in a casual way how important it is to go to the dentist, but he just don't catch the hint. I plan to be leaving him alone; he'll certainly catch *that* hint. I don't want to hurt his feelings, but sometimes, you just got to cut your losses.

Initially, I thought Murphy could be a good man for me. That is, until Myles came into the picture. Myles is my first-thug man. He's exciting and fun. Murphy is a nice guy. Hopefully he'll lose interest in me before I have to actually break things off.

I head toward the kitchen for a cup of coffee and find Payton sipping hers with a cigarette, her usual breakfast.

"Hey, friend," I greet her.

"Hey, Kennedy," she says. "So, what do you want to do today?"

"I just want to be lazy until tonight."

"I want to hit the malls before we head back home," Payton says.

"We can do that, but let's not do it today," I say. "We've got the whole week. We're going out dancing tonight, and tomorrow night is Infinity's show. After that, we can do whatever with the rest of our time here. I suppose it would be a good idea if we find out what everybody else's plans are. That way, we can arrange our activities accordingly."

"Well, I just spoke to Infinity," Tasha says, walking into the kitchen. "She wants to come over and chill with us, but she has a lot of prep to do before the show. She's got to get her wardrobe, hair, and makeup all together, especially because she'll be changing twice during her set. She's singing two songs, *and* she's making sure we have seats up front so we'll be sitting right in front of the stage. Yay!" Tasha shouts. "Oh, I'm so excited for her. I can't wait."

"Where are the other girls?" Brooke asks. "Does anyone else want coffee?"

"Everybody went back to sleep," Tasha says, giggling.

I rub my eyes. "I'm tired, too. After my coffee, I'm leaving you all right here. I'm going back to catch me some more z's."

Brooke and Payton exchange a look and little laugh. "I think Brooke and I are going back to sleep, too," Payton says. "Shit, Diamond kept us up all night."

~~~

Myles and I are having sex in his truck, and just before I climax, Diamond knocks on the passenger-side window, frantic. She looks crazy. Her hair is a mess, and she has blood all over her face and hands. She's screaming, but I can't understand what she's saying. She breaks the window and starts grabbing for me with her bloody hands. I'm so scared. I keep trying to push her hands away, and try to climb onto Myles, who is sitting in the driver's seat, screaming.

Diamond gets a hold of me and is shaking me. She keeps looking over her shoulder. She's completely out of her head. I hear footsteps coming up behind her, but I can't see a face. The voice is screaming, "Wake up!" The voice—a woman's—is getting closer, and louder...

~~~

I wake with a start. Infinity is standing over me. "Oh, hey, girl," I say and smile groggily. "What time is it?"

"It's seven-thirty," she says.

I can't believe I slept so long. I must have been more tired than I thought.

The rest of the girls appear to have been up for a while. They're doing their nails and going through their suitcases in search of what to wear tonight. I wipe my eyes and jump up to give Infinity a warm embrace. I am so excited to see her. It's been a long while since I've seen my girl.

"Infinity, you've lost so much weight," I observe. "Dieting?"

"More like starving myself," she says, grimacing.

"Well, whatever you're doing, you lookin' good, girl." I ask her how things are going, and we talk about her career, which certainly seems like it's starting to take off. We all have so much to catch up on that we talk for nearly two hours.

"Okay, it's eight-thirty, and we need to leave here by ten o'clock," Lola announces, looking at her watch. "And we still need to pick up Diamond and Renee."

Later, when we pull up in front of Diamond's house, Lola puts her foot down. "I refuse to go upstairs and get her. If we go upstairs, we'll end up spending another hour here sitting around bullshittin' before we actually take off for the night."

"I second that," Payton says. "Diamond's always got the music on when she's getting ready to go out, and she always has plenty of booze available. If we go upstairs, it'll turn into a party, and I don't want to waste any time here."

I agree with Lola and Payton. We have four of our old New York friends hanging out with us tonight, none of whom drink. And all we need is *three* designated drivers, so I can drink myself sober. I'm excited about going out, and I don't want to hang out at someone's house.

"Oh, wow!" I exclaim. "Look who's coming down the stairs now—Diamond and Renee."

"I just texted her, told her we were out front," Lola says, and winks at me.

As usual, Diamond and Renee have drinks with them, in plastic cups. They already look tipsy. Everyone jumps out to give them kisses, and then we all hustle back into the cars and go on our way.

The line to get into the bar is really long, and I have to use the bathroom. "I hope this line goes quick, girls. I really have to pee." When we finally make it in, I run straight to the ladies' room.

As I'm finishing up, I'm startled by a knock on my bathroom stall. It's Renee, and she sounds flustered. "Kennedy, they won't let Diamond into the club."

"What? Why?" I ask.

"I don't know," Renee answers.

"Wait a minute," I say. "I'm coming out." I step from the stall, wash my hands quickly, and rush back to the front door. When I ask the security guard, she informs me, "She's not allowed in here anymore."

"But, why?"

"It's personal."

"If you know and I don't, then it's not personal," I say.

We stare each other down for a minute, and then she gives in. "Last time she was in here, she was caught by the owner giving head to some guy on the dance floor."

"Oh my God." I close my eyes and shake my head. When I open them again, I can see that Diamond can hear our conversation. She's still standing outside, directly in front of the entrance.

Diamond gets my attention when she shouts above the crowd, "Kennedy, don't believe her!"

Tasha yanks on my elbow and pulls me out of Diamond's view. "Remember last night when that guy outside the bar volunteered that information to us," she reminds me. "We thought he was just being a jerk, but now I'm not so sure."

Tasha and I look at each other and say at the same time, "Oh my God."

"It all makes sense now," I say.

"That's why she took off without her coat and purse. She was kicked out. They obviously didn't even give her an opportunity to gather her things before they escorted her out of the club."

I run over to Diamond. "Are you sure the bouncer isn't right?" I ask her. "You did tell me this morning that you didn't remember anything that happened last night."

"If that happened, Kennedy, then someone put something in my drink," Diamond says in a huff. "If you're going to believe them over me, then I'm leaving."

"Hold on," I say. "Let me round up the other girls."

Tasha is still standing in the entrance. "What'd she say?"

"She said she didn't do it." I find the rest of the girls sitting at the bar. "Girls, we have to leave."

"Why?" Lola asks.

"The security guard just told me that the bar owner caught Diamond giving some guy head on the dance floor last night. That was the reason for the disappearing act." I add, "Damn, I really like this place, too." I see the owner being led over to us by the security guard I just spoke with. He approaches me with his gorgeous face and says, "I seen her with my own eyes, ma'am—no one else but me, thank God. Her nasty ass is no longer allowed in this establishment. I try to run a respectable business here. I won't have that kind of trash in here, giving my business a bad reputation. You girls are welcome to stay, but she cannot come in here."

I turn to my friends. "Are you girls ready?"

"Hell, no!" Lola says, exasperated. "I just ordered this drink. Diamond can wait till I'm done drinking it! I swear she is nothing but a damned fun-snatcher."

"I really really like this place."

"And the men here tonight are fine." Lola continues, clearly disappointed.

"Hurry up with your drink, then," Payton says. "I'm eager to hear Diamond's side of the story." But when we finally make it outside...no Diamond.

"Where the hell's she at now?" Portia asks, losing her patience.

Two minutes into the search, we spot Diamond walking up toward the next block.

"Diamond, wait for us!" I shout. We all run after her.

When we reach her, Payton asks her what "really" happened. Diamond repeats what she told me a few minutes earlier. "That's my story, and I'm sticking to it," she says, indignant. "I don't remember anything like that happening. I would never do something like that. Like I said, *if* it happened, then someone put something in my drink."

"What do you mean?" I ask. "You either did it, or you didn't."

"You know what I mean, Kennedy," she snaps.

"Well then, that indicates to me that you *are* capable of doing it. But *you* just said that you would *never* do something like that. I'm a little confused, Diamond. Which is it?"

"Well, if someone put something in my drink, then I don't have much control over my actions, now, do I?"

"You mean, like the date-rape drug?" I ask.

"That's what I'm saying, yes. I certainly wouldn't degrade myself like that under normal circumstances." She's arguing with us, but I can't help but hear the guilty strain in her voice.

"Then it's simple," I say. "You'll just have to take your ass to the doctor tomorrow and request a date-rape drug test. To see if you have any of those drugs in your system."

"Good idea," Diamond agrees. "That's exactly what I'll do."

"I think it only stays in your system for maybe three days, Diamond, so make sure you go to the doctor tomorrow. No later."

"I said I will, Kennedy," Diamond spits back. "Can we just let it go for now?" She's becoming more agitated by the minute.

I decide to drop it and try to revive the night. "Anywho, a friend of mine just opened up this bar, 95 South, right here in Brooklyn. It's over on Franklin Avenue, not too far from here. I promised him I would stop in whenever I happened to be in New York. I know he'd love to see me and meet all of you."

"Well then," Sky says, "what are we waiting for? Let's stop standing around on this damned street and go to your friend's place!"

~~~

When we arrive, the line is long. Thank God my friend is standing outside talking with his security staff. When he sees me, he does a double take and his mouth drops open. He didn't know I was in town.

"Surprise!" I say, smiling.

He saunters over. "Give me a hug, girlfriend," he says as we embrace. "I haven't seen you in centuries."

"Well, maybe not *that* long," I say. "But it *has* been a long time. It's so good to see you."

After our greeting, I introduce him to each of the girls, and he doesn't hesitate. "Do you guys want a drink, or something to eat?"

"Hell, yeah! I want a drink." Diamond, of course.

The bar is impressive—classy, elegant, unique. The crowd is mature, and his employees are all very sociable. The atmosphere is very much a reflection of my friend's personality. It's perfect.

After he seats the girls at the bar, he puts his arm through mine and proceeds to give me a tour of his lovely establishment. The bar is beautiful—and huge. It starts about thirty feet from the entrance and stops just past the middle of the building. There are just enough tables and chairs to accommodate his guests. "During the day, it's a restaurant," he boasts, "and then comedy, karaoke, and dancing on different nights of the week." Guessing
~~~

from the crowd here, my gut feeling is that he will be in business for a good long time.

"This is the kitchen, complete with full staff." He doesn't introduce me to the staff, who are all working busily and wearing chef's hats and aprons. It's just a quick tour, after all.

"The food smells fabulous," I say.

"I'll grab you a menu on the way back out. You still eat soul and seafood?"

"You know it!"

"Then you're gonna love the food. I'll even pack you and your friends some to go."

"Make sure it's a little of everything," I say, winking.

"I will, and it's on the house," he insists.

"Thank you. I feel so special." I feel like the first lady. He *is* the president of this business; a girl can dream. When we come through the kitchen, I see there is a nice-sized back patio directly across from the restrooms, behind the bar. It looks to be a perfect place to enjoy a warm evening.

"I am so proud of you" I say. "How many people can fit in here?"

"About a hundred," he answers.

"Good, I want to schedule a private party."

"Whenever you're ready, just let me know." He smiles. "You look good, Kennedy. You haven't changed a bit. What do you do, sleep in a freezer so you won't age?"

I laugh. "Funny. Thanks for the compliment. You don't look so bad yourself."

As I walk through the restaurant, I can feel the friendly vibe of the place. That's not exactly usual in New York City bars. The girls are equally impressed. Lola whispers into my ear, "I like this place as much as the other place."

I grin and say, "Good, me too!" The music is bangin'. The DJ is playing all the best stuff. If I do decide to throw a party here, I want this DJ. He doesn't disappoint. The music just keeps getting better and better. He plays all the ol' school music—reggae, rap, R&B. I look at the girls while we're on the dance floor and say, "Well, girls, this will be our spot from now on."

Brooke shouts, "Hello! This spot is off the hook." We all laugh because Brooke is always trying to sound hip. Brooke's a white girl in a black girl's body. She's got so much rhythm—she drop it like it's hot, at the drop of a beat. She never feels uncomfortable in a predominately black atmosphere. She doesn't look at the world as a color. God bless her sweet soul.

Diamond looks like she's completely forgotten about what happened earlier. She's clearly having a good time on the dance floor. Everything happens for a reason. Maybe we were meant to be here tonight but I will be going back to Chance 11 without the presence of Diamond my next visit here. I love the beauty and atmosphere in that bar, its so classy. I still don't know why Diamond even went back to that club. I would have never shown *my* face in there again. I suppose that might be why I'm inclined to believe her story—because she went back. On the other hand, she probably didn't think they would remember her. I hope it's not true. Such a shameful act—lowdown, dirty and disgusting. Well, not the act itself of course, just that she happened to do it in a public place. Anyway, I guess we'll just have to wait for the doctor's report.

"Have a drink, Infinity," I suggest. "Enjoy yourself."

"Ah, I can't, girl," she declines. "I have a big day tomorrow. And you know I don't need a drink to enjoy myself...unlike you," she chides playfully. "I'm just so glad you guys are here."

"I will always be your number-one fan," I tell her. "And I wish you nothing but success."

"Thank you, Kennedy," she says, and we hug.

It's a little after three in the morning. The club is starting to wind down and clear out. I'm totally exhausted and ready to get back to Tasha's, get some sleep. "I want to be well rested for the main event tomorrow," I say.

"Me too," Portia agrees.

"Well, let's get the rest of the girls off the dance floor so we can head out."

I excuse myself for a moment so I can go and find my friend, the owner. I want to wish him continued success and let him know I'm leaving. Who knows, maybe I'll get a chance to come in again before I leave to go back to Orlando.

When we reach Tasha's crib, I'm planning to crash without bothering to take a shower. I'm thinking that eleven-thirty sounds like the perfect waking time for a Saturday morning.

When I finally do wake up on Saturday, the first thing I do is give Diamond a call. I want to make sure she goes to the walk-in clinic across town from her place to get tested. She assures me that she's going to get dressed right away, go down there, and take care of it.

When I call her later to get the results, she tells me she didn't go because she got caught up doing something else. Now I'm not sure what to believe. If she really believes someone might have slipped the date-rape drug into her drink, wouldn't she want to make finding out a priority?

The girls and I decide to go out for a late lunch/early dinner at a place in Clinton Hills. The place turns into a club at night. The music is already playing when we walk in at 4:40. At first I think there is a DJ. Turns out, the owner is just playing a CD. The music has us in the mood for drinks. The atmosphere is definitely night club-ish. A crowd at the bar is engaged in conversation. They look as if they've been here for hours.

After our meal, we decide to stay a little while longer and have another drink. Diamond gets up and dances with a guy who looks so intoxicated, he's stumbling on the dance floor. The rest of us dive into conversation.

Twenty minutes later, I'm talking to Sky, who is sitting on my left. Brooke, on my right, taps me on the shoulder. She points to the dance floor. I turn my eyes in that direction. Diamond is still out there, but no longer dancing. I'm speechless. She is down on her knees with her hand inside the hole of the drunk guy's boxers. She's about to pull out his penis. His denim jeans are around his ankles, and he's leaning against the mirrored wall that lines the far side of the dance floor. The area is dim, but not dark. It's lit well enough so that everyone in the restaurant can see what is going on.

Out of nowhere, three guys rush over to the scene. They're screaming at their drunken friend. "Cody, what are you doing? You can't do that in New York! It's not like down south!"

We're all still in shock when Diamond walks back over to our table and kneels in front of me.

"What you gonna do, suck my penis too?" I say sarcastically. But the music is too loud, she doesn't hear me.

"Kennedy, did you see that?" she asks me.

"Did I see what?" I ask her back. Diamond asks me again if I saw what just happened. I'm starting to get pissed. "Tell me what it is you think I've seen, and I will tell you if I've seen it or not."

Diamond looks at Brooke and asks her, "Did you see that, Broo—"

But before she can get Brooke's name out, Brooke answers, "Yes, I seen exactly what you did. You're nasty. You should be ashamed of yourself."

Sky chimes in, "So it's true, what took place in the bar the other day."

The light bulb went on for me. "That's why your ass wasn't eager to go get a blood test. You already know the results." I'm thoroughly disgusted.

We leave the club quickly after leaving some money on the table to pay for our drinks and food. We're all completely embarrassed. "Diamond is not joining us for the rest of this evening," Lola says, wagging her finger in my face. "I don't care what you say, Kennedy. She is *not* going with us." Lola turns to face the rest of the girls. "I know you all think Diamond is your girl, but there is a side to her that proves otherwise, and I believe we've all just been witness to that particular side."

"You tried to warn us, Lola," Portia says. "And tonight definitely proves you were right. I was trying to give her the benefit of the doubt, but..."

"Yes, Diamond is responsible for her actions, but don't crucify our friendship with her," I plead. "She needs to be surrounded by people who love her."

"No, Kennedy, she *needs* to be surrounded by people with a penis," Lola barks.

Portia bursts out laughing. "Lola, you're crazy," she says.

"You think I'm the crazy one?" Lola replies, starting to laugh, too.

"Maybe she feels like an outcast when she's with us. Maybe this is her way of getting attention." I continue to defend what I know is indefensible.

"There are more productive ways of getting attention, Kennedy," Lola says. "Stop making excuses for her. You can be nice to her all you want, but that bitch is not going anywhere with me ever again! And especially not tonight!"

We leave the bar with Diamond in tow and get into the cars. Unfortunately for Diamond, she's riding in the car Lola's driving. Lola's nose is flaring as she gets into the car. I didn't think Diamond would ride with Lola. Girl has been making some seriously fucked-up choices since we've been here.

In my car, things are very quiet. Momma always said, "If you don't have anything good to say, then don't say anything at all." We're glancing around at each other, trying to figure out how to go on with the night. It's a very uncomfortable situation.

Lola takes the lead and pulls her car up in front of Diamond's house. Those of us in the other two cars pull up behind her. From our vehicles, we hear Lola say to Diamond, "Get the fuck out of my car!"

"I'll get out when I am good and ready," Diamond yells back.

"Diamond, get out of my car before I put you out," Lola threatens.

"I'll get *out* when I'm *ready,*" Diamond yells. "And when I *am* ready, you're going to give me door-to-door service."

Lola hits the gas and speeds off down the block. She lands right in front of a bus stop. I follow her in the car I'm driving because I know it's gonna go wrong. She stops the car abruptly and scares the passengers waiting for the bus. She gets out of the car, opens the back door, and begins pulling Diamond out of the back seat. Diamond holds onto the seat belt to prevent Lola from pulling her from the vehicle. The people at the bus stop don't know what's going on, but from the looks on their faces, you can see they don't want any part of it.

"Lola, stop!" I scream from the driver's side window of my car. I am so embarrassed.

"No!" she shouts back at me. "You think this bitch is going to disrespect me and get a ride home from me? Hell, no!" Lola grabs Diamond by the feet and continues to pull her out the car.

"Kennedy, get her off of me!" Diamond screams. But it's too late. Lola has already pulled Diamond out of the car, and now Diamond, who has managed to get up off of the ground, is standing on the sidewalk next to the people at the bus stop. Lola brushes her hands together and gets back into the driver's seat without bothering to look back in Diamond's direction.

"I can't believe this is happening," I say, looking down and shaking my head.

Sky calls my phone from the car she's driving to find out what's going on. She's still parked in front of Diamond's house. "Why'd Lola drive off like that?" she asks. "And why isn't she picking up her phone?"

"I'll explain when I get back there. Why didn't you follow us?"

"Because I thought you guys was going to the store or something. Diamond didn't get out the car, and I didn't feel like following y'all to the store. But y'all were taking so damned long, I called to see what was up. Where are you now?"

"Just around the corner," I say. "I'll be there in two minutes."

When we meet back up, I relay the story of what happened between Lola and Diamond. Sky starts laughing hysterically. She can't believe it.

"Lola, you know you shouldn't have done that," I say, trying to keep a straight face.

"Fuck y'all," Lola says. "I have no regrets. And that means, by the way, that I will do it again if I have to." Lola looks down at her jacket. "Look at this shit, her shoe prints all over my white coat. Now let's get the hell out of here before she comes back. I don't want to have to beat her down."

"Let this be a warning to whoever is riding back to the house with me," I say to the girls. "I *don't* want to discuss this anymore. I just want to concentrate on what to wear for the main event tonight, so when I get back to the house, I can just take a nap."

Chapter 9

KENNEDY
THE CONCERT

It's a full house tonight at the Nassau Coliseum. It appears to be sold out. That's good for our friend, plenty of exposure. Infinity's managers meet us in the entrance area and lead us back to her dressing room—Infinity's orders.

Infinity looks a little nervous. She's full of confidence as usual, but she's not used to entertaining a crowd of this size. She looks beautiful. She's wearing a long, winter-white, double-breasted coat-dress that falls to her ankles. She has on matching boots with rhinestones that remind me of Michael's glove. She's also wearing the most amazing diamond jewelry—earrings and a necklace. Her pearly white teeth scream perfection, and I admire her refined nose. Her hair is weaved past her shoulders, and delicately fans across her breasts.

"So, which song do you guys recommend I sing first?" she asks. "'Pick a Door' or 'Never?'"

"Please sing 'Pick a Door,'" I plead. These are the two songs on her album that will definitely make the top of the charts. They're our personal favorites, so I'm glad she's singing them tonight. She sings the hell out of both of them. We visited the studio while she was recording the album—another reason why we wanted to come and support her tonight. We were there for the birth of this baby, now we want to see her walk for the first time.

Infinity writes all of her own songs. If she somehow doesn't make it as a singer, she will damned well be recognized for her writing. The music industry is a lot different now than it used to be. Now you have to come into show biz with the whole package. You have to know how to dance, sing, write, be sexy, and most of all, you have to be youthful. If you're fortunate, you'll meet someone in the music world that will take a chance and invest in you.

Infinity is definitely someone I'd take a chance on. She has a voice that will be talked about and remembered by our great-grandchildren, and their children, and so on. Her music is creative, and devoted to love, lust, good times, and happiness. People really respond to that.

Her dressing room door has her name on it, just like for movie stars. Inside the dressing room, above the mirror, there are those large round lightbulbs. The makeup cases are all lined up and neatly placed on a pink cloth that covers the counter. We spend about half an hour in the dressing room with Infinity before heading to our reserved front-row seats.

I'm leading the girls into the row we are sitting in. We fill almost the entire row with the exception of one seat. I look over at the unfamiliar young lady seated next to me. She has a pointy *Sister Sledge* nose.

"Hi, my name is Kennedy." I extend my hand to her. "My sister is performing tonight. She's opening the show," I say excitedly. "Let me know what you think of her performance, and please be honest."

"Congratulations to your sister," the girl says.

"She's not my blood sister, but sometimes sisterhood isn't about blood."

"I hear that, girlfriend."

Lola leans forward in her seat and says to the woman, "She's really good."

The woman laughs. "I believe you."

The house lights go down and the stage lights come on, indicating the show is about to start. The seven of us start screaming. As Infinity starts to sing "Pick a Door," we sing right along with her, word for word. I can hear the girl sitting behind us say to her friend, "I've never heard this song before. Have you?"

Her friend replies, "No, I don't think it's out yet."

"Well, *they're* singing the lyrics," the first girl says, pointing to us.

I turn around and say, "It's not out yet, but it will be soon." Now, I don't know that for a fact, but I have faith. Besides, they don't have to know she doesn't have a record deal yet. Lola is singing the tune like the song is a hit on the radio already. The people seated all around us stare in wonder. I imagine they're thinking, *Who is this girl, Infinity?*

I'm sitting on the edge of my seat—literally and figuratively—waiting for Infinity to hit the high note in the song. The crowd is on their feet, going crazy. They're enjoying the song as much as we are. Tasha stands up along with the rest of the audience, turns around, points her two thumbs into her chest, and repeats over and over, "That's my sister!"

When Infinity's last song is finished, I ask the young lady next to me, "Well, what did you think?"

"She's amazing," the girl exclaims. "I love her voice. Where can I buy her album?" I pull a CD out of my pocketbook, give it to the girl, and wink. "Thanks!" she says. "I'm going to listen to it in the car on my way home."

"You're going to love it, I promise."

The people in the row behind us ask, "Can we have one, too?"

"Sure," I say, as I hand out the handful of CDs I slipped into my purse before we left for the show.

Sky leans forward and says in my direction, "You were quick on your feet, girl, thinking to bring those CDs along." After giving out the rest of my stash of Infinity's CDs, we rush back to her dressing room to congratulate her.

"Job well done, Infinity!" I say. "The people sitting around us *loved* your performance. They all wanted a copy of your CD when they happened to notice that I'd brought a few with me."

"Wow, they liked me?" Infinity exclaims. She looks so happy, and much more relaxed than before the show.

"No, they *loved* you," I say, and smile wide.

"Everybody high-five!"

We decide to watch the other performances from backstage. It's a great show. I can say with complete confidence that it is definitely the concert of the year.

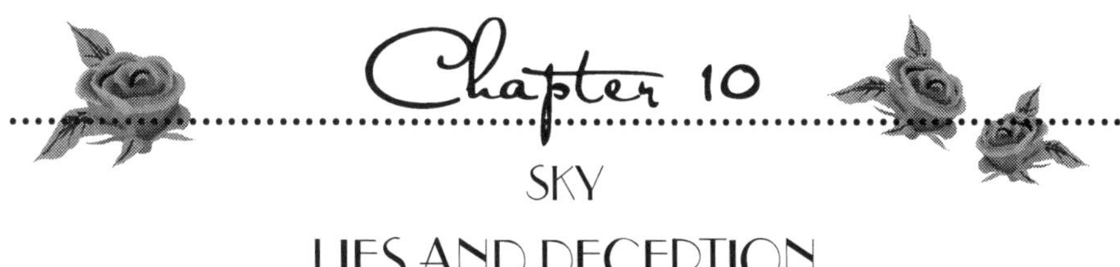

Chapter 10

SKY

LIES AND DECEPTION

It's been a month since my last physical altercation with Fuji, and two weeks since we've been back from New York. I told my boss I'd been in a car accident—I didn't want to have to explain the bruises. It took two weeks for the abrasions to heal completely. My co-workers appear to have believed my tale. No one has asked questions or seems suspicious.

I work for a criminal attorney. I have to be extra careful about my appearance when I have bruises. I suspect my neighbors know exactly what's going on, because beat-downs are not exactly quiet. I told the girls that Fuji and I were going on vacation to discourage them from dropping by unannounced. Of course, the vacation story was Fuji's creation. And just in case the girls or Dylan *did* happen to get wind of what happened, he decided it would be a good idea for him to go missing-in-action for a while.

He's been extremely affectionate and caring since the last incident, and I've fallen in love with him all over again. When things are great between us, they are truly great. Fuji is a loving and caring gentleman—the man I fell in love with.

Fuji just stepped out to the liquor store for a bottle of Alizé. I'm preparing a spectacular dinner for the two of us. Unlike me, Fuji prefers to eat healthy. He begged me to make his favorite meal tonight: salmon steaks and grilled shrimp sautéed in Mazola butter spray, roasted red onions, green and red peppers, and freshly diced garlic. Also, red potatoes, sweet corn, and tossed greens.

I love to have music going when I cook. It relaxes me, helps me think, and is a great way to escape the world for a little while. The girls and I have this in common. I decide to put on my girl Anita Baker's album, *Rhythm of Love*. I could listen to it all day long.

In a little over an hour, dinner is ready. Fuji has yet to return from the liquor store. He left just as I was starting to make dinner. At first, I'm not too concerned. I figure he's bumped into a few of his buddies and has just lost track of time. I set the table so we can sit down and eat as soon as he comes in the door. I'm famished.

Another hour has passed, and still no Fuji. I'm starting to get worried. I call his cell phone numerous times, but he doesn't answer. I make various phone calls to try and track him down—his mother, his friends, other relatives, but no one has heard from him. This is strange, even for Fuji. Now I'm thinking the worst. This can't be happening to me. Our relationship has been going so smoothly.

I'm in a panic. I don't know what to think or expect. I pick up the phone to call the girls. I want them to come over and help me stay calm and rational till this matter is settled. If I can count on anyone, I can count on the girls. When I need them, they drop everything to come to my rescue, to be with me in my time of need. I place a call to Kennedy and wait.

I have other friends who encourage me to handle my own rescues—acquaintances that masquerade as friends. These are the people who let me down when I need them the most. I haven't necessarily removed them from my life completely, but I hold them in a separate place from my true friends. Especially those friends I have always been there for, but *I* can never count on. I'm confident in my decision to put them on a different level of friendship. I doubt they even notice I make a distinction between them and my true friends. For my own sake, I simply keep them at a distance so they can't disappoint me again. Sometimes, I stay loyal long past the time that I should because I've known a particular person for a long time. But at some point, I have to put myself first. For me, friendship isn't that much different from being in a relationship with a man. If you don't share the same level of commitment, it's not going to work. Someone is going to get hurt eventually.

Indeed, it's times like this I can determine who my true friends are. Speaking of which, I see headlights in the driveway. I open the garage door so they can let themselves in. They show up, one by one, within five to ten minutes of each other. The first thing each of them says to me is, "Has anyone told you they love and care about you today? Well, I do."

I'm feeling worse now, though, because the girls are acting as if Fuji is dead. They're almost too sympathetic for comfort. They're questioning me all at once. I tell them I'm worried sick because he went out to the liquor store for a bottle of Alizé, and the liquor store is only a ten-minute walk from our house. It's been three and half hours!

"Well, I'm going to start calling the hospitals," Kennedy says, in her usual take-charge manner.

"I'll contact the precincts," Portia offers.

But no one fitting Fuji's description is found in either of those places. I make calls to his family and friends again. But they haven't heard from Fuji either, nor do they seem all that concerned about him. *Why don't they seem even the least bit troubled by this?*

Kennedy puts a voice to my new concerns. "Don't you think it's strange that no one in his family or circle of friends is assuming the worst?"

"Yes," Payton agrees. "Not even his mom."

"There's something fishy here," Kennedy says. "I'm suspicious. Particularly because of his mom. Why isn't *she* worried?"

"Fuji is definitely a mama's boy, you guys." I can't help but roll my eyes playfully, thinking of Fuji's devoted mother. "She loves her baby Jerome more than life itself. She caters to him like you guys wouldn't believe. I mean, c'mon, she still does his laundry, irons his shirts, cooks him dinner every other night. I don't have to cook most of the time because she's always at my door with food. I love her to death. I couldn't ask for a better mother in-law."

"She *is* very amusing when she calls Fuji her 'husband,'" Tasha says.

"She even moved here to Florida because she missed him something terrible," Lola adds.

Kennedy nods. "Exactly! She cares for him as if he is still her little boy. Something is *not* right."

"Yep, something is definitely not right," Lola agrees. "I hate to say it, but I suspect deceit. I mean, he asks you to cook him dinner and then just takes off indefinitely? Either something went wrong or...Fuji is not treating you very well, Sky."

I flinch. *If they only knew.*

"Sky, be honest," Lola says. "Do you think it's possible that Fuji would be so cruel and disrespectful as to go off to the liquor store and not come back?"

Kennedy puts her arm around my shoulder. "Yeah, especially when he asked you to cook him his favorite dinner."

I'm juggling these two thoughts in my head, fighting for answers. Nothing makes any sense. I feel more at peace now, at least, because I'm no longer thinking the worst. I have a strong gut feeling that Fuji is okay. For a moment, I'm relieved… until I start to feel a new emotion overtake me: anger.

"I swear if that man is disrespecting me or our marriage in *any* form, I will leave him for good," I say, resolute. The girls know what I'm getting at—the possibility that Fuji is with another woman. They are all too aware of his habits. "Well, girls, this might be a very long night. Take a seat at the table, and I'll dish you up some food." I'm not hungry anymore. But I'll be damned if *Jerome* gets one morsel of the meal I so lovingly prepared for him.

"I'll help myself, girl," Tasha says. "You don't have to serve me."

"I'm going to the liquor store," Payton announces. "If this is going to be a long night, then we'll need refreshments." She steps outside the door to leave, but a moment later she sticks her head back in and jokes, "I promise I'll be *right back*."

"Very funny," I say, and we all share a much-needed chuckle.

"You guys don't have to stay until he gets home," I say. "You might be here all night. I know you guys have a life."

"You know we'll stick it out with you for as long as it takes," Lola insists. "We have your back like a jacket, girl."

I backtrack in my thoughts. I'm trying hard to make sense of Fuji's actions. I realize I can't make sense out of something that doesn't make sense. It's just not logical.

"Let's just relax and wait for Fuji," Kennedy says as she sits down by the window in the family room.

"Do you guys mind if I turn off the stereo?" I ask.

"Of course not, Sky," Kennedy replies.

"Thanks." I'm no longer in the mood for music. It isn't so much soothing as it's impairing my ability to think clearly.

"I'm back!" Payton says, walking through the door. "I have a bottle of Hennessy—was thinking we probably need something a little stronger than wine."

But I don't really care what she's brought back. I'm running out of patience. I have so much I want to say to Fuji, but I can't because he's not picking up his phone.

"Okay, girls, I'm starting to lose it," I say. Hours have passed. "Sitting here waiting for him is making me crazy." I'm so *angry*. Each minute that ticks by is making it harder for me to hold my composure. "I can't help but think he's

Reagan's obsession with Fuji has always been completely over the top, abnormal—and obvious to everyone. Fuji has always been well aware of Reagan's fixation with him. Although he told me it bothers him, I've always gotten the impression that on some level he gets off on it—a real ego boost.

He doesn't respect me at all. After everything we've been through together, why would he put a stupid fling with an infatuated girl ahead of *me*, his wife? Fuji's not a man, he's a syndrome. What the hell would he have told me if Infinity hadn't clued me in? Does he even care? I don't know who this man is anymore. Maybe I *never* knew him.

Infinity tells me again how bad she feels for having to be the one to break the news to me. "I am so sorry," she says again. She can hear my muffled sobbing. I assure her that she has no reason to apologize, that she hasn't done anything wrong. Fuji *put* her in this situation. She didn't *ask* to be in it.

"Thank you, Infinity," I say, and we hang up.

I feel too ashamed to go out there and face the girls with what I've learned. I take a few minutes to dry my eyes and compose myself. I need answers. And I need to hear them straight from the horse's mouth. I dial Fuji's number again. He doesn't pick up. I'm more pissed than ever. I decide I need to drive to Virginia. I call Infinity back and get the details on where she's staying. "I'm coming up. Lay low till I get there."

"No problem, girl." We hang up for the second time tonight. I want to shock the shit out of the bastard. How dare he treat me like this? I demand respect from him. I pump myself up pretty good while still in the bathroom. It's time to let the girls in on what I've learned. I grab the brass knob on the bathroom door and hold onto it for about thirty seconds before I gather the courage to turn it.

"Mystery solved!" I shout, coming out of the bathroom. They'd all nodded off, but that got their attention.

Kennedy looks at my eyes. "Baby, have you been crying?" I can tell by their faces they think Fuji is dead.

"He's not dead, girls...at least, not yet. Get your things together. We're driving to Virginia. We're going to pay a little visit to Fuji who is apparently 'on vacation' *with Reagan*." The girls look at me and then each other with stark blank faces. Lola's jaw drops wide open. Before anyone can ask me any questions, I say, "I'll explain everything on the way down."

Thank God Payton has her SUV, because we're all able to fit comfortably in one vehicle—*we*, meaning me, Kennedy, Lola, and Tasha. Portia and Brooke can't just pick up and leave town, being a wife and a mother.

"Promise to keep us posted," Portia says before we pull out of the driveway.

"And please, try not to get into an altercation," Brooke warns.

"I'll try," I say, "but I can't promise you anything. You know Lola." Lola is the loudest and most obnoxious of us. She has a tendency to react strongly when it comes to defending herself and her friends.

The mood in the car is tense and anxious. The girls know all about my previous episodes involving Reagan. Things got physical with us a few times, and I beat her ass each time. But she didn't let that stop her from attempting to undermine my relationship with Fuji. There was a point at which he was seeing both of us at the same time—until things got out of hand. Reagan kept showing up at my house claiming that Fuji was *her* man. For a while, she was going around saying that they were engaged—a flat-out lie. She had this gold ring of his that had Fuji's name on it, and she tried to tell people it was an engagement ring. She was also in the habit of threatening me whenever I happened to pass her on the street. Seemed I couldn't even run to the store without bumping into her. I felt like I was being stalked.

Finally, I couldn't take it anymore. I gave Fuji an ultimatum—her or me. He claimed he loved me and couldn't live without me. He told me he was going to leave Reagan. I remember it like it was yesterday. We were all living in Brooklyn at the time. Fuji lived around the corner from me, and Reagan lived around the corner from Fuji. The day he broke it off with her to be with me, Reagan lost it. Fuji was walking back down the street to my place after having told her it was over between them, and she was two steps behind him, crying, pulling at his coat, begging him to stay. She looked and sounded like a complete idiot. He restrained himself from hitting her, but kept shouting repeatedly at her to "go home!" She finally stopped carrying on when she saw me standing in front of my house, waiting for Fuji. She pulled herself together quickly.

I couldn't believe her reaction. I'd always thought she was a tough chick with at least a *little* integrity. Later, I heard she moved to Virginia to get away, and to help herself get over him. I haven't seen her since she moved. I assumed Fuji hadn't, either. I really thought my problems with Reagan were in the past. Obviously, I was wrong.

We make it to Virginia in eleven and a half hours. Payton drove the entire way. She drove like a bat out of hell—at least a hundred miles per hour at points during the trip. We pull up to the Comfort Inn, which is where Infinity told me they were staying.

"There's his damned car." I feel my blood pressure begin to rise. I dial Infinity. "Hey, girl, we made it. What room are they in?"

Lola yells from the back seat, "Yeah, what room is that bastard in?"

"Room 256," Infinity says.

"Have you seen him at all today?"

"Nope," she confirms. "They haven't come out of that room all day."

"How do you know that?"

"Because I'm right next door, in room 254. The walls between rooms in this joint are paper thin. I can hear everything that's been going on in there.

"Have you heard them having sex?" The question escapes my mouth even though I don't really want to know the answer.

"Sky, please don't ask me that," Infinity pleads. But her reply is enough for me to know the answer. I feel like someone is driving a knife straight through my heart.

"I hate him! *I hate him!*" I bang my fists on the dashboard.

Lola snatches the phone from my hand. "Infinity, what just happened? What did you say to her?" Infinity apparently replays our exchange to Lola, who looks at me sympathetically and nods. "I don't know what you're planning to do, Sky, or what's going to happen between you and Fuji. But I can tell you one thing for sure: I will never be speaking to that sorry-ass excuse for a man again. Do you hear me, Sky? I will never speak to him ever again."

"Lola, you can't just throw people away because they disappoint you," Kennedy points out.

Lola's eyes go wide. "Oh yeah? Watch me. I am surely going to throw his ass away for good."

Payton pulls her SUV into a parking space, but before we all get out, they give me a group hug. I can tell by the way they're squeezing me that they feel my pain. "What would I do without you, girls?" I ask, choked up.

Brooke and Portia have been calling to check in the entire ride down. I remember that I told them I would call as soon as we arrived at our destination, but decide to put the call off until later.

"I want to confront him alone, if you girls don't mind," I say.

"Okay, girl," Kennedy agrees. "We'll wait for you next door in Infinity's room."

"I just feel like I need to do this alone."

"It's fine," she assures me. "We totally understand."

I'm standing in front of the door to room 256, feeling so many emotions at once—anger, hurt, anxiety. My hands are shaking. The tremors are so bad

I can barely knock on the door, but somehow I find the courage. No answer. I knock again. I think I hear moaning, but it could be my imagination. I put my ear to the door and try to listen. Finally, I hear Fuji asking from the other side of the door, "Who is it?"

"Room service," I lie.

"Hold on," he says. "I'll be right there."

When the door opens, Fuji's eyes go wide. He gasps and chokes on his own spit. He's coughing uncontrollably. Before he can catch his breath, I grab his throat with my left hand and dig my fingernails into his flesh. Then I throw a powerful right hook that sends him back and down to the floor. "I suspect I'm the last person you expected to see on the other side of this door, huh? Didn't think I would go to the trouble of driving six hundred miles just to bring you down, did ya?"

He's still on the floor, and before I even know what I'm doing, I'm smacking the crap out of him. He tries to cover his face with his hands, but he's still in shock and just flailing. I stop, put my face down in front of his, and ask, "Where's my Alizé, Jerome?" With that, I leave him lying in the doorway and step over him, walking into the room.

Reagan is in the bed, naked save for a white sheet she's wrapped around herself to cover her breasts. She looks nervous, but she has a smirk on her face that I find extremely irritating. This is obviously payback for her. My impulse is to beat her, and that is exactly what I do. It's a sudden impulse, and it even catches *me* off guard. The blows she's receiving are brutal and full of rage. All the drama she's pulled through the years up till now is going through my mind. I feel righteously justified. Poor, defenseless Reagan didn't see it coming. She tries to grab my hair, but her grip isn't nearly enough to subdue me, much less overpower me.

In the middle of the fight I realize I'm no longer alone. Kennedy, Lola, Payton, and Tasha have showed up and have joined me. Fuji doesn't even come to Reagan's defense. He's standing there like a fool. He's trying to tell me he didn't do anything wrong. "It's not what you think, Sky."

I look at him and say, "If you can even draw an honest breath, I want to be there to see it." My daddy used to tell me, *Don't believe anything you hear, and only half of what you see.* But this fool is crazy.

Infinity starts pulling us off of Reagan one at a time, shouting, "Stop! You're going to kill her." I know Infinity is right; she's saving us from catching a case. Once up and away from the action, I motion for the other girls to stop.

Blood is coming from Reagan's nose and mouth. Her eyes are wild and she looks traumatized, and I think, *good*. Still huffing and puffing, I stick my finger in her face and say, "This is your last warning. You won't be so lucky next time, so you'd better stay the hell away from my husband."

"Tell your husband to stay away from me," she spits back, holding her hand to her mouth.

"I would shut up if I were you," Lola says.

Reagan is standing now, dazed and completely naked—she's left her sheet behind on the bed. I begin to walk out of the room, and the girls follow me, breathing hard and fixing their hair. When I walk past Fuji, he grabs my arm. "I'm sorry, baby. Please forgive me." I stop, look straight into his eyes, and shove my wedding ring into his hand.

"Baby, don't do this," he pleads. "Please put the ring back on. You're my wife, and I love you."

"A wedding ring is a symbol of love and commitment, *Jerome*. So why would I keep it on when we have neither?"

I turn to leave, and Fuji grabs my arm again. The girls step between us. "Let go of her," Kennedy speaks up. "You should have thought about *loving* your wife instead of *disrespecting* her."

I walk about fifteen feet down the hall, drop to my knees and begin to cry out of control. I'm screaming and in excruciating pain. My girls drop down and huddle around me. They console me with tears in their eyes. They tell me everything is going to be all right. I know they will help me get through this.

I hear Tasha answer her phone. "Hey, Portia. Yep, he's here with Reagan. We beat her ass. I'm gonna have to call you later, though. Sky needs us right now. Okay, girl. We'll talk soon."

I hear Fuji down the hall, shouting. "Sky, baby, I'm sorry. Please forgive me. I messed up, baby." His voice is getting closer. "Please, baby, let me hold you. I'm the only one who can fix this. Your friends can't fix this."

Lola gets up and walks over to Fuji. "Back up, and get the hell away from her." She's trying to keep her cool, but she's seething.

I look at Fuji and say, "What are you gonna do, Fuji? Huh? Make me some soup?"

Fuji has a look of deep sorrow on his face. I feel almost sorry for him, but I snuff out the impulse as quickly as it arises. He knows he's lost me. There's no going back from this. A woman will take abuse from a man for only so long before she understands that her love for him alone will never be enough. We all have our limit, and this is mine.

I turn my back on the man I thought would be my eternal lover, friend, and husband…and my tears resume. It's hard to imagine life without Fuji. I can't shake the feeling that my time with him isn't up yet. There is a part of me that wants to cling to our relationship, wants it to continue. *What's wrong with me?*

I resolve to find the courage to break free from the vicious cycle that our marriage has become.

Chapter 11

PORTIA
HE IS MY FAVORITE ACCESSORY

The answering machine is blinking, indicating I have messages. I sit up in bed, wipe my eyes, and stretch before getting up. I go to the bathroom, wash my face, brush my teeth, and say a silent prayer to God. *Thank you for my family and for blessing us with all that we have.* I still haven't quite grasped the fact that I'm living in this beautiful mansion. My son, Dante, is coming home for the weekend. He's only seen pictures of the new house, and he's excited to see it in person.

I press the playback button on the answering machine. The first message is from Lola, filling me in on Sky and Fuji's drama. I *knew* he was cheating on her. That's probably what was going on the night the girls spent the night here. Sky was constantly leaving the room, trying to get in touch with Fuji. *The bastard.* She loves him so much, and he just takes her for granted. Yes, she has cheated on him, too, but it was only for revenge. She always feels awful afterward.

She's tried getting involved with other men. She's even threatened to leave Fuji on several occasions—she's knows he's not good for her—but she never follows through. I hope this incident is enough to open her eyes. I hope she can finally find the courage to leave him for good. She is such a wonderful person. She doesn't deserve this. And she could do so much better than the likes of Fuji. She deserves a good man.

I pick up the phone and call Sky. No answer, so I leave a message. "Hi, friend," I begin. "Has anyone told you they love and care about you today?

Well, I do. I know things are tough right now. I'm here when you need me, girl. Call if you feel like talking. Love you."

I hang up and continue listening to my messages. The next is from Dylan. He's asking me to have lunch with him at his office at one o'clock. I give him a call. "Hi, honey." There must be someone in his office. He tells me to hold on, and I can hear him excuse himself from the room to take my call. He's so cute—he sounds genuinely excited to hear from me. He always makes me feel like I'm the only woman in the room. To the casual observer, it would appear that Dylan and I are only just now falling in love. I feel so lucky to have him.

"Hey, baby, did you get my message?" he asks. "You were sleeping like an angel this morning. I didn't want to wake you."

"Of course I got your message, baby."

"Well, do you have any plans today?"

"Even if I did, I would cancel them for you."

"Perfect. See you at one o'clock then?"

"Sounds good, sweetie. See you then. I love you."

"I love you, too."

Thankfully, I'm able to use the reserved parking when I visit Dylan at work, because there is rarely parking in this area. His dental practice is located within a large shopping district in the busiest part of downtown.

When I walk into the reception area, I find his secretary is away from her desk. I assume she must be using the restroom. I look around the office for any signs of life. "Where the hell are his patients?" I say out loud to myself. It's like a ghost town in here. "Yoo-hoo! Where is everybody?" I call as I look at my watch to confirm the time. "It's only ten after one." I sigh and head for Dylan's office, which is in the back.

When I open his office door, I see lit candles covering every surface of the room. A large red-and-white checked picnic blanket is spread out on the floor with a beautiful basket filled with food. Dylan is sitting on the blanket next to the basket, pouring champagne into glasses. He's wearing a white button-down shirt with the sleeves rolled up, and black slacks.

"Honey, this is stunning," I say. "I'm speechless." I'm still standing in his office doorway, taking it all in.

"Come have a seat." He smiles and pats the area next to him on the blanket.

"Baby, you are so sweet... and a hopeless romantic, I might add. I feel like the luckiest woman in the world." I kneel down and join him on the floor. I place my hand on his cheek and kiss him softly, passionately.

"You touch me so deeply, baby," he says. "I feel like I have an entirely different set of emotions reserved just for how I feel about you."

"I feel exactly the same way about you, baby."

"So, how has your day been so far?" he asks.

"It's been fine. Thanks for asking," I say. "So, where is your staff?"

"I gave them the afternoon off, with pay, of course." He smiles.

"What about your patients?"

"I only had two patients this morning. That's why I decided to do this for you today."

I change the subject and get him up to speed on Sky and Fuji's situation. I told him she was preparing dinner for the two of them, and that Fuji stepped out to the liquor store. But instead of coming right back with a bottle of Alizé, the fool drove to Virginia to be with his ex-girlfriend.

"Unbelievable!" Dylan says. "You don't just get up and walk out on a woman like Sky. Why would he do something so cruel? She's his *wife*, for God's sake. Sky deserves better." Dylan pauses, and a mischievous smile appears on his face. "I have the perfect man for her. But I don't dare hook her up with him until her divorce from Fuji is final."

"Look at you, divorcing them already," I chide. "Don't be too sure she's really going to leave him. Girl has taken him back plenty of times before, for much worse offenses."

"I know there's a possibility she'll take him back. But eventually she'll leave him...or he'll leave *her*. Their relationship is toxic. Fuji lives like he's single. That will only fly for so long before it destroys their marriage completely. Just be there for your friend, baby, as much as you can. She's going to need you."

I smile. "I'm glad you said that, baby. I feel guilty for not being there for her in Virginia, but my first priority is always my family."

"I know that, baby. That's one of the reasons I love you so much. But it's okay to be with your friends when they need you. You and your friends are like sisters, and they're as much my family as they are yours. I could never drive a wedge between you and your girls."

"Oh, honey, you're the best," I tell him. "I love you. Now, just what do we have in here?" I begin digging through the contents of the picnic basket. "When did you find the time to do all of this?"

"Well, I got a little help from my receptionist, Lucy. She was gracious enough to run out and pick up a few things for me."

He leans over and kisses me passionately. I stop him and say, "Honey, you are going to be so mad at me."

"Why?" He looks at me quizzically. I give him my best puppy-dog look and turn out my bottom lip. "It's that time of the month, isn't it?"

"Yes, honey. I'm sorry."

He chuckles softly. "That's not exactly your fault, baby."

I look at him, smile, and take a bite of my sandwich. My phone rings. On the other end of the line, Tasha is practically out of breath. "Sky and Fuji almost got arrested!" she says.

"What?" I ask in disbelief.

Dylan is looking at me, concerned. "What's happening?"

I ask Tasha to hold on a moment. "It's Tasha. Sky and Fuji almost got arrested." Dylan nods and waits patiently while I get the rest of the story from Tasha.

When I finally hang up from Tasha twenty minutes later, I do my best to relay the details to my husband. "Bear with me, baby, while I try to keep this story straight," I say. "I guess Fuji came over to Infinity's room after all the drama yesterday and begged to speak with Sky. Sky, of course, went back with him to his room." I roll my eyes. "While they were in Fuji's room, someone knocked on the door. Fuji just assumed it was one of the guys he does business with, so he turned the knob on the door and pulled it ajar and then directed his attention right back to Sky without paying attention to who he was letting into the room." Dylan nods and tells me to go on.

"Apparently, earlier yesterday before the girls arrived in Virginia, three guys came to Fuji's room. Fuji knew and was cool with two of them, but he didn't know the third guy. Anyway, these guys dropped off a package in Fuji's room that turned out to be a briefcase with a hundred thousand dollars inside." I pause to think. "My guess is that we were right about Fuji. He is definitely into something illegal."

"Well, it's not all that difficult to conclude, given Fuji's general attitude," Dylan agrees.

"Well, after the drop, they invited Fuji to some party that was taking place later that night. Apparently, Fuji doesn't like mixing business with pleasure, so he declined. Then, this morning, when Fuji and Sky were talking in his room, the one guy Fuji didn't know from the day before was the one that knocked on the room door. He had a gun, Dylan!" I stop and take a deep breath. "Anyway, this guy demanded that Fuji give him the money from the briefcase. Fuji was taken completely off guard. And poor Sky, she was terrified. Still *is* terrified, according to Tasha. In fact, all the girls are pretty freaked out right now."

"Portia, this just isn't our scene at all."

I nod. "Here I was feeling guilty for not being there, and now I'm grateful I'm not. Anyway, the gunman told them not to scream or say a word. He told Fuji that if he just handed over the money, he would leave and no one would get hurt. So Fuji did what the guy asked him to do, holding Sky behind him the entire time.

"But instead of leaving right away like he said he would, the gunman started saying things to Fuji like, 'You think you're a big shot here on my turf, don't you?'

Sky told the girls that Fuji started to say something back to the guy, but then I guess he thought better of it. Then the gunman said, 'This is *my* town, and I am the man. I catch you down here again, I rob you. So take your ass back to Florida and become king on *your* streets.' Or something like that. Anyway, I guess the guy started getting all pumped up at that point, saying things like, 'I don't like the way you're looking at me, punk,' and, 'I don't think it would be smart for me to let you and your lady go.'" I can't imagine how scared Sky must have been. I realize that my heart is pounding. "After that, the guy cocked his gun, but Fuji *thankfully* acted fast. He was able to grab Sky and run into the bathroom. Luckily, the gunman's pistol jammed or something.

"While they were in the bathroom, they could hear the guy trying to fire the gun, but it was still jammed. I guess they could see his shadow pacing back and forth through the crack at the bottom of the bathroom door. Creepy. Then the guy stopped pacing and just stood still in complete silence for what must have felt like hours to Sky and Fuji. Then he just walked away." I shrugged. "Just like that, he was gone.

"Of course they were relieved when they heard the room door close. I guess Sky tried to leave the bathroom at that point, but Fuji pulled her back in and signaled for her to stay quiet. He wasn't in any rush to go back out into the room. I mean, I guess he was right. How could they be sure the gunman was really gone?

"At that point, Fuji remembered that his cell phone was in his pocket, so he called his boys to let them know what was going on. But instead of coming to back him up, his buddies called him back and told Fuji that they'd called the police."

Dylan shakes his head, amazed. "I never would have thought criminals would call the police for backup."

"Apparently, neither did Fuji. But I guess Sky was getting pretty desperate by this point, because she called the girls from Fuji's phone and told them to knock on Fuji's room door. She told them to be careful because there might be a gunman in the room. They didn't believe her at first, but they went ahead and did it. When Sky heard the knock, she ran from the bathroom, opened the room door, and ran into the girls' arms." I'm starting to tear up just thinking about how terrified Sky must have been by then. "Tasha said Sky was shaking like a leaf.

"They didn't really know what went on, but the girls didn't waste any time. They ganged up on Fuji and started screaming at him, asking him what in the hell they did to Sky. He didn't even respond. That's when the girls realized he was just as scared as Sky was. After she calmed down a little, Sky was able to tell the girls what happened. But as she was trying to explain everything that had gone on, two uniformed police officers showed up at Fuji's room. They said they'd received an anonymous call complaining of a disturbance." I roll my eyes. "Well, Fuji *apparently* found his voice at that point and told the officers there wasn't any problem. But the officer didn't believe him. I guess he went back and forth with one of the officers for a while, and then the officer insisted that they search the room. Fuji just said to the guy, 'Knock yourselves out.'

"So the officers searched the room. According to Tasha, they left no stone unturned. Their search didn't turn up anything, though, so the officer looked at Fuji and said, 'We both know why you're here, and we're not going to allow you to dirty this town with your filth.'

"Then the guy's partner stepped up to Fuji and said something like, 'My partner and I are going to escort you to the highway so you can get the hell out of this state. And if we catch you here again, we're taking you in.'

"Fuji started getting his things together at this point, and Sky said to the girls that she was going to go with him." I shook my head. "I guess I understand why she'd want to do that. He is still her husband, after all. No wonder she hasn't been answering my calls."

Dylan gets up from our picnic and walks over to the window. He looks troubled and deep in thought. "Sky doesn't need to be tangled up in this street life bullshit," he says. "She's too much of a lady for this. She needs to get out of this relationship before she gets hurt, or worse. And y'all are going to have to help her."

"I totally agree, Dylan."

"I can't believe she left with him after all that," Dylan says. "How much does she have to take before she realizes Fuji is no good for her?"

"But Dylan, I can imagine how she felt. She thought she was going to lose her husband to a gunman. No matter how terrible Fuji has treated her, he is still her husband. It's probably very difficult for her to imagine him gone."

Dylan turns to face me and smiles. "Hey, I have something for you." He walks over to his coat hanging on the coat rack in the corner of his office and reaches into the pocket. He pulls out a gorgeous diamond bracelet, gently takes my arm, and clasps it around my wrist. "For my lovely wife."

"Thank you, honey!" I scream, wrapping my arms around his neck. I am once again overwhelmed by his love and generosity.

"You're welcome, baby. Now let's get out of here and go home."

"Oh baby, I'm so sorry for putting a damper on our romantic lunch—making you listen to my friends' problems."

"You're forgetting, they're my friends, too."

I look at the bracelet and smile, then look up at him and wipe a bread crumb from the corner of his mouth. "*You* are my favorite accessory."

Chapter 12

DIAMOND

BACK IN NEW YORK CITY

I was in the liquor store one day when in walked Gerald, talking to Fuji on his cell. I happened to overhear the first part of their discussion because Gerald had Fuji on speaker. They were talking in code, but I knew what they were saying.

"Hi, Fuji!" I said into Gerald's phone when I realized who he was talking to.

I heard Fuji say, "Yo," on the other end, but he didn't know it was me. "Who is that?" Fuji asked Gerald.

"That's Diamond," Gerald answered.

"Take me off speaker," Fuji said, sounding annoyed.

I heard Gerald telling Fuji something about a package in Virginia being ready for him. "You need to hurry up there and pick it up for me, Fuji. And be careful. The cops in Virginia are pretty swift. They know a street transaction when they see one."

I continued to listen to Gerald's end of their conversation. I learned that the police in Virginia pay very close attention to out-of-state license plates. They're all too aware of the drug trafficking that goes on, and the shit that goes down with it. It's crucial to get in and out as quickly as possible.

"You have to leave right away, Fuji," I heard Gerald tell him. I didn't hear what it was that they were purchasing or profiting from, but I had enough information to suit my own purpose. "There's a motel room already reserved for you at the Comfort Inn, room 256. My guy's already got a room, but he'll be leaving today, right after the pickup." Gerald gave Fuji exact directions to the Comfort Inn, of which I made mental note. "My man is leaving a key inside the fire extinguisher cabinet down the hall from the room. So, go on, get! Time is money, and money is time!"

Bastard! Didn't even say hi or bye to me. Nothing. But I decided not to get angry with Fuji. I'd get even instead. It was time to move on. I wasn't going to let any sort of guilt over having slept with him interfere with my normal functioning. I'd get his ass. Man can't treat me like a disease and get away with it.

I grabbed my phone from my pocketbook and placed a call to a friend of mine who lives in Virginia. He controls the streets down there. He's big time. I relayed to him what I could of the conversation between Gerald and Fuji, and gave him the information on the hotel and the room Fuji would be staying in. *Damn, I'm good.*

I also told him how Fuji was making a shitload of money from drops in Virginia, that Fuji was taking money out of *his* pocket, and that he shouldn't take that from no one. The one thing I couldn't provide was an exact time. He'd just have to use his best judgment.

He thanked me for the heads-up and said, "I got something for you as soon as the deal is sealed. I'll give you a shout-out when it's a done deal."

"Okay," I said.

After we hung up, I pictured Fuji's deal turning sour, and a big, broad smile broke across my face. "Sucker," I whispered to myself.

I paid for my booze and headed home to celebrate and look forward to my big payoff.

Chapter 13

LOLA
YOU PUT ON QUITE A SHOW

It's been two and a half weeks since our showdown in Virginia with Sky and Fuji. I can't believe she's back with him. But I can't spend my time worrying about Sky when my own life ain't right.

I've been trying to get my mind off Winston for a couple of hours. I really put that guy on a pedestal. I thought that man had been put on this Earth just for me, but he turned out to be just like the others—if not worse.

Our relationship was like the perfect storm: rain, snow, sleet and wind. I wore my heart on my sleeve. I didn't play games with him. And what I thought was true love turned out to be a catastrophe. Winston let me down in a major way, and in doing so, created the monster I have become toward men. I hate him. And I will never trust another man. I'm not planning to turn to women, but I don't have faith in men anymore, and it's all because of him.

I started getting suspicious of Winston's loyalty when the holidays came around. I noticed him conspicuously absent on family holidays like Thanksgiving and Christmas. But he was also missing-in-action on couples' holidays like New Year's Eve, and even Valentine's Day. He always had a justifiable excuse—had to work overtime or some such. If he did show up, it would only be for a short time, and then he'd be off again. But I trusted him fully. I never questioned it. I believed he loved me and that he was sincere.

One day, he showed up at my house with a magazine. I happened to notice a woman's name on the mailing label, and while I was mildly curious about it at the time, I didn't really think that much of it. Perhaps the magazine originally belonged to an associate of his. He happened to leave the magazine behind when he left that day, and without thinking, I tossed it on top of a stack of my own magazines.

There was another day when I called him to tell him I was in the neighborhood and was about to do a drive-by—a quick stop-in for sex. I let myself into his house and immediately noticed that all the pictures of me were missing from the walls. I was curious and did some hunting around, and found them stacked up on his night table. I got curious, and upon further investigation, I found that the lingerie I kept in one of his dresser drawers had been removed, put into a plastic bag, and placed up in his closet behind the blankets.

I approached him and asked, "Why did you take all my pictures down?" He gave me some lame excuse about wanting to buy new frames for them. And I believed him! Then, when I asked him about my lingerie, he said he was just making room for *his* clothes, that he'd had run out of space. I believed that, too. Sort of. In any case, I masked my concern and decided to let it slide.

On Tuesday of the last week we were together, the day started out pretty typical for a day at Winston's house. Usually, when I'm over, I cook dinner and then make love to him after we eat. On this particular evening, we decided to use my vibrator, which I kept in his nightstand drawer. When we were finished, I went into the bathroom to do a quick bird-wash and clean my vibrator. When I was walking over to put the vibrator away, I caught a look of alarm on Winston's face. I didn't know what to think. As I set the device back inside the nightstand drawer, I vaguely noticed a blue box in there, but I didn't think too much of it and closed the drawer.

But as I climbed back into bed, I was puzzled. I didn't understand that look on Winston's face. I decided that as soon as he left the room, I was going to look inside that drawer again, a little more carefully this time. A couple of minutes later, he got up to go to the bathroom. I quickly leaned over his side of the bed and pulled open the drawer. And there it was—the proof. In that one instant, all of my love and trust for Winston vanished.

I was so grateful to have this man in my life. I showed appreciation to God every day that we were together. I thought God had sent him to me. But it was all a lie. How disgusted and disappointed I felt in that moment. A brand new box of condoms from Rite Aid, unopened. I just stared at it for what seemed like hours, trying to register what was happening. We hadn't used condoms in nearly a year now, so they were definitely *not* for us.

I waited for him to come back in the room. I wanted to whip his ass.

Instead, I kept my composure—for a moment—until I threw the box at his face. It hit him square in the forehead. He was completely caught off guard. Then, very calmly, I asked him, "What are you doing with those?"

He looked like a deer in headlights. You would not believe the lame excuse he gave. He insulted my intelligence by telling me his nephew had come over the other night and gave out condoms to him and his friends. Now, I don't know if men give lame excuses because they don't have the ability to come up with a better one, or because they are operating under the assumption that their women are dim or simply not paying attention.

I said, "Okay, fine. Then you won't have a problem calling your nephew and letting me speak to him."

"Fine," he answered, and then proceeded to call his mother and ask for his little brother…instead of his nephew! Can you believe that? He called his mother to ask for his brother, instead of calling his sister to ask for his nephew. He was stalling, and at the same time, he was managing to make a complete ass of himself. *Hello, jackass! Your nephew doesn't live with your mom!* Men are so not good at getting caught. They are simply not smart enough to get one over on us—unless we let them.

So, I'm listening to him on the phone with his mom, asking her for his little brother, who has absolutely nothing to do with any of this. Now I'm confused, so I ask, "What the hell are you calling your mother for?" I can hear his mother through the phone, informing Winston that his brother is asleep.

"All right then, tell him to call me when he gets up." He continues talking with his mother for a few minutes and then finally asks after his nephew. Of course, he only asked for him because I was damned near breathing down his neck, reminding him why he called in the first place. His mother then informed Winston that his nephew wasn't at her house.

When he hung up the phone, I asked him again, "Why did you call your mother?

"Because my nephew was over there earlier today."

"Well, he's not now. Call his cell phone," I demanded.

"I don't have his cell number." A lie.

"You had it before."

"He has a new number."

"Well, why didn't you ask your mother for the number? Better yet, why don't you give your sister a call? She's his mother. I'm pretty certain she would have her son's cell phone number.

"My sister's at work."

"Whatever," I said. At this point I was so agitated that I decided to leave well enough alone. If it wasn't for the way he was acting, I probably would have believed his lies. But the way he was reacting to my questions, I knew something was wrong—very wrong.

His face was blank. He just stood there by the bed looking stupid. I couldn't stand to look at him, so I excused myself to the bathroom. This man had deceived me, and I just kept wondering to myself how he could be so cruel. Why would he not be faithful to me? I did everything right, or so I thought. I finally came to the conclusion that Winston was simply not the man he portrayed himself to be.

A few moments later, I could hear him yelling from the bedroom, "Honey, I'm not cheating on you. Now, come back to bed." The sound of his voice made my skin crawl. I was disgusted by him. I gathered my things and stormed out of his house with the intention of never coming back. I could still hear him calling my name in the background until I slammed his front door on my way out.

My heart turned to ice. I rushed home because I wanted to cry, but I couldn't shed a tear. I was hurt, but I was also completely numb. I even tried to force myself to cry, but the tears just wouldn't come. I never realized just how much I loved and trusted Winston until that moment.

I kept wondering, *Is this normal?* I wanted to cry so I could release the pain, but my mind seemed no longer able to make contact with my heart.

~~~

Two weeks later, I was sitting on my couch, reminiscing. There had been warning signs, but I'd chosen to ignore them. Then I remembered the magazine with the woman's name on it. It had been sitting on the entertainment center for months by that time. I felt something that day he'd left the magazine behind, but I'd shoved the uneasy feeling to the back of my mind.

I decided that I needed to investigate further, for my sanity—and closure. Normally, it wouldn't be my style, but this was something I felt I had to do. The time I invested in this relationship was compelling me to find the missing parts of this confounding puzzle.

I called up a friend of mine who's a private investigator and gave her the name and address from the magazine's mailing label. Twenty minutes later, she called me back with a phone number. I hesitated for a day or two. I wasn't
~~~

sure if I was ready to hear the worst. If I heard the worst, I'd have to leave him for good, plain and simple. I deserved better, and I wasn't about to accept anything less. On the other hand, ignorance is sometimes bliss. What I didn't know couldn't hurt me, right? But I knew I'd never be able to trust him again with all these questions going around in my mind.

Two days later, I gathered the courage to call the woman from the magazine mailing label. I decided that if I was able to gather proof that Winston was cheating on me, I would leave him.

I picked up my phone and placed the call. After the second ring, I nearly hung up because I started to lose my nerve. But before I could decide for sure, I heard a woman's voice on the other end of the line. "Nicole speaking."

"Hello, my name is Lola."

"Yes, do I know you?" the woman asked.

"No, you don't know me, and I don't know you," I said. "But I believe we have a friend in common. Do you know Winston?"

"Yes, Winston is my fiancé. How may I help you?"

"Fiancé?" I repeated, nearly choking on the word. I felt dizzy, and thought I might be sick. My brain was having trouble comprehending what she'd just said. My heart was most certainly breaking. But somehow I regained my composure.

"Well, it might interest you to know that I've been in a relationship with your *fiancé* for several years."

She remained polite and calmly said to me, "Winston and I have been together for twenty years. We've been engaged for three."

I swallowed hard. I felt like I might pass out. "WHAT?" I screamed into the phone. "Well, that man might as well just lie down on the floor and stop breathing because *he's dead!*" I recaptured my composure after releasing those words, and instantly, I was full of regret. She had been so polite to me and was obviously extremely well-spoken. I could well understand why this woman would interest Winston.

My worst fears came true when she said she and Winston had two children together, ages twelve and fifteen. All this time he'd been making me feel like I was number one, and it turned out that *I* was the other woman. My blood was boiling, but somehow I found it within myself to move forward with our conversation.

"So, when are you planning to marry?" I asked her.

"Sometime in the next couple of months," she answered.

"Um, do you mind if we meet? I want to show you some pictures of

Winston. I want to be absolutely sure that we're talking about the same man."

"Yes, you can meet me at my home, if you'd like," she offered. "If you'd feel more comfortable meeting in a public place, I'm open to that also."

"Your home sounds just fine. Thank you."

"You can come over now, if you'd like. Winston and I don't live together yet—we're waiting until after the wedding. Here, let me give you my address."

As I was writing her address on a piece of paper, it occurred to me that her reaction to all of this seemed a little unusual. In fact, I was quite stunned by her demeanor. She seemed way too calm for a woman who'd just found out that her man of twenty years—*her fiancé*—had been in a relationship with another woman for years. "Can I ask you a personal question?"

"I suppose."

"Are you at all bothered by the information I just shared with you?"

"To be sure, I'm angry. But I make it a habit never to lose my cool. I am a woman of high social position. I was brought up to handle things tactfully no matter how disturbing they might be."

I was perplexed—and a little impressed. "Okay, I'll see you in a few."

I wanted to call the girls, but I needed to make sure Nicole and I really were talking about the same man. My gut feeling was that we were, but there was still a part of me holding out hope for a miracle, some kind of crazy coincidence.

When she opened the door, she gestured for me to come inside. As I walked in, she checked me out from head to toe. I was taken aback when she said, "Yeah, you look like his type." I didn't know what she meant, being that she was the exact opposite of me in both appearance and attitude.

She was petite, about four foot eleven, and skinny as hell. Her complexion was dark, and she was pretty, but in an unusual way—her eyes set far apart. She wore glasses. She seemed uptight. And she was definitely a snob. I almost felt like a nerd.

"Come into the living room and have a seat." There were framed photos covering the walls—pictures of the two of them, pictures of their kids, pictures of the two of them with their kids. Most of them looked to have been taken at different vacation destinations, but the thing I noticed more than anything else about all of those photos was that the people in them looked happy.

I was frustrated all over again. I'd thought that by changing my taste in men, I would get the man of my dreams, like Portia. But I was wrong. Winston had concealed his true identity from me, but at that moment I could no longer deny his deceit. His secret life was revealed by the images in those frames. Of course, it wasn't his *secret life* at all. It was his real one. His life with me was the imposter.

"Yes," I said, "this is the same man I am in love with." I paused. "Oh, how could I have been so blind?" I muttered, fully aware that I was berating myself in front of this exceedingly proper woman. "Am I that naïve?"

I shook my head. I felt like a shell of my former self, totally deflated. And yet, I felt like I could have exploded at any moment. But Nicole was so calm. Her reaction to all of this was becoming more disturbing with each passing minute. She appeared as if she couldn't care less, and yet we were talking about the man she was scheduled to marry in just a couple of months. Was she devoid of emotion? Her face was expressionless. I was finding myself becoming more and more annoyed. I was also planning just how I would deal with Winston once I got my hands on him.

"I'm going to call him," she said. Before I could respond, she reached for her cell phone on the coffee table and dialed Winston's number. At this point, I happened to notice that I wasn't quite sure of her ethnic origins, and that I smelled curry.

"Hi, honey," she greeted him calmly. "There's someone here with me who would like to speak to you. Hold on..." Then she offered the phone. I was shocked. I wasn't prepared for this. She hadn't even discussed it with me. She just decided all on her own to go about it her way, with her cool ass. I took the phone from her, my hand shaking.

"Hi, Winston."

"Who is this?" he asked. No sign of alarm.

"It's me, Winston. Lola."

A pause, and then, "What the hell are you doing there?" he spit out, upset.

I glanced at the phone as if I was communicating with a stranger. Winston had never in our years together raised his voice to me. He had always been the perfect gentleman.

"You are the last person I would have thought would ever do this to me," he said. "I thought you were more mature than this." I was stunned—the nerve of his slick ass trying to make this about me. "You couldn't come to me and just ask? Instead you go off and try to *bust me*? Who are you? I thought you were different from other girls, Lola. But you've proven you're just the same as all the rest."

I was so taken aback by his comments that I just sat there, silent. I couldn't think of how to respond.

"Now, get off my phone!" he shouted.

The phone dropped from my hand. I watched it fall and hit the hardwood floor. The Winston I knew had a soul. He was warm, gentle, and considerate. But I didn't know the person on the other end of that phone line.

"Are you okay?" Nicole asked as she reached down to pick up her phone. But before I could give her an answer, she put the phone to her ear and said, "Hello? Are you still there? What did you say to her, Winston?" But I could tell she didn't bother to wait for him to reply. "No, I don't want you to come over here. It's over. We're through. Whatever we had together is done. If you come over here, I'll call the police." She hung up the phone and asked me again, "Are you okay?"

"He's never talked to me like that," I said, staring at her blankly. "The Winston I know is kind and gentle."

She smiled at me with genuine sympathy. "That man you just spoke to? That's the *real* Winston." She pointed to a large hole in the wall above the television. "Lola, that's an imprint of my head—from when Winston tried to kill me."

"Huh?" I was in shock.

"He thought I was cheating on him," Nicole explained. "Isn't that a laugh?"

"I have never seen that side of him," I said. "He's always been so kind. I've never detected one ounce of anger in him."

"He'll be coming over soon to plead his case, Lola. If you wish to confront him, you're more than welcome to stay."

"But I just heard you tell him to stay away. Did he say he was coming over anyway?"

"No, but I know my man. I've been dealing with him for decades now, after all. I'll understand if you'd like to leave before he gets here."

I paused for a moment and thought about my options. "I'll stay. Thank you."

After a few moments of silence between us, I asked, "Were you at all suspicious of him cheating on you?"

"I was. But whatever is done in the dark eventually comes to light. In truth, I've waited for this day with a certain amount of patience. I was about to give this man the other half of my life…then you came as a warning. You see, I think of you as a blessing, Lola, not a threat. I was about to make the biggest mistake of my life. I had my doubts, and I asked God to send me a sign. And here you are.

"My family and friends have always told me there is something 'not right' about Winston because he doesn't spend much time with us during the holidays. He always claims to be working or something, always some justifiable reason why we can't be together."

"Why have you put up with this for all these years?" I asked her.

"I wish I had a logical reason. Over time, it's just became a way of life for me. And then, of course, our children."

I'd given her the courage to walk away from this man that I thought was mine. But he was never mine. He was just an intruder. And he'd worked his way into my heart without an invitation. He made me the *other woman* without my consent.

Fifteen minutes had passed when we heard Winston attempting to open Nicole's front door. She had the chain pulled across it, so his attempt failed. A moment later, he tried entering through her kitchen window. Nicole screamed because she was so startled. "Winston, if you don't leave, I'm going to call the police!" But threat or no threat, a moment later, Winston was standing in her kitchen.

"I'm not going anywhere till you understand that me and this woman do not have a relationship," he yelled. "She's someone I dated very briefly, years ago. And because she can't seem to move on, she's been stalking me."

I looked at Winston in disbelief and turned to Nicole. "Do you mind if I smack him?" I asked her. "I'd like to hit him, and I don't want you jumping in."

Nicole stepped aside. "Go right ahead," she said kindly.

I walked up to Winston and hit him with my fist—square in the nose. He attempted to hit me back, but Nicole jumped between us. "If you hit her, we'll *both* jump your ass."

"Baby, do you seriously think I would jeopardize our relationship right before we're supposed to get married? I love you. I want to be with you."

"You honestly want me to believe this woman is crazy?" Nicole spat back. "Are you really trying to tell me she's making all of this up?"

"Yes," he says.

"Are you serious?" I asked. "Who *are* you? Where is the man that loves me?"

But he just kept up. "Lola, please stop lying. Tell my fiancée the truth. This is my life you're destroying."

"The truth?" I repeated, incredulous. "You wouldn't know the truth if it smacked you square in the face." I couldn't help but smile to myself at the fact that "the truth" *did* just smack him square in the face—*literally.* I turned to Nicole and thanked her for her time. Then I walked out. After I closed Nicole's door behind me, I looked up at the sky, sighed heavily, and said out loud, "God, this relationship was all make-believe. I need you to help me walk back into reality…because I can't do it alone."

As I walked away from the house, I could hear Nicole and Winston arguing. My intention was to walk to my car and get the hell out of there, but I walked past my vehicle absently and continued walking across the street to the park. When I reached the sidewalk surrounding the park, I said a silent prayer: *God, if you're listening, please send me a man who is capable of genuine love.* I was about to go on, but I got sidetracked by the attention I was getting from men in passing cars. One guy actually doubled parked, got out of his car, and started walking toward me. *Thank you, God.*

"Excuse me, do you have a minute?" he asked.

"No," I answered.

"Well, I have *two* minutes," he began. "Would you like to borrow one?" Then his face broke into a mischievous smile. He seemed polite enough and was very good looking. I had to give him points for such a unique comeback. I decided to give him my full attention.

"Now that's original," I said to him, smiling back. "I've never heard that line before."

"It's not a line," he said. "I have a lot of time on my hands." He paused and observed me curiously. "You're blushing."

"Truthfully, I've been having a horrible day," I said, "and you just helped to make it a little better. So, thank you."

"I'm glad to hear that. Um, may I offer you a ride somewhere?" he asked, gesturing to his double-parked car.

"No, thank you. My car is parked over there," I said, pointing to my car still in Nicole's driveway across the street. "But if you'd like to join me here in the park for a bit, you're welcome to. My name is Lola, by the way."

"Jeremy," he said as he held out his hand for me to take. I was so emotional I starting tearing up right in front of this perfect stranger.

"Well, I hope you were honest about having a lot of time on your hands, Jeremy. Because I've got a lot to talk about…"

~~~
~~~

The entire time I was talking to Jeremy, his eyes never left me. It was beginning to make me a little uncomfortable, so I paused my story for a moment and asked him, "What is this look you're giving me?

"I'm trying to figure out why I'm so attracted to you," he said. Then he asked, "Would you have dinner with me tomorrow night?"

I chuckled, and answered, "Yes."

"I didn't take you to your prom," he added sweetly, "but I promise to take you to the moon if you'll let me."

I looked at him and smiled disbelievingly. "Does the right thing to say always come natural for you, Jeremy, or have you rehearsed these lines before? The way you talk...well, let's just say that I'm extremely wary of taking you too seriously."

"Okay, maybe I'm taking it a little too far," he conceded, "but the reason is totally sincere, I swear. I just really want to make a good first impression here because I would love to see you again."

What am I getting myself into already? I thought. I hadn't even taken time to process all that had gone on with Winston. And I'd already agreed to go out on a date with someone new? *Oh well, why not? That's how the cookie crumbles, and Jeremy is here to pick up my crumbs.* My mom always told me, "The only way to get over a man, Lola, is to get under another one."

Just then, my phone rang. Winston's name popped up on the screen. My heart started to beat faster and harder, and I suddenly felt uncomfortably warm. Before I could decide whether or not to pick up the phone, I heard myself saying, "Hello?" I excused myself from Jeremy and walked down the sidewalk a few feet.

"Can I talk to you?" Winston asked. I was completely silent; I couldn't get a single word out. "Lola, are you there?" he asked, sounding a little desperate.

I took a deep breath. "Yes, I'm here, and yes, you can talk to me."

"Where are you?" he asked.

"I'm across the street from Nicole's house, at the park."

"I'm coming over there now."

I realized that I wanted him to see me talking to Jeremy. I placed my hand on his knee. "My ex is going to be meeting me here in a few minutes—to talk." I grabbed Jeremy's hand. "I need closure."

"I understand," he said. "Just promise me you'll call me."

"I most certainly will," I promised. Out of the corner of my eye, I saw Winston crossing the street. I knew he could see me talking to Jeremy, and it made me laugh inside. I gave Jeremy a peck on the cheek, and he walked off before Winston approached me.

"Who was that?" Winston asked.

"None of your business," I answered flatly. "What do we have to talk about, anyway?"

"I want to apologize to you, for disrespecting you," he said. "I was angry."

"If you think I'm going to believe that bullshit, you're out of your mind. What happened, Winston? Did Nicole kick you to the curb, and now you want to make things better with me?"

"No, ba—"

I cut him off. "Don't you even think about calling me 'baby.'" Tears started to form in my eyes. I stared at him without blinking. "What kind of man pretends to be with me, spends time with my friends and family, holds me in his arms, assures me I'm safe with him, and it all turns out to be a lie?" The tears started to spill down my cheeks. "The person I've been having this relationship with doesn't even exist." Hearing myself say those words was a bitch slap of truth. "You convinced me we were going to live our lives together forever."

"I love you, and that is no lie," he said pleadingly.

"Are you telling me the truth now?" I asked. "Because the man back there obviously loves Nicole." I stopped and took a long breath. "You treated me like a stranger, Winston! Like some crazy, obsessed old girlfriend." I was incensed. "How could you do that?"

Winston just stared at me, mouth open.

"Answer me, you bastard!"

"I'm sorry," he said. "I never meant to hurt you. I messed up."

"I wish I could take back the years you stole from me," I hissed.

Then he had the nerve to say in a smooth tone, "Shut up and listen to me. Sometimes I feel like another person."

"Oh boy, here we go," I said, and rolled my eyes.

"Just listen to me. I'm trying to do the right thing now." He paused. "It's almost like I leave myself most of the time. Like I'm dressing up and playing a part. Like I'm living as my alter ego."

"So, today you're dressed up in guilt?" I said sarcastically.

"Lola, I'm just trying to explain. To make sense of my actions."

"I don't need an explanation, Winston. I had a front-row seat for the live show." I got up and started walking away from him. Then I noticed a woman approaching us.

"Winston, baby, is that you?" the woman asked him.

Winston looked at me, panicked. He didn't know how to get out of this one. "Honey," he stammered, "what are you doing here?"

"Excuse me," I interjected, "and who might you be?"

"I'm his girlfriend," she said. "And who are *you*?"

"Well, up until about an hour ago, I was his girlfriend, too," I answered. "I hate to burst your bubble, but this man also has a fiancé and two children."

"What?" Her eyes went wide. She looked at Winston and turned to me. "Well, we've been together for two and a half years, *exclusively*."

"Woman," Winston interjected, "you cheated on me, so shut up."

"I did, and I apologized," she said. "And you accepted my apology, remember?" She gave him a look of disgust. "You made me feel like what I did was the worst thing in the world." The woman paused. The truth was clearly sinking in. "And you were cheating on *me* the whole time—with *two* other people?" She was standing there, indignant, in tight jeans and high heels. She'd been walking through the park with club gear on—who *does* that?

"I never took you seriously after you cheated on me," Winston said arrogantly. "You're damaged goods now."

I stood there in disbelief. I couldn't believe his twisted way of looking at things. What the hell was with the double standard? I had to get out of there. "Well, three's a crowd," I announced, and hurried off to catch up to Jeremy.

~~~

KENNEDY

I tried to convince Lola not go out with Jeremy so soon after her breakup with Winston. But talking to Lola is like talking to a brick wall. Her strategy was to date as much as possible, as soon as possible, to keep her mind off Winston. She told me that her heart would heal more quickly that way.
~~~

Chapter 14

BROOKE
BAILEY IS MISSING IN ACTION

Someday, I'm going to kick the habit, once and for all. I've been smoking for over twenty years. My daily cigarette tally has grown with each passing year. It's so bad now that when I get up in the middle of the night to pee, I light up before I go back to bed. I *did* change from Marlboro Reds to Marlboro Lights a while back—my version of a cigarette diet.

Randy thinks I've quit. He despises cigarettes—and smokers. I don't blame him. It's not exactly a pleasant odor, nor is it a very attractive look for a beautiful woman such as myself. It's a harmful addiction that I can't seem to kick. Lord knows I've tried. Every day I tell myself this is my last pack. Then a birthday, holiday, or a vacation comes up that requires drinking. When I drink, I smoke—just no way to separate the two. Cigarettes intensify the high from the alcohol, and I can't resist that combination. And being around others who smoke doesn't help.

Today I'm preparing a calm rest-and-relaxation day at my house for me and the girls—to help us all blow off a little steam. I hired a party planner to bring "Hawaii" to my backyard, and I'm going to throw a few steaks and burgers on the grill. The girls and I have been going through some tough life changes lately. It's time for a little stress release.

Lola is *still* dealing—or not dealing—with the fallout of Winston's deception. Sky found out Fuji is not only a cheater, but also a criminal. And I continue to have problems with my daughter, Bailey, and the young man down the block. I use the term "young man" loosely. Recently, I found out Bailey is still sneaking over there after school to see him.

I chose to be a stay-at-home mom because I feel it's important to be here for Bailey full time. It's how my mom raised me. Thankfully, Randy and I share the same parenting philosophy, and through his financial support (and a little help from my parents) we've been able to honor our beliefs. I was helping Kennedy with the phones at her office because her business has been picking up so much lately. Unfortunately, this meant I was rarely home anymore to greet Bailey after school. But with her behavior becoming more and more difficult, I decided to cut back on my hours.

I've been hearing stories about Bailey and Cory continuing to see each other behind my back. I feel like I'm losing control of her. Sometimes I have to keep the fear in my child's heart. It's the only way I can keep her respecting me.

The doorbell is ringing. It must be the girls. It's 8:30 on Saturday morning. They agreed to arrive early to help me prepare for the barbeque. I'm good at making pasta and finger foods because of my Italian background. Kennedy always makes her famous lo mein. Portia makes the best potato salad. Lola is making Mexican rice and beans. Lola's food tastes better than at a Mexican restaurant—she has the magic touch. Payton tends to keep things basic, so she's preparing a tossed salad and providing the spiked punch. Sky is making oxtail, Jamaican style. She learned to cook Jamaican dishes from being around Winston, when Lola and Winston were still together. And Tasha…well, Tasha doesn't cook. Unless you count peanut butter and jelly sandwiches. I've assigned her to grill duty. I open the door, and they all say together, "Has anyone told you they love and care about you today? Well, we do!"

"Aw, group hug, ladies," I say.

Tasha has on a T-shirt that reads: *I'm stress free cuz I don't have a boyfriend.* I can't help but chuckle when I read it. We all head into the kitchen and begin the preparations for our afternoon vacation.

"Diamond called me the other day," Sky mentions right off. "She wanted me to tell you guys she misses you. She was also telling me she feels like she's falling into a depression, that she needs an escape. I was thinking maybe we can all chip in and send her a roundtrip ticket to Orlando for a week," she suggests. "What do you guys think?"

"Yeah, let's do it," Kennedy agrees. "I kinda miss her crazy ass, too."

"I told her about the Fuji episode in Virginia," Sky continues. "She was beating herself up for not being there," Sky says, and sighs. "Anyway, I tried to cheer her up, but she seems really down, girls."

"Well, I cut back my hours at Kennedy's," I announce. "I'd be happy to go online this week and look for a plane ticket."

"Why did you cut back on your hours?" Payton inquires.

"Girl, Bailey's been sneaking off to see that guy again," I say, obviously frustrated.

"I knew something was up with that kid when I talked to her the other day," says Lola. "She was all sly and secretive. I just figured she was getting to that age where she needs her privacy—no time for her auntie anymore." Lola rolls her eyes playfully.

"Where is the little brat?" Portia jokes.

I chuckle. "She's over at her dad's house. He's bringing her over in a bit to join us." The doorbell chimes. It's my party planners, ready to set up. I direct them to the backyard. Two hours later, the yard is ready. It's magical—I really feel like I'm in Hawaii.

My parents entertained all the time when I was a kid. In fact, they still love to throw parties. I come from a wealthy family. My parents moved from New York to Beverly Hills a few years ago. My dad is a cosmetic surgeon, and my mom owns a fabric store. My mom and I are close, but I'm a total daddy's girl—don't have to ask for anything. When I moved to Orlando, Daddy made sure I had plenty of credit cards and an account set up where he could deposit money for me if I needed it. He doesn't want me to depend on a man for anything—well, unless that man is him.

Randy is here dropping off Bailey. He didn't realize we were having a Hawaiian-themed spa day. "What is going on here?" he mused.

"Oh, I decided to get the girls together and make believe that we're on vacation at a Hawaiian resort."

"At *your* expense, or Daddy's?" he says, laughing.

"Later, Randy!" I grin and wave goodbye to him.

We're having a blast, enjoying our massages and discussing the various happenings in our lives. The masseuses rub and knead, and we're all becoming more relaxed as the minutes tick by. I can tell the four masseuses are intrigued by the stories of our lives, even adding their two cents every once and a while. Their feedback intrigues us. It's always interesting, and often very helpful, to get an outsider's opinion. The day is just as relaxing as I planned it to be.

After our massages, I begin to wonder why Bailey has been so quiet. Back before all of this new behavior started up, she would have insisted on joining us. "I'll be back, ladies," I say. "I'm going upstairs to check on Bailey."

In Bailey's room, I see her school uniform on the floor next to the bed. Her closet looks like it's been ransacked. Her book bag is on the closet's doorknob. But Bailey is nowhere to be found. I don't panic at first, just assume she's just gone outside. I walk downstairs and step out the front door to have a look around, but I don't see her anywhere. My stomach lurches, but I remain calm. I go back inside and tell the girls what's happening. I make phone calls to her cousins and her friends. No one has heard from Bailey. I call Randy. He doesn't waste any time in getting here. He shows up with a friend of his who's a detective for the state of Florida. Whoever said, *It's not what you know but who you know,* was really onto something.

Randy's friend has a team of searchers on the ground and a helicopter. The girls and I are doing whatever we can to help. After searching the neighborhood, I decide to go home. If she happens to call, I want to be by the phone. The girls don't want me to be alone, so they come with me.

Meanwhile, Randy, Dylan, Myles, and Fuji continue the search for my little girl. I never forgave Fuji for what he did to Sky, but *she* did. And I'm sure glad he's here today.

By six the next morning, there is still no sign of Bailey. We're all thinking the worst. My resolve to remain calm is weakening. I'm crying now, and the girls are trying to be strong for me.

It's Monday, so the guys are on their way to Bailey's school to see if she might show up there. No luck—she doesn't show. According to the police, Bailey is now officially a "missing person."

At seven that evening, the phone rings. It's the police department from a neighboring town. They tell me they have Bailey at their precinct. I drop the phone, get in the car, and drive. In the meantime, Portia calls Randy and tells him the news. Randy and I arrive at the station almost simultaneously, and are shocked to find that Bailey has blood smeared all over her blouse and scratch marks on her face. Her earlobe is torn where an earring has been ripped out. Her shirt is torn down a little ways past her breasts. I want to run to her and hug her, but my intention is thwarted when Randy and I are approached by a woman who turns out to be a detective.

"Are you Bailey's parents?" she asks us.

"Yes," we answer together.

"Please follow me." Randy and I obey. Moments later, the three of us arrive at a private office. "Please, have a seat," she says, motioning for us to use the chairs opposite her desk. "I want to relay to you what Bailey has told us about her situation. I should warn you that what I'm about to share may be difficult to hear." She takes a deep breath. "Bailey told us she was walking to the store about a half mile from your house yesterday afternoon when a white van pulled up and two boys jumped out of the cargo area and grabbed her. She said they threw her into the van and that there were two more boys inside, a driver and a passenger.

"She said they drove for about an hour and eventually pulled over into a deserted area, where they proceeded to rob, beat, and fondle her. She described them all as teenagers, black, ages roughly fifteen to nineteen."

Randy puts his arm around my shoulder and guides my head to his chest. He can see that I'm horrified, and he's trying to console me. But I'm having none of it. I get up and run out of the office in search of my child. Randy follows me. I want to make Bailey feel safe again. When I reach her, I see that the girls are already there sitting with her and trying to comfort her. Lola looks at me with a strange expression, and shakes her head. I'm curious. I step closer and ask, "Lola, are you okay?"

"Brooke, she's not telling the truth," Lola blurts out.

"Lola, how do you know?" Tasha asks. "She was obviously attacked."

"Just give me five minutes with her," Lola pleads. "I'll get to the bottom of this."

The detective, who has apparently been listening to our discussion, steps in and says to me, "I'm sorry, but I think your friend might be right." She turns to Lola. "You're welcome to use the small office across the hall."

The space is more the size of a closet than an office. Lola walks over to Bailey, who has her head buried in Randy's lap. "Honey, can I speak to you for a moment—in private?" Bailey, her eyes red and swollen, stands up and follows Lola. I follow behind them, but I don't enter the room. Tasha and the girls are going on about the way Lola is treating the situation. They sound angry.

"Hush!" I scold them. "I want to hear what's going on with my daughter." Lola's voice is loud enough that I can hear them even though they are now inside the office.

"Okay, Bailey," Lola begins, "I *know* you're not telling the truth. So, what really happened? And don't go wandering those eyes all around the room," she scolds. "Bailey, you're stalling." I can hear Lola sigh heavily. "Okay, let's try this, then: I'll start and then you take over." Lola takes a deep breath. "Number one, those scratches on your face look self-inflicted. Number two, the blood on your blouse looks smeared, as if you wiped it on yourself. It's time for you to come clean, girl, because you are making some very serious accusations here. And if you're lying, you'll be wasting the taxpayers' money, and the police department's time.

"I'm not trying to scare you into telling me the truth…or more lies, for that matter," Lola tells her. "I realize it's possible that this happened. The thing is, I don't believe it really did." Lola sighs again. "Okay, Bailey, your turn. Tell me what really happened."

I can hear Bailey break down. She's starting to cry. "Auntie, you're right. I made it all up," she confesses. "Do you hate me?" My heart feels like it stops beating for a few seconds. I'm disappointed and angry about what I just overheard. Tasha covers her mouth in disbelief, but no one says a thing. We just listen.

"Bailey, baby," Lola says, consoling her, "I just want you to tell me the truth."

"Okay, Auntie, I will. But I don't want to disappoint Mommy and Daddy."

"Bailey, I think it's a little late for that. But you have to remember that no matter if you disappoint them or make them angry, they will *always* love you, no matter what. I'm not going to lie to you. They'll be upset, but it's better to come clean now before this police investigation gets underway."

"Okay," Bailey begins, "me and a few girls from school met up to go over to a friend's house whose mom wasn't home—she's on vacation for the week. Anyway, we were just listening to music and dancing. Her older sister was supposed to be there looking after her and the house, but she ended up spending the night at her boyfriend's house.

"At first, there were just four of us, but more kids kept showing up, and before we knew it there were ten of us. So we made it a party…and it spun out of control. I lost track of time."

"Bailey, what do you mean it 'spun out of control'?" Lola interjects.

"Well, her mom has a mini bar in the living room…and we started drinking," Bailey says sheepishly. "I only took a taste, I swear. I didn't drink any more than that because I didn't like the taste. When I looked at the time, it was past midnight, and I panicked. My curfew is seven o'clock. So I spent the rest of the night with my friend trying to come up with a good excuse to tell my mom. That's when we decided on the robbery and kidnapping story. My friend told me we had to make it look like an attack."

"So, she scratched your face," Lola concludes.

"I told her to do it when I wasn't paying attention. I called the house to listen to Mom's voice, to get an idea of what frame of mind she was in. She sounded upset, so I hung up fast."

I nod at the girls and whisper, "I did get a hang-up call." Outside the little office, our ears are glued to the textured glass door.

"My friend was able to catch me off guard," Bailey continues. "She scratched my face and ended up ripping my earring out of my ear by mistake. I cried really hard because it hurt so much."

"So the tear-stained face, that's at least real," Lola says, sounding somewhat relieved.

"I'm so sorry, Auntie," Bailey apologizes. "I didn't know what else to do. I was too scared to come home. I didn't want to disappoint my mom again."

"You could have blown this situation up to another level had you stuck to your story," Lola scolds.

"I know, I wasn't thinking," Baileys admits. "But I was desperate."

"I'm proud of you for telling me the truth," Lola comforts. "Now it's time to apologize...to everyone—the officers, your parents, and all of the people who were out looking for you." Then Lola adds, "And remember, if you're ever in a jam again and you feel you can't go to your parents, you can always come to any of us. That's what we're here for. We're family. Do you understand what I'm saying, Bailey?"

"Yes, Auntie Lola. I'm so sorry." Bailey sniffs. "Auntie, can I ask you a question?"

"Of course," Lola answers.

"How did you know I was lying?"

Lola smiles. "Because I did the same thing when I was your age. Although my story isn't quite as extreme. There were and scratches and blood, but I wasn't nearly so creative as getting the police involved. I just told my parents that I got jumped by a bunch of bullies after school, and I was afraid to come home because they were following me, that I didn't want them to know where I lived." Lola pauses. "And don't you ever think about telling my parents the truth," she jokes. I hear laughter explode between them.

They're both still giggling as they step through the door of the office. I grab Lola and give her a big hug. "Thank you, friend," I say to her tearfully. I look at my daughter and say, "I'm so angry with you." Bailey's laughter dissolves.

Randy decides to jump on board. "That goes for me, too," he says to her, wagging his finger in her face. "You're grounded for three weeks, young lady.

And no TV! And no company. And no going outside after school. It's straight up to your room!" I've never seen Randy so angry—or so scared. The idea that his little girl isn't a little girl anymore is clearly hitting home. Just when I think he's done, he starts in on her again. "Oh, and one more thing: you're going to write a letter apologizing to all these good people who were out looking for you. That should take you about three weeks, come to think of it."

Randy turns to Lola and says, "She had all of us fooled—but not you. Thank you." Lola just smiles at Randy and pats his shoulder.

"I don't know about you guys," I say, "but I need a drink."

~~~

KENNEDY

Bailey is causing my friend Brooke nothing but stress. Before this most recent incident, Bailey had gone out with a friend on a school night and stayed out way past her curfew, until daylight. I guess Bailey didn't expect the consequence of getting her ass kicked by her mom that day. Her mom had never disciplined her so harshly before.

Brooke called to tell me Bailey had been gone since early evening. I called the girls to help with the search. Randy and Dylan joined us as well. Brooke stayed home. We felt it best for her to be there in case Bailey called or came home. We'd been searching most of the night when Brooke called to tell me Bailey had been calling and hanging up on her all night. We were getting nowhere with our search, so we went back to the house for the rest of night.

We tried to sleep, but no one was convinced Bailey was okay, so there wasn't much point in trying. At six in the morning, Bailey finally came in the door. I'd never seen Brooke react to Bailey the way she did that morning. She's usually a talk-it-out type, the typical white girl solution. But not this time. By the time Bailey walked through that door, Brooke had been stewing an awfully long time. She was pent up—full of worry and rage. She attacked Bailey right off. She just couldn't take the disrespect anymore, I think. Enough was enough. She didn't beat her, but she definitely manhandled her—pushed, grabbed, and shoved her. She yanked Bailey's arm so hard at one point she bruised her wrist.

It was because of me Bailey went to school that day. I yelled at her and expressed that she would still be going to school. No one cared how tired she was. I drove her there myself. After dropping her off, I went home, called my
~~~

office, and told them they'd have to manage things without me for the day, then went to sleep.

At 2:45 that afternoon, Brooke called to tell me that Bailey had reported her to social services. Brooke was so nervous. She practically screamed at me, "Come over here. I'm so scared." Bailey apparently told her teacher and the dean that her mom had physically abused her, and that she had the bruises to prove it.

I grabbed my keys and my purse from the table by the front door and rushed out to help my friend. I was pissed at Bailey—could have killed her. When I arrived at Brook's house, Randy was there. The police and the social worker were on their way out the door...without Brooke. Randy and Brooke were able to convince the authorities that Brooke was not an abusive parent. It helped to explain the circumstances and inform them that Bailey was in counseling.

Bailey eventually admitted to the social worker that she'd lied about the abuse because she was angry with her mother. The school had no choice but to report the abuse of course, and while they didn't find anything to charge Brooke with, they did suspect that there were ongoing problems between her and Bailey, and required Brooke to attend parenting classes for two months.

Brooke hated going to the parenting classes, and who could blame her? The first day of class, she told the teacher, "I have to attend these classes, but I will not be raising my hand to ask questions or turning in homework, because I don't really belong here." Eight long weeks later, she was finally free of the humiliation.

Bailey lived with Randy during that time. Brooke couldn't stand to look at her. Every time she looked at her daughter, she was reminded of what Bailey had done and why she had to attend parenting classes—three days a week, three hours a day.

Brooke allowed Bailey back into the house eventually. She couldn't take being in the house alone all the time. Bailey never apologized.

Chapter 15

DIAMOND

THE BALL ALWAYS FALLS IN MY COURT

My doorbell rings. To my surprise, it's Fuji. I spy him through the peephole, and now I'm so nervous I'm struggling to get the door open.

"What's up, Diamond?" he asks.

"What the hell are you doing in New York?"

"I'm only here for a couple of hours, have to take care of some business."

"Does Sky know you're here?"

"No, I'm only here for the day," he informs me. "I'll be home before she even notices I'm gone."

He steps inside, and I help him with his coat. I get down on my knees—and do exactly what he came here for. That bitch can't please him the way I do. That's why he keeps coming back. Eventually, he'll leave her, and I'm going to be right here waiting with open arms. It's just a matter of time.

After we're through, I ask, "How are you and Sky doing?"

"That's none of your business. Every time I come here, you ask me about Sky. But you don't give a damn about her, Diamond, so stop pretending like you do."

"I care about Sky," I told him. "I just hate that she don't appreciate what she has."

"Yeah, but *you* appreciate what she has."

Fuji gives Sky anything she wants. But she complains all the time about every little thing. If my man gave me everything I wanted, I wouldn't even care if he cheated on me. “Things between us are just fine,” he finally says, “couldn’t be better.”

“So why do you stop by my house every time you’re in town?”

“It wouldn’t be right if I didn’t,” he says, like he’s God’s gift to women. He acts as if everything between them is fine, but I know better. Fuji may refuse to discuss their personal life, but Sky doesn’t.

After he leaves, I call Sky. Because it’s long distance, I get my daughter to call her and tell Sky to call me. “Hi, Diamond,” she greets me when I pick up the phone.

“Hey, girl, what’s going on?” I ask.

“Same old, same old. Fuji and I have been struggling. Nothing major—I’m sure it’ll work itself out.”

“What, did he cheat on you again?”

“No, nothing like that. He’s just got some jealousy issues. He always thinks I’m out messing with somebody else.” As she says this, I feel rage building inside me. I want to curse her out, but I maintain my composure. I wish I was the one Fuji was jealous about. I decide to fill Sky’s head with reasons she should leave him.

And her dumb ass is agreeing with me. “I’m serious, Sky, you need to leave him. You don’t need him.”

I have to do something to get rid of this bitch. I want this man to myself. I got a trick up my sleeve. I’m just biding my time, waiting for the right opportunity to bring it out. The ball always falls in my court.

Chapter 16

BROOKE

SHE'S NOT A VIRGIN ANYMORE

It's two hours past Bailey's curfew, and she still isn't home. I don't want to call her dad prematurely. But I'm upset and worried so I call my girl, Kennedy, who also happens to be Bailey's godmother. "Kennedy, can you come over? Bailey isn't home yet, and I'm getting concerned. I don't want to call Randy unless I have to."

"Wasn't she supposed to be home hours ago?" Kennedy asks. "Do you want me to call the rest of the girls?"

"No, no. She may just be late. I don't want to involve them unless it's absolutely necessary."

Kennedy arrives about twenty minutes later and enters through my back door.

"Hello? Brooke? Where are you?" she calls.

"I'm in the kitchen on the phone," I answer back. When she steps into the kitchen, I cover the receiver and say quietly, "I'm on the phone with a friend of Bailey's." Kennedy nods and gives me a short hug while I continue talking with Bailey's friend. A moment later the front door opens. We get to the foyer just as Bailey is closing the front door. I'm relieved—and angry.

"Bailey, where the hell have you been?" says Kennedy. "You've had your mother scared to death!" Kennedy has a different approach than I do. Nonetheless, I'm standing behind Kennedy, silently rooting her on.

"I was just hanging out with some friends," she explains. "Time got away from me." Bailey shrugs, making me even angrier. "Gosh, you don't ever let me breathe, Mom. All my cousins are able to hang out, and *their* parents don't go crazy."

"Who? Who of your cousins are we talking about here?" I ask, thoroughly annoyed. Of course Bailey names the ones who are raised by a mother who's usually drunk, and parties most the time. When she's not hung over, that is.

"So you'd be happy if I was a drunk and a fool? You think that'd make me a better mother, huh?" I ask, disgusted.

Kennedy turns around to face me. "Let me handle this," she whispers. "She'll open up to me before she opens up to you. It doesn't matter how close the two of you are, you're still her mother, and Bailey is almost a teenager, which makes her almost instinctually directed not to trust you." Kennedy smiles sympathetically.

"Okay." I walk back to the kitchen, pouting. But I can hear their conversation from where I'm sitting at the table.

"Come have a seat, Bailey," Kennedy begins. "Let's sit here on the stairs for a minute and talk. I have a question. We've always been able to be open with each other. And you know you can trust me, right?" Kennedy pauses. "Can you tell me where you spent this evening? And please be honest, Bailey. If you were somewhere you weren't supposed to be, then it's even more important that you tell me the truth."

"I was at Cory's house," Bailey admits.

"Okay." Kennedy pauses. "Then my next question is very important, so listen carefully. Bailey, are you having sex with Cory?"

There's a long pause. "Yes," Bailey says, her voice barely audible from where I'm situated in the kitchen. I drop my head to the table. Tears form in my eyes. I continue listening.

"Was tonight your first time?"

"Yes."

"Did the two of you use a condom?"

"No."

I'm sobbing quietly now. My baby is no longer a baby.

I hear Kennedy sigh heavily. "Oh, Bailey. How could you be so irresponsible?" She's genuinely concerned. "We'll discuss this more later. I'm not through with you yet. But I do appreciate your honesty. You realize you have to share this with your mom, right? You can tell her yourself, or we can go into the kitchen right now and tell her together. What's it gonna be?"

"No, Auntie, I can't tell her," Bailey whines. "I don't want her to be disappointed in me."

"Bailey, it's going to disappoint her," Kennedy tells her. "She's going to be angry, but she'll get over it. Do you want to do this together?"

"Yes," Bailey says in a rush.

"Okay, let's go." I hear them coming toward the kitchen. Kennedy is reassuring Bailey that everything is going to be okay. When they walk into the kitchen, I can see Bailey is too frightened to talk to me. Kennedy has her arm around Bailey's waist, and she says, "Brooke, we have something to tell you." I decide to play dumb. I don't want Bailey to know I've been listening in, because I don't want her to trust me any less than she already does.

"What is it?" I ask. I realize knowing what they're going to tell me doesn't make me any more prepared to hear it firsthand. Bailey sits down beside me at the kitchen table, but remains silent.

Kennedy, seeing that Bailey can't get the words out, decides to take over. "There's no easy way to say this, Brooke, so I'm just going to say it. Bailey was with Cory tonight, and they had sex."

I want to deny it, was secretly hoping that I'd overheard wrong. I stand up from the table and drop to my knees on the kitchen floor. I repeat over and over, "God, no! Not my baby!" My cries are as though someone just told me my little girl died. And in a sense, she has. Kennedy kneels down beside me and motions for Bailey to join us. We all cry together for what seems like hours.

Later, after we've calmed down, Kennedy explains to me that this is just a part of life. She keeps reminding me that it could have been worse. I hug Bailey and ask her to tell me what happened. Before she starts explaining, I ask, "Did this take place at Cory's mother's house?"

"Well, yes, but I didn't go inside the house."

"What does that mean?" I ask, confused.

"I called to let him know I was outside," Bailey explains, "because I didn't want his mom to see me. A little while later, he came out the front door with a pillow and blanket. At first I didn't know why. Then he said, 'I want to make love to you.' I told him I was scared, but he just said, 'Don't be scared, this is what all the girls your age are doing. As a matter of fact, I'm surprised you're still a virgin.'

"Then he told me to lie down. I told him that I wanted to go home. He just kept saying, 'Bailey, it's okay. I know you're scared, but we can be scared together. It's my first time, too.' What he said made me feel more comfortable, so I went ahead and lay down…and had sex with him."

"Did it feel good?" Kennedy asks.

"No, Auntie. It hurt," Bailey confesses.

"That's why girls your age shouldn't be having sex," Kennedy lectures. "At this age, sex doesn't benefit you, sweetie—only him. When you become a woman, you'll understand what I'm saying."

I take Kennedy's hand and we walk into the foyer. Bailey is again sitting at the kitchen table. "I'm pressing charges against him," I announce to my friend. "And I have to tell Randy. But first, I'm going to have a little chat with Cory and his mother. Will you stay with Bailey?"

Kennedy disagrees with my plan. "Hell, no! You are not going over to their house, Brooke. You're either going to call the police or call Randy."

I sigh. I know she's right. I walk back into the kitchen and explain to Bailey that Cory has deceived her into having sex with him. "Do you understand what I'm telling you, Bailey?"

"I'm not sure, Mommy."

"Cory manipulated you into having sex with him," I explain for the second time. "And he needs to be punished for it. But before we call the authorities, I want to be sure—did you *want* to have sex with him?"

"No, Mommy, I swear I didn't," she tells me. "But I didn't want him to stop liking me." My heart is breaking for my little girl.

"Okay, I need you to know, I'm going to press charges against him."

"But, Mommy, will he get in trouble?"

"Yes, Bailey. What Cory did is against the law. There are consequences. He took advantage of you, and you're an under-aged girl. And he's probably done it before."

"No, Mommy. He told me he was a virgin, too."

"Bailey, trust me when I tell you he lied about that to get you to trust him. As you mature, you'll understand what I'm telling you." I pause and take a deep breath. She's not going to like what I have to say next. Kennedy is kneeling down in front of Bailey with her hand in her lap. "Sweetie, we have to tell your father."

"Mommy, no," Bailey whimpers.

"Honey, I have to."

She starts to cry. "Mommy, *please* don't," she pleads.

"I have to, sweetheart," I say. I pick up the phone and call Randy. I don't want to tell him over the phone, so I just tell him we're having a family emergency and to come when he can.

When I hang up, Kennedy says, "I'm going to leave now, okay, Bailey?"

But Bailey whines, "Please, Auntie, don't leave."

Kennedy is a sucker for Bailey's tears. "Okay, I'll stay. But just until your dad gets here."

Less than an hour later, I hear the key in the front door. I'm nervous. I can only imagine what Bailey must be feeling. When Randy walks into the kitchen, Bailey gets up and run into his arms. "I'm sorry, Daddy. I promise I'm still your little girl."

"Of course you are, sweetheart," he soothes. "You will always be my little girl." He turns to me, confused. "What is all this about?"

I'm having trouble getting my mouth to form words.

"Brooke, tell me what's going on before I start tossing tables and flipping chairs," he says sternly.

"Randy..."

"Yes?" he answers, raising both of his distinguished eyebrows.

My voice starts to crack, but I manage to blurt out, "Bailey had sex with the guy up the block. His name is Cory. He's nineteen years old."

"*What?*" Randy barks so loudly it startles me.

"Now, Randy," I say slowly, "don't do anything stupid. Let's let the police handle this. I already called them," I lie. It's the only way I can think to keep him from just walking up the street and killing the boy. "You'd better sit down," I say, concerned for his well-being. He looks like he might faint.

"No, Brooke," he says angrily, "I'm a man. I can take it. Just tell me what the police said," he demands, banging his fist on the wall.

"We have to go down to the precinct to file charges," I explain.

We all leave the house together. Kennedy gets into her car and heads home. Randy, Bailey, and I drive in one car to the precinct. Randy is still furious. He's barely talking to me. Bailey is telling an officer her story. After we've been there about twenty-five minutes, Randy finally breaks his silence. "How damned long has this been going on, Brooke?" he asks me.

"A while," is all I can manage to choke out.

He looks at me, his eyes full of rage. He starts to say something, pauses, then says, "You kept this from me."

Randy is scaring me. I have never seen him so angry. The officer notices our uncomfortable exchange. "Now let's just settle down, folks," he warns. "You guys need to know we can pick this kid up. But in order for the charges to stick, Bailey has to tell a grand jury that this guy raped her. Do you think she's capable of that?"

"She'll do it," Randy says, giving Bailey a threatening look.

"I'll do whatever you want me to do, Daddy," Bailey says, grabbing Randy's hand.

Randy melts in his little girl's arms, and to my surprise, starts to cry. I'm afraid if I try to console him, he'll reject me. But I grab my man anyway and huddle with my family. Even the officer looks emotional. "I'll leave you all alone for a minute."

We complete the necessary paperwork and will wait for the phone call from the police informing us the bastard has been arrested. We leave the precinct and head straight for the hospital so that Bailey can be examined, treated, and tested for sexually transmitted diseases. The doctor will also gather evidence for a rape kit.

Bailey's scared; she's never had a pap smear. I stand beside the exam table and hold her hand. "This is what you'll have to go through when you start having sex. Doesn't feel good, does it?"

"No, Mommy," she says. "I'm never having sex again."

"You're damned right, you aren't!" Randy yells from the hallway, apparently overhearing our conversation.

Back at home, Randy decides to stay the night. I go to my room and lie down, while Randy tucks Bailey into bed. A few minutes later, he approaches my bedroom door. "Don't you ever keep a secret like that from me again," he scolds before storming down the stairs to sleep on the couch.

I scramble from the bed and follow behind him. "I'm sorry, baby. I will never keep anything like this from you again."

"This never should've happened, Brooke."

He is so mad at me.

~~~

Four days later, Bailey is testifying in front of the grand jury. Randy and I decide to stay outside the courtroom. We don't want to make Bailey any more uncomfortable than she already is. Besides, we can barely tolerate hearing the details again.

Randy isn't saying much to me, but I keep trying to make some kind of meaningful contact with him. I walk over to him, hold his face in my hands, and say, "Baby, I am *so* sorry."

He looks at me. There are tears in his eyes. "That's my baby," he says, and squeezes me tight. *God, I love this man more today than I did yesterday.*

We're still embracing when Bailey and the arresting detective exit the
~~~

courtroom. The officer looks at us and pats Randy on the shoulder. "We got him," the officer assures us. "Now go home and take care of your family. Kid's going away for a long time. Turns out—not surprisingly—he's already got a rap sheet a mile long."

"I didn't want him to get in trouble, Mommy," Bailey pipes in. The poor girl is just too young and immature to understand what's happened. Once home, I check the mailbox. There's a letter from the hospital with the results of Bailey's exam. Randy hears me scream from where he's sitting in the living room and comes running.

When he reaches me, I look up at him. "Oh my God!" I exclaim.

"What is it?" Randy asks, concerned.

"That dirty motherfucker gave our baby chlamydia!" I don't know what the hell chlamydia is exactly, but I do know it's a disease.

"Baby, calm down," Randy consoles me. "It's not as bad as you think. It's totally curable."

Bailey walks up behind Randy. She'd heard my screams from her bedroom.

"Mommy, Daddy…I'm sorry I'm not a virgin anymore."

Chapter 17

BROOKE

THE SURPRISE PARTY

It's been two months since Bailey testified before the grand jury. Today is her thirteenth birthday. We're throwing her a party. Randy helped me plan the celebration. Since the incident with Cory, we've started to become a real family again. I'd even go so far as to say that Randy and I are back together.

Randy still has his house, but he sleeps here at least six nights a week. Cory is in prison, but I'm not sure how much longer he'll be there. I never went to the trial, with the exception of the day Bailey testified. I felt bad my baby had to get up there and testify against the guy she thinks she loves. My conscience was killing me for taking it that far, but it was the right thing to do. As her mother, I had to set a good example. It was all those prior arrests that made the police want him so bad. Maybe something good will come out of this for him. I'll pray for him.

For the sake of any other girls he should happen to have sex with, I called Cory's mother and told her to take him to the doctor because he'd given my child chlamydia. Chlamydia is a silent disease that can't be detected through symptoms. You have to be tested for it. His mother tried to deny that her son was a carrier. She was either embarrassed or too private to share—understandable. But I couldn't live with myself knowing this young man is walking around with this disease and not tell him or his mom about it.

Unlike most women, boys and men just aren't in the habit of going to the doctor every year to get checked out and tested. If it's not burning, leaking, or required by a higher authority, they simply will not go in for a physical. I believe it's the obligation of responsible women to clue them in when necessary. This is, of course, why Kennedy asked Bailey if Cory used a condom.

Luckily, I know for a fact that Bailey was a virgin before she had sex with Cory. I'm great friends with my gynecologist, and started taking Bailey for regular exams after her eleventh birthday. My doctor-friend assured me that Bailey's hymen was still intact as late as her last appointment, which was just a few days before the incident with Cory. Having sex for the first time is not information most girls volunteer to their parents. So I took it upon myself to stay as informed as I could of her sexual activity, or lack thereof.

I do think Cory deserves another chance. He's really just a boy. He still has time to mature. The detective on the case said that he'll keep me informed of Cory's release from jail.

My relationship with Randy has improved drastically. We've reached a whole new level of understanding for each other. The incident with Bailey brought us closer together and has shown us we really belong together. This time around, we're determined to make it work. Randy has always been a good father, but now he's much more involved in Bailey's daily life. We've also been engaging in plenty of family activities and weekend getaways. It's been just wonderful.

~~~

I can't believe Diamond and Renee will be here for Bailey's birthday bash.

Infinity is coming as well—she visits at least twice a year. Renee and Diamond only come down when we girls combine our resources to pay for their plane tickets. Diamond has never worked a day in her life. Renee works, but it's a dead-end job that barely pays her bills. They're not as fortunate as Infinity or the rest of us, but they're always invited to our events.

Sky and Fuji left a bit ago to pick up the New York girls from the airport. The rest of us stayed behind to finish preparations for Bailey's big celebration. Guests are beginning to arrive and are milling about the house and chatting on the patio.

There is plenty of animated conversation and laughter, and everyone seems to be enjoying themselves.

Renee and Diamond arrive. Diamond looks as if she's put on some weight, and Renee is still in the habit of wearing heavy mascara.

"Hey, girls!" I greet them.
~~~

"Hi, Brooke." Diamond and Renee appear happy to see me.

"Girl, those jeans are mighty tight," I say to Diamond.

"I know," Diamond says, rolling her eyes. "So I put on a few pounds."

Randy walks over with a plate of food. It smells good. "Honey, taste the rice and beans," he says, putting a spoonful into my mouth. "They're delicious."

"Mmm," I declare, and smile knowingly. "Lola made this."

A bit later, I happen to notice a lot of whispering going on between Randy and the rest of the girls. I guess they're planning a surprise for Bailey. Bailey doesn't notice what's going on, though. She's too busy in the pool with her friends. She's showing off her pink one-piece bathing suit. The kids are playful and loud, talking over the music.

A few moments later, Randy cues the DJ to turn off the music, and he walks over to the microphone. "Bailey, why don't you get out of the pool?" I say. "Come listen to Daddy's speech."

"First," Randy announces, "I would like to thank all of our friends and family for coming out today to help us celebrate Bailey's thirteenth birthday party. I would also like to wish my little girl a very happy birthday." He looks over at Bailey and winks. "Honey, your gift hasn't arrived yet, but it's coming soon, I promise." He told me he bought her diamond earrings and a matching necklace. "Brooke, will you come over and stand by me, please?" I walk over to him, wondering what he's up to. He grabs my hand. "Honey, I know we've been through a lot over the years. It's my feeling that we've spent far too many years apart. I want to try to make up for that today." Randy gets down on one knee and presents me with a diamond ring. "Marry me, Brooke."

Without hesitation, I jump up and down on my four-inch heels and scream, "Yes! Okay! I'll marry you!"

"So that's a 'yes' then?" he jokes.

I'm shocked. This is now officially the happiest day of my life. I'm shaking and crying, and Bailey is attached to my every move, attempting to hide her happy tears. Everyone's clapping as we seal the deal with a kiss. The diamond is huge and sits high in the setting. After our long up-and-down journey together, Randy and I will finally be together for the long haul. It's a dream come true. I take hold of the microphone and say proudly, "I got my man back!"

The girls are looking on and throwing tearful kisses when Bailey takes the microphone. "Daddy, thank you," Bailey says through tears. "This is the best birthday present I've ever had." There's not a dry eye in the house.

Barely a minute later, Diamond shouts, "Well, since this party is full of surprises, I have something to tell you guys." She's so loud she doesn't even need a microphone. Everybody quiets and turns their attention to Diamond.

I can tell Lola is irritated because she's rolling her eyes. She's hasn't had much to say to Diamond since the incident in New York. "I'm pregnant!" Diamond announces.

Sky hugs her first because she's standing the closest. "Congratulations, baby. Can I give you a baby shower?"

"I would love for you to give me a baby shower," Diamond says.

"How much time do I have?" Sky asks.

"I'm about four and a half months, so there's still plenty of time." Diamond smiles and winks at Sky.

Something feels fishy to me. Diamond lacks credibility. She has a tendency to smile and say the exact opposite of what she means. There is definitely something up, but I decide now is not the time to mull it over. I'm not going to let Diamond interfere with my happy day. Infinity resumes the party-like atmosphere by singing "This Ring," by Shalamar. Randy and I smile at each other. This certainly has been some surprise party.

~~~

DIAMOND

What I *wanted* to announce at the party is, "Yes, that's right, Sky, I'm pregnant. Fuji and I are having a baby. He's leaving you for me." Fuji's freckles practically fell off his nose when I made my announcement.

I'm on my way to the bathroom, but before I can get there, Fuji comes up behind me and yanks my elbow. I turn around to face him. "So we meet again," I say.

"What the hell do you think you're doing?" he asks angrily.

"Relax, Fuji. It's not yours, so get your hands off me."

"So when you told me you were pregnant a few months ago, you were lying?"

I lie and tell him I got rid of that seed. He exhales with relief and walks away, which really pisses me off. I want to take back what I said, tell him the truth just for the satisfaction of wiping the look of relief from his face. I'll tell him when the baby is born. Or even better, I'll tell Sky at the baby shower she's planning for me.
~~~

The first time I slept with Fuji was at their wedding. Yes, you heard right. I snuck into the men's bathroom, followed Fuji when I saw him leaving the main ballroom. I couldn't help it because he looked so good walking back up the aisle. Sky was beautiful, too—better than I had ever seen her look before.

Don't get me wrong, I love all the girls. It's just that it's not fair that they have everything and I have nothing. I love them for their personalities; they're fun people to be around. But I hate them for what they have. I don't want to feel like this toward my friends, but I can't help the way I feel. Why can't I be just as successful? I would definitely appreciate it more than they do. I guess you could say I have a love-hate relationship with them. I know if I work hard I could achieve anything, but I shouldn't have to work hard. Why does nothing in life come easy for me? Why do I always get the short end of the stick? Most of them have good men who give them everything they want. I attract losers who always end up leaving. Or, I end up with men who are already involved with someone else. *Why, God?*

Anyway, Fuji was a little tipsy from all the toasts. Almost everyone gave a toast wishing them well, including me. He didn't know I was in the bathroom till he came out the stall. Before he made it completely out, I pushed him back in and got right down on my knees. His money fell out of his pocket from the force of my push. But he didn't even notice because he was so tuned in to my performance. I held his manhood with one hand, and scooped the hundred dollar bills up off the floor with the other, and slid them into my bra. That's what I call "skills." I used my tongue to play with the tip of his penis, and then began sucking it and groping his balls. I took him so far into my mouth the tip of his penis hit the back of my throat. I never gag—this is my specialty. *After this performance he'll be hooked,* I thought. *It never fails.*

When I finished the job, I congratulated him on his marriage and walked back into the celebration a few hundred dollars richer. I made sure I saved some of Fuji's juices for when I kissed Sky on the cheek. I liked the idea of kissing her with the juices from sucking off her new husband still on my lips. I was testing Fuji. I wanted to see if he was a changed man, one who wouldn't cheat on his wife. Needless to say, he failed the test. Better me than a stranger. It was really the best wedding gift I could have given Sky. She needed to understand the dog she married.

I'm looking at myself in the mirror in Brooke's bathroom and considering my options. *Should I tell Sky about Fuji and me, or no?*

Chapter 18

LOLA

FORGIVENESS

Michael Jackson's "Off The Wall" was playing before Randy made his speech and proposed to Brooke. I love that song. And I loved that moment. So I think I'll always remember it was playing that day.

I still can't believe Diamond tried to make Bailey's birthday celebration all about her. Wait, I *can* believe it. Taking the attention away from Bailey and Brooke with news that she's pregnant—she should be ashamed of herself. I wouldn't be surprised if she's pregnant by someone else's man, because she'll sleep with just about anybody.

Diamond acts like she loves us when she's with us, but when she's not, she talks to other people like she hates us. She talks about what we have and how we're somehow not responsible for our own accomplishments. I don't get it. None of us has ever done anything but treat her like a friend., and all she does is talk bad about us to anyone who will listen. The girls don't see it, but I have twenty/twenty vision. She is what most people call "a hater." She came up to me at Bailey's party talking about how we should just forget what happened in New York and call a truce. I agreed—for now, anyway. But I don't trust her because I know what she's capable of.

Toward the end of our stay in New York, we went to see Infinity perform at a little hole-in-the-wall bar in Brooklyn. One of Diamond's sidekicks was there. He came over to me while I was at the bar ordering a drink. He and Diamond were no longer seeing each other, so he asked me how Diamond was doing. Keep in mind this was only a few days after I'd kicked her out of my car. "I don't speak to that girl," I said to him, still full of rage for what she'd pulled on the dance floor of that club.

He said, "Good."

"Why do you say that?" I asked.

"Let me tell you why I stopped seeing her," he replied. "For one, I think she's crazy. And when I say crazy, I mean *really* crazy." Needless to say, this guy had my attention. "When I used to go over to her house, she'd always be telling me how much she hated you all. I mean, *really* hated you. But whenever she was around you guys, she'd act as if she loved y'all to death." He was clearly still trying to figure it out. "When we'd come to your house for drinks, she would peck you on the lips and say, 'I love you.' I was confused. And frankly, scared that I was dealing with a real nutcase. It was like dating Dr. Jeckle and Mr. Hyde."

"Weird," I said.

"Like I said, the chick is crazy," the guy said again. "So, I left her alone." Then he smiled and said to me, "but I've always had a crush on you." I gave him a look that said, *Don't even go there.*

"All jokes aside," he said, "you all need to watch your backs, 'cause crazy-girl is definitely *not* your friend."

As long as I stay one step ahead of her, she can't hurt me. When she made her announcement about the baby, I wanted to grab the microphone and say to her right then and there, "Diamond, why don't you click your heels three times and just go home?"

~~~

I've continued enjoying Jeremy's company since we met that day in the park. Well, Jeremy and *others.* One of the guys I'm dating lives in Atlanta. I only bother with him when he comes to Orlando to visit his mom. I actually met him through his mother who I met at a bar in my neighborhood while out alone one night. She had just gone through a dragged-out, angry divorce. We struck up a conversation and started swapping stories. She's much older than me, but you could tell she was a fox in her younger days. And she still had a little fire burning. Our discussion was so intense we decided to exchange numbers and eventually became friends.

Soon after, she started playing matchmaker for her son. I was skeptical at first, but when I finally agreed to meet him, I was pleasantly surprised. I was instantly attracted to him—he's definitely my type. I also appreciate the
~~~

fact that he lives in another state, so we won't get tired of each other. Serious relationships and marriages are no longer part of my agenda. I'm dating and I don't want to get caught up with spending too much time with one guy. I don't plan to fall in love ever again.

Winston still hopes we'll get back together, but it will never happen. I forgave him, but my head and my heart will never forget. Forgiveness is accepting what happened and moving on. That's what I'm doing. When the breakup was still new, the bad feelings took over like a destructive burning flame that struck my heart without warning. But I don't hate him anymore. We still speak and sometimes even go out to dinner. He thinks he'll eventually be able to break through and worm his way back into my heart, and I let him think that. What he doesn't know is what we have right now will be the extent of our relationship, period.

He even has the audacity to ask me if I'm sleeping with someone else because I'm not giving him any. He tells me I need to have sex more often—meaning I should be having sex with him. Who is he to be asking me when we're going to do it? As if I could ever believe he isn't having sex with Nicole, and probably that woman from the park, and who knows how many others. I just let him think that I believe his bullshit.

The girls are wondering why in the hell I'm speaking to him at all. This is why you can't tell your girlfriends your problems; they will forever have an opinion about it. I still love Winston, but not in the way you might think. It's hard to quit him cold-turkey. He's like a drug I need to wean from gradually. But I imagine the relationship will eventually self-destruct. Then I can walk away, free of any feeling for him.

Chapter 19

SKY

THE LAST STRAW

Even after everything that happened in Virginia, I still haven't made up my mind about leaving Fuji. I've decided to stay with Kennedy until I can make a decision.

When I went to the house to gather my things, Fuji was there begging me to stay. He tried to mask his anger, and did manage to restrain himself, thankfully. Sometimes I think he has a hold on me, and so do the girls. But they don't even know the half of what goes on behind closed doors in my home.

My phone's been ringing off the hook since I moved in with Kennedy. Fuji has been calling me constantly. When I don't answer my phone, he acts even crazier. I'm thinking about changing my number. He's even been calling Payton and Lola, trying to explain the circumstances and begging them to put in a good word for him with me. But that didn't fly with them; they were witness to what happened in Virginia.

Kennedy and I are on our way to a bar in downtown Orlando in an attempt to help get my mind off Fuji. The bar is a little hole in the wall. The room is no bigger than my 27x20 bedroom. The bar itself takes up most of the space. It's long and narrow. The average age of the crowd looks to be about forty. There is a painting on the wall of a woman with her T-shirt hanging off her shoulders, her left breast hanging out. She's holding her crotch with her right hand. The tall windows at the front entrance extend from floor to ceiling and are covered with deep purple curtains that match the purple-tinted walls. The fragrant oil burning on the bar fills the room with the scent of coconut.

We grab two seats at the end of the bar, next to the dance floor, where there's a group of about ten people dancing. Kennedy spots an old fling of mine. I haven't seen or slept with him since the last time Fuji messed up. He's happy to see me, and I do look good, I must say. I realize I'm happy to see him, too. He has no idea at this point that he'll be wandering up my skirt later tonight. Although he's been my boy-toy for years, Fuji doesn't know about him. Thankfully, their paths have never crossed.

"I guess I'll be going home alone tonight, huh, Sky?" Kennedy jokes.

"You know it," I say excitedly. He's walking toward me, wearing a see-through white shirt that outlines his sculpted chest.

"Hi, Tank," I say to him.

"What's up, girl?" he asks. "Where have you been hiding?"

"Hiding?" I repeat, with a confused look on my face. "Where have you been, mister?"

"I've been around," he answers coolly. He leans down and puts his lips next to my ear. "So, Sky," he says, "what are we getting into tonight?" This is me and Tank's way of feeling each other out—to find out if we'll be getting it on tonight.

"Let's have a few of drinks with Kennedy," I say, winking at him. "Then we'll see. You wouldn't mind joining us for a while, would you?"

"Not at all." He gives me a flirty smile and takes the seat next to me. His pearly white teeth compliment his brown skin. Two drinks later, we leave the bar and walk Kennedy to her car. She couldn't have gotten into her car fast enough. I'm eager to get into Tank's car.

We head to a nearby hotel on the strip. I don't care if I'm seen or not—tonight I consider myself single. The room is beautiful and cozy. There's a king-sized bed with a mirrored headboard. In most hotel rooms I've seen, the walls are usually white, but this room is painted mint green. The color adds to the coziness. A flat-screen television hangs on the wall across from the foot of the bed, and the furniture is the color of sand on the beach.

I step into the bathroom to freshen up. I never leave home without the items I need for an emergency quick-fix. I make my usual grand entrance for Tank because I know he's anticipating it. His face tells me he likes what he sees. I'm wearing a pink bra with matching panties. I always wear matching sets because I never know who I might run into at a bar. Tank is sitting on the bed in his boxers, looking like he's wrapped up in a bottle of lord-have-mercy.

He meets me in the middle of the room and greets me with a wet, sloppy French kiss. I can feel him rubbing something warm and wet on my back. Between kisses I ask, "What is that?"

"Just lie down on your stomach," he says, "and let Daddy take care of you." Apparently, the hotel has left us complimentary oils on the nightstand. I do exactly what "Daddy" told me to do. He unhooks my bra and begins to massage my skin with the cherry-scented oil. It feels so good oozing down my back. His massage is just what the doctor ordered. *Lord, how I need this after everything I've been through.*

Tank slowly kisses down the small of my back and removes my panties with his teeth. Once they're all the way off, he uses his tongue to lick between my buttocks. *This is new.* It's nasty, but I like it. Either he's been getting some practice with someone else, or he's missed me. Just then, he flips me over and says, "Damn, I've missed you."

"I've missed you, too." He picks me up, carries me to the dresser that sits below the TV, and sets me on top of it. He kneels down and pulls me toward the edge. As he's consuming me, I experience a sudden and violent release. My orgasm is so intense that it actually squirts fluid like a man's. This has never happened to me before. It sprays right into Tank's face, and he moans to express his gratitude. My legs won't stop shaking, and I have chills. I almost feel faint. I've been having great sex since my thirties, but this orgasm is amazing beyond anything I could ever have imagined.

Tank can't wait a moment longer. He throws me onto the bed, eager to get it. He climbs on top and sticks his average-sized penis inside me. Low and behold, I feel myself about to cum again. "Wow, what's happening?" I say.

"Damn, baby, you're having a good time," he answers, obviously happy with himself. "When's the last time someone made love to you?"

"Shut up and just fuck me." *This ain't love, fool.*

"Anything you say."

What I love about Tank is I never have to tell him to put on a condom. He does it without a request. It says a lot about his character. Too bad I can't say that about all men. I can't believe in this day and age, with all we know about sexually transmitted diseases, people still hook up and don't bother to use protection. That's why I always pick Tank as my go-to guy whenever I need some space from Fuji.

We're having sex in a sitting position when Tank releases the babies. Then we fall back on the bed together. We rest for about two hours before we decide it's time to leave. I'm ready to get back to Kennedy's place so I can knock out without interruption. I'm not sure if Tank still has a girlfriend, and I don't want to know. If I ask him, it will ruin things. This night lacked for nothing, and I don't want to feel guilty about it. It's bad enough that someone is sleeping with my husband. How could I turn around and do the very thing that tore my own heart to pieces?

We're stepping off the elevator and about to head to the front desk to return the room key when I hear a familiar voice around the corner in the hall. I'm stunned and halt in my tracks, then begin walking again. I hope my ears are just playing tricks on me. But once around the corner, I can't deny what I heard, because I can see Fuji at the desk checking in with another woman. He's *still* cheating on me!

I gasp when I see him. Fuji looks up, and we lock eyes. Tank is glancing from me to Fuji and looking to have a fairly good idea of what's going on. "That's my husband," I confirm. At the same time, I see Fuji whisper to the woman he's with. I think I hear him tell her that I'm his wife.

"I'll bring the car around," Tank offers. He's clearly uncomfortable and looking to get out of the lobby as quickly as possible. Is that a punk move or what? I trot along behind him until I feel Fuji yank my arm.

"What the hell you doing here, Sky?" he demands. Tank keeps it moving without hesitation.

"I suspect for the same reason you're here, Fuji," I answer back spitefully.

Fuji is speechless—at first. I take that as an opportunity to get the hell out of dodge. I snatch my arm back and run after Tank. "I bet he won't be able to bust a nut tonight," I say to myself. "But I damn sure did." I let out a giggle.

I see Fuji and the girl getting back into his car as we drive by in Tank's BMW. He notices me. I feel good because not only is Tank fine as hell, but we're driving in a top-of-the-line vehicle. The girl Fuji is with doesn't look too bad. She's cute, but so am I. It bothers me that he was going into the hotel with her, but there's nothing I can say or do about it this time, because I did the exact same thing.

I tell Tank to pay close attention in case Fuji decides to follow us. I'm particularly concerned because Fuji doesn't know where I'm staying, and I want to keep it that way. "Did you guys break up or something?" Tank asks as we're leaving the parking lot.

"Yes."

"Really?" he says with a satisfied look on his face. "So, what's up with me and you?"

I can't answer him. My thoughts are still stuck on what just happened. I'm looking in the side and rearview mirrors, making sure we aren't being followed. I admit I'm sort of disappointed he's not following us. I swear, either love doesn't make sense, or I don't know what love is. Sometimes I think this marriage is a life sentence with no possibility for parole. Then other times I'm obsessed with thoughts about where Fuji is, what he's doing, and who's he doing it with. I see bright headlights in the rearview mirror, which could indicate Fuji is behind us. But it's probably just wishful thinking.

When we pull up in front of Kennedy's building, I look at Tank and say, "Thank you for a memorable night, Tank."

"My pleasure," he answers. "I'll call you later in the day."

I get out of the car and walk around to the driver's side. I plant a huge kiss on Tank's lips. He watches as I let myself in. I open the door again as I hear him drive off and take another peek outside to make sure Fuji didn't follow us. I run upstairs to Kennedy's place and into her bedroom. I shake her awake and fill her in on the details of my night. Her jaw drops as I tell the story.

The next morning, Kennedy comes into my room and wakes me up. "Was I dreaming," she asks, "or did you tell me you and Fuji busted each other at a hotel last night?"

"You heard right," I say, wiping the sleep from my eyes. "Before we get into this discussion again, let's put some coffee on." I definitely need a pick-me-up before rehashing the details of my long night.

The doorbell rings as Kennedy is heading to the kitchen. I hear her press the intercom. "Who is it?" she asks.

A familiar voice answers back, "It's me, Fuji."

He's figured out where I'm staying. I jump up out of bed and yell to Kennedy, "Oh my God! Kennedy, you can't let him in."

"Well, Sky, he knows I'm here," she says, "what am I supposed to say to him?"

I keep forgetting that the girls don't have a clue that Fuji hits me. Nervously, I say, "Just tell him you have company."

Kennedy presses the talk button, "What can I do for you, Fuji? I'm not dressed."

"Well, put on some clothes and buzz me in," he demands.

"I can't do that, Fuji. I have company."

"Have you seen Sky?"

"No, but I spoke to her yesterday afternoon."

"Where is she? I need to see her."

"I can't tell you that. She doesn't want you to know."

"Please, Kennedy, I need to see her. Not seeing or speaking to her is driving me insane."

"I'm sorry, Fuji. How about I call her and tell her to call you."

"Okay," he agrees. "Can you do it now?"

"Okay, okay." Kennedy takes her finger off the talk button and looks at me. "Now what do you want me to say to him?"

I pause. "Tell him I didn't answer my phone."

Kennedy counts to twenty, then presses the talk button again. "She's not answering, Fuji."

"Did you leave a message?"

"Yes. I told her to call me. When she calls me, I'll tell her to call you."

"Okay, Kennedy, thanks…Take care."

Later in the day, Kennedy and I go to the supermarket for some groceries. We shop for nearly an hour. On our way back home, I notice Fuji standing in front of Kennedy's building. "Kennedy, stop the car," I yell. "We can't go in while Fuji is standing there."

"We can enter through the back entrance," Kennedy suggests. But when we approach the back of the building, there's a friend of Fuji's standing there, stationed as a lookout. He sees me and Kennedy trying to sneak in the back door. Before he can finish dialing Fuji's number, we're already inside.

We aren't inside twenty seconds before the phone starts ringing. Kennedy presses the speaker button and answers, "Yes?"

"Can you please tell Sky to come down here so we can talk?" Fuji says. "I know she's there."

Kennedy takes the phone off speaker and looks at me questioningly. I sigh and say, "I'll go see what he wants."

"Are you sure you want to do this, Sky?"

"Yeah. Tell him I'm coming down."

"She's on her way down, Fuji," Kennedy says, and hangs up the phone.

I'm nervous but not scared, probably because he only beats me behind closed doors. He wouldn't dare get physical in public. Maybe I can charm him into leaving before the neighbors come out. This is a quiet neighborhood.

The moment I open the front door of the building, he pushes his way in with unbelievable strength. He attacks me with a swift punch to the left side of my face. I fall straight back and onto the floor of the lobby.

Fuji reopens the door and drags me by my ponytail outside to a grassy patch next to the building. He pulls a leather belt from his back pocket and proceeds to beat me like I'm his child. It's obvious he planned this, because no one carries a belt in their pocket. He whips my body till I feel the stinging through my jeans. He has a vacant stare in his eyes. He isn't speaking. I realize at this moment that this man is crazy.

He starts to pull at my clothing. We have a tug-of-war with my clothes. I shout through tears, "What are you doing?" I'm scared for my life. "Jerome! Snap out of it!" It doesn't work. His face remains expressionless. I don't know how much longer I can hang on. The more I tug back on my clothes, the more he whips me.

He stops when he hears Kennedy yelling, "Fuji, get off of her!" Kennedy is on the phone, shouting her address. Jolted out of his trance, Fuji runs to his car and jumps into the passenger seat. I can see him yelling at his buddy, who is in the driver's seat. Within seconds, they pull away from the curb and speed off down the street.

I can hear the neighbors shouting, "Is she all right?" I'm embarrassed. Kennedy helps me to my feet. Tears are rolling down her cheeks. She looks devastated. I know she's never seen this sort of behavior firsthand.

Fuji is still calling Kennedy's home phone and leaving threatening messages on her answering machine. I guess beating the shit out of me wasn't enough; he has to finish me off with threats. He always warned me that if he ever caught me with another man, he'd kill me. And he tried. But I'm still standing.

This was indeed the last straw.

Chapter 20

KENNEDY

SKY'S SECRETS ARE STOLEN FROM DEEP INSIDE

I'm still trying to comprehend what happened between Sky and Fuji. I had no idea that my friend was in an abusive relationship with a man. I guess you never know a jackass till you really know a jackass.

Upstairs, Sky cries for what seems like forever. I'm speechless. I don't know how to comfort her. I'm still in shock. I cry along with her. She's like a sister to me, and I feel her pain. There are two things I can think to say to her to soothe her grief and fear. "Has anyone told you they love and care about you today? Well, I do." And, "I'm going to call the girls."

She looks at me, still weeping, and says, "I just couldn't bring myself to tell you guys."

"How long has this been going on?" I ask.

"It started right after we got married," she confesses.

"Sky, why did you stay with him?" I'm trying to understand, but I can't.

"I thought he'd change," she offers weakly. "We've started counseling. He always promises that he won't hit me again." Sky shrugs.

"After every time he beats you, I'm guessing?"

"Yes."

"That sounds pretty typical."

"Please don't do that to me, Kennedy. It's exactly why I didn't want to tell any of you."

"Don't do *what* to you?"

"Judge me."

I put my arm around her. "I'm sorry, sweetie. I didn't mean to. I'm just so angry. Not at you—at *him*. He was beating you with a belt, like you were his child." The image sends chills up my spine. "I will never get that image out of my head." I pause. "Is he always so... *severe* in his beatings?"

"The pain is always the same, but that was the first time he's ever used a belt. That was the last time he'll ever be putting his hands on me. I have no intention of going back to him after this."

"Well, thank God for that, friend. You do know how much I love you?"

"I love you, too," she says, blowing her nose into a tissue.

"I never want to see you go through anything like that again. You deserve better." I pick up the phone to dial Lola, and it rings. It's Myles. A sudden smile on my face appears whenever he calls. "Can I call you back, baby?" I say.

"You're so busy you can't talk to me?" he asks, sounding hurt.

"Yes, very busy. Sky is here."

"You always put your friends before me," he complains.

I walk into the next room. I don't want Sky to hear our conversation. "Baby," I whisper, "I'll fill you in later."

"No, fill me in now," he says.

"Okay, Fuji just beat the shit out of Sky," I blurt out.

"*What?* Do you need me to come over?" His tone has changed from irritated to concerned.

"No, he's gone. She just needs me and the girls right now. I was just picking up the phone to call them when you rang."

"Okay, baby, call me if you need me. I love you."

I'm stunned. This is the first time he's ever said that to me. "I love you, too." I realize I've wanted him to know this for a long time now. I was just waiting for him to say it first. *He loves me.* I hang up the phone, and it immediately rings again. Murphy. What the hell does *he* want? I told Murphy I didn't want anything to do with him anymore. I push ignore and send his call directly to voice mail. A few moments later, I'm curious, so I listen to the message. It makes my skin crawl. He actually called me "baby." *Delete.*

Finally, I dial Lola.

"Hey, Kennedy," she says.

"Lola, I need you to round up the girls and get over to my place, *quick*."

"What happened?"

"Just call the girls. I'll explain when you get here. Sky is already here."

"Okay, now you're scaring me. Is this about you or Sky?"

"It's about Sky."

"What did Fuji do now?"

"Just get here."

"I'm on my way."

I turn off the phone and look at Sky.

"Kennedy," she says, "I am so sorry I kept this from you guys. I just didn't want to involve anyone until I was ready to walk away for good."

"No worries, girl, you had to do what was right for you," I tell her. "But listen to me, Sky, you're allowed to make mistakes. Just don't put too much focus on them. Just remember, if you ever find yourself heading in the wrong direction, just make a U-turn."

The girls walk in without knocking. Payton has a spare key to my home. "So what's going on?" she asks.

"You guys have been crying," Brooke observes.

"Have a seat, ladies. I'll get us some wine." I'm handing out glasses and pouring while Sky recounts the events—or shall I say, series of events? Everyone is stunned. No one can believe what's been going on for her all this time. Shit, I saw it with my own eyes and I *still* can't believe it.

"You must have felt so alone, Sky," Portia says.

"Are there any police reports on this fool?" Lola asks.

Sky shakes her head. "No, I thought I could deal with him."

"I called the police when Fuji was attacking her, but I didn't wait for them to show," I admit. "They called my cell phone back a few times, but I didn't answer. I was busy comforting Sky."

"Well, time to get up, dust yourself off, and pack your things, Sky," Lola says resolutely. "You're closing this chapter today. Let's go."

Half an hour later, we pull up into Sky's driveway. Fuji's car is here. The storm door has been left open and is hanging ajar. Lola jumps out of the car first. We follow suit and storm into the house together. "That punk-ass woman beater is here, girls," Lola yells, loud enough for Fuji to hear.

"Don't bust up in my house like that!" The sound of Fuji's voice startles me.

Lola takes off her shoes. "Fuji!" she shouts piercingly. "Don't make me beat your ass in front of Sky. Because then she'll know how much of a punk you really are." The house looks as if it's been ransacked. There are photos of Sky's family torn and strewn about. Sky's favorite CDs have been broken in half and thrown onto the floor. We're all on our guard, waiting for Fuji to make his move.

"Do we need to take her out of here?" Tasha asks, motioning to Sky.

I turn my attention to Sky. She looks haggard, but okay. "I just want my clothes and my things for now," she says. In the bedroom, Sky sits on the bed and points to the things she wants us to pack.

Lola goes to get a glass of water for Sky, who is dehydrated from all the crying. A moment later I hear Fuji say to her, "You all are not taking my wife out of here. This is none of your business. It's between me and Sky, so get the hell out of my house!"

I yell from the bedroom, "We're not going anywhere without Sky!" I step out of the bedroom, where the girls are packing Sky's things, and head down the hall to back up Lola. I get there just in time to see Fuji picking up Lola's shoes. He walks to the door and flings them outside onto the lawn.

Lola steps up and gets in his face. "You'd better take your ass outside, pick up my shoes, and put them back in my hands, Fuji."

"I'm not picking anything up for you, bitch," he spits back.

Lola takes a seat on the couch and crosses her legs. "Well, I'm not going anywhere till you pick up my shoes. And I got *all* day." A wicked smiles breaks across Lola's face, and she yells, "Do any of you girls have anywhere to be today?"

The girls step out of the bedroom and walk down the hall to the kitchen. "We don't have anywhere to be but here," Tasha says on behalf of the group.

Sky steps into the living room behind the girls. "Come on, guys," she says, "let's just get my things and get out of here. He's not worth it."

Sky's words enrage Fuji. Out of nowhere, he picks up the living room end table and hits Sky over the head with it, nearly knocking her out. It looks like a classroom brawl. Lola leaps across the room to confront Fuji, and he punches her in the face. The rest of us jump on him.

While we're doing our best to subdue Fuji, Lola's crazy ass goes into the kitchen, grabs a knife, and charges him like a crazed lunatic, aiming straight for Fuji's chest. Before she can get to Fuji, I step between them and grab Lola's hand in an attempt to stop her. Thank God I was quick on my feet, because otherwise, she'd be headed to jail for murder.

I succeed in stopping her initially, but I make the mistake of letting my guard down. Fuji reaches across us and slaps Lola hard on the face. Lola resumes her previous track and ends up stabbing Fuji. The blade slices his thumb—cuts clean through the flesh, exposing the bone. Fuji screams in pain and launches at Lola again. But this time when he tries to hit her, he ends up stabbing himself by running into the knife with his arm.

We take advantage of his weakened state, jump on him again, and tackle him to the floor. Sky is standing off to the side, silent. She looks terrified. The knife cut deep into Fuji's bicep, and there's a lot of blood. It's everywhere—the place looks like a slasher film. I rush to the phone and call the police before the situation gets any more out of hand. I'm reeling by how quickly things escalated. We were just coming to get Sky's belongings. I can barely comprehend what's happening.

Sky is still standing off to the side but is now screaming, "Oh my God! This is why I didn't want to get you guys involved! What am I going to do now? You guys are my best friends, and he's my husband."

"Sky, this is his fault," Tasha explains, "not yours or Lola's. Do you hear me?"

"Yes, Tasha," Sky answers, "I hear you."

"Why would you stay in this abusive relationship with him for all these years, Sky?" Payton asks. "I'm not trying to pick on you. I just really want to understand."

"I stayed in this relationship because we had good times," Sky explains. "He can actually be very romantic. And I love him."

I hang up the phone. "The police are on their way," I announce.

"Good," Portia and Payton say in unison. Fuji is tending his wounds in the kitchen. He's holding a rag around his thumb. I wrap a towel around his upper arm and secure it with a belt—the same one he used to beat Sky—to apply pressure to the wound. I hate what he's done, but I don't want to see him die. And I surely don't want Lola to be responsible for his death.

Just then, Sky runs into the bedroom and closes the door behind her. Lola turns to Fuji and says, "Now, go and pick up my shoes."

He looks at her, dumbfounded, and says, "How am I supposed to pick up your shoes when you wounded my arm and my thumb?"

"Use a pair of pliers, punk," Lola suggests. Fuji gets up and skulks out of the room. "I don't feel sorry for you," Lola yells after him.

A moment later, we hear screams from the bedroom. Fuji is in there and has used his good arm to grab hold of Sky's ankles and is pulling her from the bed. When she lands, her head hits the floor with a thud. "I'm calling Dylan!" Portia shouts.

"I don't care who you call!" Fuji shouts back.

But before Portia can dial her husband, the police arrive. They take a look around the house. “What happened here?” one of the officers asks. “Is this a homicide we’re walking into, or what? Somebody has a lot of explaining to do.”

I’m frantic to explain before Fuji can start telling lies. “Arrest this man,” I say, pointing to Fuji. “He beat up his wife and assaulted my friend.”

Fuji points his finger at Lola. “I want charges brought up on her.” Then he says directly to Lola, “You assaulted me! I was just defending myself.”

“Okay, everybody calm down,” the other officer says. “Now, who is the woman of the house?”

“I am,” Sky says meekly.

“Are you okay, ma’am?” he asks. The bruises on Sky’s face are clearly visible. “How did you get those bruises on your face?”

“This bastard right here,” Sky says weepily, pointing to Fuji.

“Does he live here, too?”

“Yes, he’s my husband.”

The first officer—a middle-aged woman—says to Lola, “I have to arrest you, ma’am,” she explains sympathetically, “because he’s pressing charges and you *are* in his home. Please put your hands behind your back.”

Portia looks disgusted. “Had I known you guys were going to come in here and arrest Lola,” she says, “I would have called my husband instead.”

“Talk to your friend,” the other officer says to me. “See if she’ll press charges against her husband. If she agrees to press charges, I’ll arrest him right now.”

“*I* want to press charges against him,” Lola says, indignantly.

“Well, you can,” the female officer explains, “if he assaulted you.” The officer winks her eye and motions for Lola to walk with her to the police cruiser. Fuji has to go straight to the hospital.

“We’ll meet you down there, Lola,” I assure her. “Don’t worry, we’re right behind you. We got your back like a jacket.”

Sky is still weeping. “This is my fault,” she says. “If I’d just kept it to myself, none of this would be happening.”

Everyone but Sky follows Lola to the precinct. Sky wants to make sure Fuji is okay, so she escorts him to the hospital. I’m put off that Sky went with Fuji. But she’ll have to work that out with God on her own. I can’t concern myself with her actions right now. My loyalty is to Lola.

Surprisingly, Lola isn’t angry with Sky for going with Fuji to the hospital. She understands that he is Sky’s husband and he did get hurt pretty badly. The question is now, will Sky *stay* with him?

Portia calls Dylan as we're leaving Sky's house, and he makes it to the police precinct before we do. When we arrive, he's engaged in conversation with an officer, and they're both laughing. Portia walks up and they hug, but he's clearly upset to see a handcuffed Lola coming in behind them, being led into a cell. "I know an excellent lawyer," he reassures her as she shuffles by him. "We're going to get you out of here."

"Thank you, Dylan," Lola says, sounding sad and defeated.

In the waiting area, I notice the officers are being extremely polite to Lola. They're doing their best to make her feel comfortable, asking her if she needs anything drink or eat. The woman officer hands a candy bar through the bars of Lola's cell, "Do you want a Snickers?" she asks, but Lola just shakes her head. A few minutes later, the same officer receives a phone call from the officer at the hospital who is guarding Fuji. She walks over to Lola. I can tell by the expression on her face something is wrong. "I have some bad news."

"How bad?" Lola asks.

"He has to have emergency surgery. Your charges just went from a misdemeanor to a felony."

"I don't understand," Lola says.

"A misdemeanor is a lesser offense," the officer explains. "It's like a slap on the wrist. But a felony is much more serious charge. A felony charge involves serious time…and it will follow you the rest of your life." The officer sighs. "Unfortunately, the crime you're being charged with now is attempted murder. I suggest you get yourself a lawyer." The officer pauses. "You have a good chance of beating this case. This guy's got two prior convictions for assault and abuse involving other women, and you acted in self-defense."

"How long do you think I'll have to be in here?" Lola asks.

"Depends. They can't make a formal charge or set bail until they know the outcome of the surgery."

While the officer is giving Lola a lesson in law enforcement, my phone rings. It's Sky. I don't answer because I'm still angry with her for following Fuji and not Lola, who stood up for her. She leaves a message: "Kennedy, it's me, Sky. I just wanted to let you girls know I'm okay. Fuji is in surgery. I'll be staying here at the hospital till he comes through it." A pause, then, "I know I must sound like a fool, but he's my husband. I just couldn't leave him like this." She's chokes up. "I am so sorry for getting you guys involved in this. I'll give you a call again later. Tell Lola I love her. Bye."

~~~
~~~

Three days later, Lola is out of jail on $20,000 bail. She's craving all the things she loves. We drive all the way down to South Beach for seafood and drinks. It's a three-and-a-half hour drive, but Lola needs to get as far away as she's allowed for just one night. We haven't heard from Sky since her last voice mail. She's not answering her phone, and I'm assuming that she and Fuji are still together. She's still my friend, but I'm very upset with her reaction to the situation. I can't comprehend her tolerance for Fuji's ongoing abuse. When it comes to Fuji, Sky is weak. I realize this now, but also that Sky needs to find her own way. I can't help her if she's unwilling to help herself. Lola is pissed. In my opinion, she has every right to be. She gave Sky the benefit of the doubt initially, but is hurt that Sky didn't make any contact with her while she was in jail.

"Girls, I will never speak to Sky again," she declared on her second day behind bars.

Going on a girl trip without Sky feels strange. We try our best to take Lola's mind off things while we're here. We made a pact not to mention Sky or Fuji's names, or anything about the incident. It appears that Lola has a long road ahead of her. Fuji refuses to drop the charges. The case is going to trial. Lola ends up consuming more liquor on our overnight trip than all of us combined. We have to practically carry her back to her room.

Who would have thought that Fuji was abusing Sky? I know he's not exactly a saint, and I *have* heard him get upset with her in the past—use some pretty coarse language, insult her, and so on—but I would have never pegged him as a wife-beater. Sky's secrets are now stolen from deep inside.

Chapter 21

LOLA

I THOUGHT SHE WAS ONE OF MY BEST FRIENDS

It's the first day of the trial. The girls, Dylan, Randy, and even Winston are here to support me. My family is home in New York, so my friends are all I have right now. I'm not planning to tell my family about any of this unless I have to.

The courtroom is brightly lit. It's sterile and offers absolutely no warmth. I feel an uncomfortable chill. The walls are eggshell, the hardwood floors impossibly shiny, almost glaring. A plaque on the wall behind where the judge will sit reads, IN GOD WE TRUST. There are rows of seats on both sides behind the mahogany desks where the lawyers will sit. I've never been in a courtroom before. It looks like something out of a movie.

I spot Fuji. Sky is sitting right beside him. I almost lose my religion. I can't believe I'm here fighting for my freedom because I defended someone who isn't even here to support *me*. It's a shock to me—and to everyone else. Seeing her in the courtroom sitting next to the man who put me here really hurts. Kennedy assures me everything will be okay. She is always trying to keep the peace. "Lola, put yourself in Sky's shoes," she tells me. "Keep in mind, he *is* her husband, for better or worse."

Dylan walks up to Fuji and pleads with him to drop the charges. "Hell, no!" Fuji snaps. "She's going to pay for what she did to me."

"You're not embarrassed that a woman whipped your ass?" Randy asks.

"And you actually want to advertise it by letting this case go to trial?" Fuji stares straight ahead and says nothing. Dylan scoffs and walks away.

My lawyer, Ted Braxton—I call him Braxton—walks into the courtroom. "Can I have a word with you, in private?" he asks me.

"Sure." We walk to the front of the courtroom, which remains empty for the moment. "I know this judge, Carlton Moore," Braxton says. "He used to be a prosecutor. I also happen to know that his daughter was in an abusive relationship at one time. There's a good chance he'll be sympathetic to the circumstances of this case. He also happens to be a friend of mine." Braxton winks at me. *I hope he's right.*

We all take a stand when the judge enters the courtroom. I wait for my case to be called. The judge is handsome, black, and young, in his early forties. He looks at me and smiles. It's the most confident I've felt all day. Braxton nudges me with his elbow.

"Quiet in the courtroom," says the court officer. "We will now address the case of Jerome Smith verses Lola Santiago."

Braxton stands up and gestures for me to stand with him. "Your Honor," Braxton begins, "this case is really about a man by the name of Jerome Smith, who attacked my client, Lola Santiago, in the home of one of her closest friends. Sky Smith, the wife of Jerome Smith, invited my client, along with several other friends, to help move her belongings out of her house, which she shares with Mr. Smith. She was moving her things because Mr. Smith had beaten her with a belt in front of the residence of her friend, Kennedy Owens, an event to which there were several witnesses.

"Mrs. Smith was staying at the home of Ms. Owens due to previous physical altercations between her and her husband. After the incident in front of Ms. Owens's home, my client, Ms. Santiago, was invited to accompany Mrs. Smith to her home to help collect her things. My client wasn't aware that Mr. Smith would be home at that time."

"Is Mrs. Smith in the court room today?" the judge asks.

"Yes, she is, your honor," Braxton answers, and points to Sky.

"I object, your honor," the prosecutor says.

The judge turns to the prosecutor and asks, "What exactly are you objecting *to*, Mr. Johnson?"

"Mrs. Smith is the wife of my client. She isn't listed by the defense as a witness."

"Overruled," the judge declares. "Mrs. Smith is a witness and thereby relevant to this case."

"Mrs. Smith, please stand," the judge directs. Sky obeys. "Please come forward and state your full name and address." Again, Sky obeys the judge's orders. Then he asks her, "Do you stand by the facts of this case as stated by defense attorney, Braxton?"

I thirstily wait for Sky's answer. The room is so quiet you can hear a pin drop. "Everything Mr. Braxton has stated is true, your Honor. Mr. Smith has been beating me for all of the years of our marriage, and I'm finally at a turning point. My friends were supporting me that day when Fu... *Jerome* attacked my friend, Lola, without provocation." Sky is speaking with such sadness. She sounds thoroughly exhausted.

My heart goes out to Sky in that moment. I let my guard down. She looks over at me, and we make eye contact. I mouth the words, *Has anyone told you today they love and care about you? Well, I do.*

She smiles weakly. *I love you, too,* she mouths back. The prosecutor is clearly annoyed by our discreet exchange, but he makes no comment.

"Mrs. Smith, are you here today to support your husband or your friend?" the judge asks.

"Judge, I'm here to support my friend, Lola Santiago," Sky answers. "And with your permission, I would like to switch seats and sit with my friends."

"Go on ahead, Mrs. Smith."

The girls welcome her and make room for Sky in the row where they're sitting. I blow her a kiss from my place at the front. I glance at Kennedy. She winks and mouths the words, *I told you,* and we both smile. Whenever any of our relationships seem to be breaking apart, Kennedy is the glue that bonds us back together.

The judge turns his attention to Fuji. "Mr. Smith, it is my opinion that you do not have a case here," the judge says. "You are the cause of your own injuries. Had it not been for your actions, none of this would have happened." The judge turns to me. "I am hereby throwing out this case. All charges are dropped, Ms. Santiago," the judge says, looking me straight in the eye and smiling. Then he turns his attention to Sky. "Mrs. Smith, I hope you know you deserve better."

"Yes, thank you, your Honor," Sky says, and bows her head.

"Well, Ms. Santiago, you are free to leave," the judge tells me.

I'm practically bursting with relief. "Thank you, your Honor," I say, smiling wide.

Fuji shouts out as an officer ushers him out the courtroom, "Sky, I want you home tonight!" But Sky doesn't acknowledge him. He tries to walk back toward her, but the court officer restrains him. "You hear me, Sky? Do you hear me?" Fuji repeats the question all the way out into the corridor until his voice eventually fades.

"Mr. Braxton, may I have a word with you before you leave?" says the judge.

"Sure, Judge."

Sky heads toward me, smiling through tears. We hug tightly. "You really frightened me, Sky," I told her. "I thought our friendship was over."

In the corridor outside the courtroom, Fuji is waiting for Sky. "Okay, Sky, I forgive you for what you did in there," he says. "I promise I won't hit you again. Now let's just go home."

"Damned right you'll never hit me again," she says, "because I'm never going home with you. Our marriage is over."

Fuji's mouth drops open slightly. He looks stunned.

Sky looks up at the ceiling. "Damn, that felt good."

Fuji gets his voice back and keeps yelling for her, but Sky ignores him.

"At least we know he won't attempt to hit her while we're in *this* building," Kennedy says. We walk down the long hallway toward the elevators. I can't help but giggle to myself when I see that Fuji decides to take the stairs.

"I am so very proud of you, Sky," I tell her. "You did the right thing."

Kennedy adds, "It won't be an easy road, but we're here for you. And you can stay with me as long as you like...or until I kick you out."

Sky laughs. "Thanks. I needed that."

Braxton calls my name from the other end of the hallway. He gestures for me to meet him halfway. "Go ahead, ladies. I'll meet you downstairs."

When I reach him, he tells me, "Well, I don't know what happened in there," he says, smiling, "but you left quite an impression on the judge. He's interested in you and would like to take you out."

"You mean, like, on a date?" I ask, surprised.

"I'm pretty sure that's what he meant," Braxton says, laughing. "Here's his number. He's expecting a call at eight o'clock tonight."

"Tonight?" I repeat with a shocked smile. I grab the sticky note with the judge's private phone number from Braxton, quickly turn around, and start running back toward the elevators, shouting, "I hit the jackpot! The judge wants to take me out on a date!"

I stop short and nervously look around to make sure the judge isn't close by, listening in. Thankfully, the hall is clear of people except for me and Braxton, who is laughing and shaking his head. Once downstairs, I breathlessly fill in the girls.

"You're kidding me!" Tasha says. "Some people get all the luck."

"Do I detect a touch of jealousy, Tasha?"

"Yes, damn it! I'm jealous," she jokes.

"It would have been even more perfect if he'd asked *me* out," Sky adds. "Girl, he is fine as hell."

I forgot Winston is standing here with us. But I'm kind of glad he is. He needs to know that a man as important as a judge is interested in me. He messed up big time. Now I'm happy he did. I'll definitely be giving "your Honor" a call.

"Can you see Winston's face?" Portia whispers, giggling. "Good for his ass."

"Couldn't have said it better myself, girl," I whisper back, winking.

"Let's get out of here, girls and dudes," Dylan says. "This calls for a celebration! Let's head to that bar down the street."

"Good idea," Randy says.

Winston can't join us; he has things to do. "Lola, I just want to say congratulations. Good luck to you."

"That sounds like goodbye forever, Winston," I say.

He smiles. "No, it's not goodbye forever, Lola."

"Are you sure you can't join us for a drink?" I ask him.

"No, I really have to go."

"Well, thank you for coming and supporting me," I say. "It means a lot to me that you were here."

"It means a lot to me that you would say that, Lola. And you're welcome." He tilts my chin up and kisses me. "You might not believe this, but I will always love you."

I can honestly say now that I forgive him.

~~~

I dial the judge at 8:30. I don't want to seem anxious. He's everything I'm looking for: good-looking, smart, important, well dressed. Most of all, he has money. Hello—he's a judge! I don't need his money, of course, but it's always good to have a man who has it.

We agree to a late dinner together. He insists on picking me up rather than me meeting him at the restaurant—very gentlemanly. The restaurant is very
~~~

impressive. The food smells delicious. It's an upscale place with well-dressed guests. There are candles and fresh roses on the tables which are each draped with two white linen cloths that overlap. Soft jazz is playing, which helps drown out the humming sound of the air conditioner.

"I see you know your way around the kitchen," I say to him with a grin.

"As a matter of fact, I get around the kitchen very well," he answers. "Maybe I'll cook dinner for you at my place some night. If you're interested in going out with me again, that is."

In the corner of my mind I'm thinking, *He is eight notches above perfection.* "I guess we'll have to just see how tonight goes, and then we'll see," I say, winking.

The conversation is easy with Carlton. Everything is more perfect than I could have imagined. The food is good, the man is strikingly gorgeous, and the company desirable. He's breath-taking. I feel my emotional walls beginning to crumble. This man is inspiring me to take a chance on love again.

I learn during our conversation that he is indeed in his early forties—impressively young to hold such an accomplished position. We have a few common interests, too. I decide to put Carlton on a trial basis. I like dating around, but life is so much more worth it when you have someone special to share it with. I'm scared of repeated failure and disappointment, but I think I'm ready to take a risk again.

From my experiences, I have learned three things about love. One, you have to learn to forgive and forget. Two, you have to take the good with the bad. And three, love is not a game—it's not about winning or losing. It's too early to tell with Carlton, but I have a good feeling about him, and us. I've never felt so relaxed with someone this early on, have never shared this strong of a connection on a first date. And I'm not just saying this because he has money.

"I was born here in Florida," Carlton tells me. "My parents are both doctors."

"Ah, so you were born with a silver spoon in your mouth," I chide playfully.

Carlton smiles. "I guess you can say that," he confesses.

I definitely like him, but I'm going to enforce the ninety-day rule. He isn't getting any for ninety days. If I didn't like him so much, I'd probably give him some tonight. But because I truly like him, I want him to respect me.

"So, Lola, are you available…or is there someone special in your life?" he asks.

"Funny you should ask that. There's no one special, but up until a few moments ago, I wasn't exactly *emotionally* available," I admit. "But after spending time with you, I'm beginning to rethink that."

"You're making me blush, Lola," he says sincerely.

At midnight, Carlton pulls up in front of my place and we begin to say goodnight. Lord knows I don't want the date to end. I can tell he doesn't, either. I give him a kiss on the cheek. He kisses me on the forehead. I'm determined to be a good girl.

I walk inside, smiling to myself. Carlton feels like the prize of a lifetime. I see potential for love again. I decide I will stop seeing the other men I've been dating. As usual, I'll be honest with them—via text. I can't wait to tell the girls what a wonderful time I had with Carlton. This day has certainly turned around from how it started. I didn't go to jail; I reunited with my dear friend; and I met a beautiful man.

This whole experience has taught me a lot about myself. For one, I need to learn to control my temper. No more going from zero to sixty in a matter of seconds. I can't afford to go through something like this again, and I certainly don't want to end up in jail again.

I'm so grateful Sky came through. I should have known she wouldn't have abandoned me. I love her. And I love my life right now.

Chapter 22

DIAMOND

THEY'RE ALL GOING DOWN ONE BY ONE

Portia called to tell me Lola was in jail. Then she told me why. I was shocked. Not that Fuji was a woman-beater so much, but that Sky put up with it for so long. These bitches walk around like their shit don't stink. Sky was always acting like her relationship with Fuji was perfect, and the whole damned time, the bitch was getting her ass whipped. I feel kind of sorry for her...but not really. I don't purposely wish the girls any bad fortune, but it's high time they start getting some of my bad luck.

Portia thinks her marriage is perfect. But I know Dylan must be messing around. There's not a man who doesn't cheat. Dylan may have been faithful for a time, but I know he's getting his groove on with some other women by now. And whatever is done in the dark must always come to light. He'll be found out eventually.

When Portia was done filling me in on Sky and Fuji, I said, "Wow, you never know what's going on behind closed doors. You know, Portia, I've always wanted to ask, do you think Dylan is faithful to you?"

She got all defensive. "Of course my husband is faithful to me, Diamond. Why would you ask me that?"

"Because I don't want you to be a fool," I said. "You're my friend. I care about you."

"What are you saying, Diamond?" she asked me. "Do you have something to tell me?"

"I'm just saying, Portia, don't be stupid. Every man cheats," I taunted.

"My husband would never cheat on me. He loves me too much."

"Portia, do you really believe that?"

"Yes, I do," she insisted.

"Well, I'm just saying that I know a lot of women who start out thinking that…until their man is busted." I was on a roll. "Then they feel stupid when they're the last to know."

"Diamond, I'm going to ask you one more time. Do you have something to tell me?"

"No, Portia, I just don't want you to be stupid," I said. "You have too much trust in Dylan. Just remember, no matter how much you give yourself to him, you'll never be enough. Expect the worst. That way, when it happens, the pain won't be as severe. I always keep a wall up. I never totally trust them. "

"Diamond, if you feel like men can't love and respect you, it's probably because you haven't earned their respect."

"See, that's the difference between you and me, Portia. Love is not earned, *money is.*" I could feel my emotional blackmail starting to kick in. "Portia, I love you so much. I thought you respected my opinion?" I would love to take her down a notch by threatening to expose him, but I had no evidence of Dylan being unfaithful. My intention wasn't to cause strain on their marriage, but to help her understand she can't underestimate the cheating habits of men.

She was trying hard not to take the bait. It was starting to piss me off. She's so damned naïve. So I just said, "Portia, I gotta go," and hung up the phone. That's all right, she'll figure it out. Now I just have to work on Dylan.

~~~

TRAFFIC LIGHTS & TRESPASSING

KENNEDY

After everything Sky's been through, the girls and I decide she needs a night out. We check out a new spot in downtown Orlando that everyone has been making a fuss about. We meet up in my condo's parking lot at nine o'clock. The girls are all wearing their little black dresses. I'm wearing my little white one. We're standing in a huddle waiting for the limo I reserved to pick us up and take us to the club. "You bitches look cute," I say.

My phone rings. I don't answer because I don't recognize the number.
~~~

The caller leaves a message, so I take a moment to listen. Murphy. He's trying to get me to answer by calling from another number. "Kennedy, when I call you, could you *please* pick up the phone?" He's just not getting it. I delete the message.

A tall, lanky woman passes us in the parking lot and stops to compliment our shoes. She says she can tell we're from New York by our sense of style. We all laugh and say thank you as we climb into the car, which has now arrived, and head off for the evening. When we reach our destination, I open the glass partition that separates us from the driver and ask if he can provide us with a number to call him when we're ready to leave. "No problem," he says, "just give me about a half-hour courtesy time."

"Deal," I say, and shake his hand.

At the entrance of the restaurant, two hostesses stand behind a podium. The DJ isn't visible from where we're standing, but the music is playing. The atmosphere is tropical. Parrots and other colorful fake birds dangle from the ceiling, with a net just below to catch them if they fall. The lighting is set for romance. The bar is located in the middle of the restaurant so customers can order drinks from every side of the room. We're seated on the outskirts of the bar in the middle of the room, which draws a lot attention. After about twenty minutes, the waitress finally comes over to take our order. It's a full house. We're not ready to order dinner, so we just order drinks for now.

"A round of Jack Daniels shots and Coronas, please." This used to be our drink back in the day. We used to drink and drive—I'm talking, tore up from the floor up, needing a check up from the neck up. I can't believe how stupid we were. We're much wiser now. We wouldn't dream of getting behind the wheel after drinking.

Our shots and beers arrive. We hoot and holler loudly and end up catching the attention of an acquaintance of mine, a friend of a friend. "Kennedy, how are you?" she asks me.

"Good, Stormy, how are you?" I reply.

"I'm fine. Long time no see."

"Girls, this is Stormy," I say, "an old friend of mine."

"Stormy, what a unique name," Tasha observes.

Stormy smiles. "My mom named me that because I was born while a storm was passing through."

"I never knew that," I say. "Stormy, these are my sisters: Brooke, Lola, Tasha, Payton, Portia, and Sky."

"Hi!" the girls sing together.

"Stormy, would you like to join us?" I ask.

"Oh no, dear. Thank you for asking, though. I'm here with some friends." She gestures to a table across the restaurant. "In fact, Kennedy, why don't come over and meet them?"

"Sure," I say. "Excuse me ladies, I'll be right back."

"It was nice meeting you, ladies," Stormy says to the girls.

As we approach her party of four, Stormy introduces me. "Ladies, this is Kennedy. Hey, where's Trina?" she asks, looking around.

"Oh, she's on the phone with Myles," one girl says, rolling her eyes and gesturing to their friend, who is standing just outside the entrance to the restaurant.

"Yeah, he's giving her a hard time about going out with us tonight," explains another of Stormy's friends.

I feel my stomach lurch. "Myles?"

"Oh yeah, girl," Stormy says. "You know there's only one Myles."

"Well, there'd better be two," I say, feeling my blood start to boil.

"Oh my," she exclaims. "I thought you and Myles were no longer dating." She looks concerned. "At least, that's what he told Trina. Do you even know that he and Trina are engaged?"

"You're kidding me, right?" I'm stunned, and getting angrier by the minute.

"I'm completely serious," she says.

I walk away from their table and head back to my girls. "You all are not going to believe this," I say as I sit down. "Myles has a fiancée."

"*What?*" they all scream together.

I nod. "It's true. Do you freaking believe this bullshit? I've got to go. I can't sit here."

Brooke asks, "Did his fiancée tell you this herself?"

"No, Stormy did," I say. "His *fiancée* is outside talking to *him* on the phone."

"Well, honey, you can do one of two things," says Brooke. "You can approach her and get details so he can't lie his way out of it, or you can confront him directly."

"What do you want to do, girl?" Lola asks.

"I want to go out there and confront *her*," I say. "I want answers. I didn't say anything to you guys, but I've heard rumors about this on two different occasions now…from different people."

"You heard he's engaged to someone else?" Payton asks, eyes wide.

I sigh. "Yes."

"Why haven't you said anything?" Portia asks.

"Because...I confronted Myles and he *apparently* lied his way out of it," I say, feeling defeated. "And I believed him." I take a deep breath. "Well, ladies, you ready? Let's go."

"Go ahead," Payton says. "I'll catch up to y'all after I pay the bill."

Brooke says, "Give me the number so I can call the limo."

I push through the exit door, and there she is, standing on the sidewalk, turning off her phone. Damn! I wanted to catch Myles red-handed on the phone with her. I tap her on the shoulder. "Excuse me, can I speak to you?"

"Sure," she says. She's polite enough, and obviously curious.

"My name is Kennedy. My boyfriend's name is Myles. Do you happen to know him?"

"Um, yes, he's my fiancé," she says, showing me her ring.

"How long have you two been engaged?"

"For about two years."

"Bastard!" I exclaim.

"He's coming to pick me up." Not a moment later, Myles is pulling up in front of the restaurant. But he sees me standing next to his fiancée and keeps on driving.

I turn to her. "Are you going to call him, or should I?"

We both try calling him, but of course he's not picking up. I am so hurt. I can't stand around here any longer. I have to leave. What a coward; he doesn't even have the balls to come to us.

A player is a man who dates multiple women at once but is open about it. Often, the women even know each other and get along just fine. Myles is not a player—he's an asshole. I walk over to my girls, who've been giving us some space to talk. Before I walk away, I turn and ask Myles's fiancée, "It's Trina, right?

"Yes."

"Yeah, girls," I say, "that's the name I heard before."

The good news is, it's *she* who's stuck with a cheating bastard. The bad news is, I will definitely miss sexing him. But I won't stand for feeling like number two. Even if I'm not number one, I need to at least feel that I am. Meeting Trina face to face changes everything between Myles and me.

~~~
~~~

Later the same evening, Myles is calling my phone constantly, leaving one voice mail after another. He says he can't believe I acted like a child, trying to set him up. He told me the girl was crazy and asked why I would stand there and listen to her lies. Do you freaking believe this man? Does he think I'm an idiot? He thinks he can hand me some bullshit excuse, and I'll just accept it? Well, he's wrong. I dial his number. When he picks up, I say, "Do me a favor. Don't call me ever again. Stay away from me, you two-timing nasty asshole. And stop leaving messages on my phone!" I hang up.

The way this man put my entire body in his mouth—including my asshole—makes me wonder. *Does he do that to both of us?* If he is engaged to her, then I have no choice but to believe that he does the same to her. *Nasty! Just nasty!*

He's called twenty times, and there are twenty messages begging me to pick up the phone and talk to him. He's pleading, saying he can't live without me. I'm getting tired of hearing my phone ring, so I give in and pick it up. "Yes, Myles," I answer, "what the hell do you want?"

"Kennedy, baby, I cursed that woman out for lying to you. Those girls were trying to set you up. Stormy don't like you."

"So why the hell didn't you stop when you saw Trina and I standing in front of the restaurant together? You could have just addressed the situation right then and there."

"I was looking for parking," he says. "When I finally found a place to park and walked back to the entrance, you were gone. I tried to call you but you wouldn't answer your phone."

"Okay, Myles, if what you're saying to me is true, then why don't you, me, and Trina meet up like adults and talk about this."

"Kennedy, I don't know where to find that chick," he says. "I don't even know her."

"You said you loved me, Myles." My voice starts to crumble. "You lied."

"I *do* love you," he says emphatically. "And I never loved anyone before you."

"Myles, I don't believe you." My resolve strengthens. "If you love me and you want our relationship to continue, then you'll bring her to me so we can clear the air." I hang up the phone.

He calls back again, this time crying. "Kennedy, please don't do this to me," he pleads. "I need you right now. I'm not going to let you walk out of my life like this."

I can't believe what I'm hearing. Myles is actually crying. Maybe he really does love me.

"Hearing you cry for me is making me feel closer to you," I say.

"Can I come over, Kennedy?" he asks, sounding nearly desperate.

"No, I'll come to you." He's lucky. I was about to call Murphy.

When we meet, I can't look him in the eye. Deep down inside, I know this man is manipulating me into believing his bullshit. We have sex, but it's not good. I feel empty, and images of Myles making love to Trina are running through my mind the entire time we're making love. Finally, I push him off of me. I jump up and tell him I need time to sort things out. He grabs my arm as I try to leave, and I yank it away from him. "Please, Myles, you need to give me some time."

"No, Kennedy, I can't give you the space you're asking for," he says. "I know how you operate. If we don't see each other, you'll leave me. You need to give me a chance to fix this."

"It's not up for negotiation," I tell him. "I'm *telling* you I need time, not *asking* you." I walk out of his apartment and slam the door behind me. The girls are calling, but I don't answer my phone. I'm not up to speaking to anyone tonight. I need time alone.

I hear Myles scream through his door without opening it, "When will you call me?"

"I don't know," I yell to the closed door. "It will probably be a while." As I walk further away from his door, I mumble, "Not until tomorrow, at least."

As I get in my car, I happen to notice a black car parallel-parked across the street with its headlights on. As I drive off down the street, the car does a U-turn and follows me. Two blocks later, I'm stopped at a red light. The car is still behind me. When I look into my rearview mirror, the driver flips on the car's high beams, making it too bright for me to identify the driver. The light turns green, and I drive straight through the intersection. It's about three miles to the highway. Three blocks later, another red light. I stop. The car following me still has its high beams on, but I see someone, a woman, get out of the car and begin walking toward me. The light turns green before she reaches my car, and I drive forward. In my rearview mirror, I see the woman run back to her car, jump in, and continue following me.

"Who is this crazy woman, and what does she want?" I ask myself out loud. I drive a few more blocks. I can see that she's catching up to me. After another three blocks, I come to a stop at another traffic light. The woman jumps out of her car again. She's holding something in her hand. I'm saying to myself, "Come on, light, change! Hurry up and change!" The light seems to be taking forever.

I hear a loud crashing sound, and scream. This woman is breaking through my passenger side window. "Stay away from Myles!" she shouts. "He's my man! You better leave my man alone!" She points the object in her hand at me. It's Trina—the polite woman from the restaurant who claimed to be engaged to Myles. She's acting like a maniac. I hit the gas and drive right through the red light like a bat out of hell. I can see her in the rearview mirror, running back to her car and jumping in to continue the chase. I'm scared. I can't even dial for help. My car skids and almost turns over because I take the highway on-ramp at too high a speed.

On the highway, I drive about a mile, thinking I might have lost her, until I see a car behind me, swerving in and out of traffic. My heart starts pounding again. I floor the gas pedal. Seeing her getting closer is making my heart pound. I'm so scared. I'm relieved when I see her get caught up in some traffic. She's driving in the middle lane now. There are cars on either side of her, and she's boxed in. *Thank God.*

I'm shaken up, but relieved. I keep my speed up till I don't see her in my rearview mirror anymore. I drive past two more exits, exit the highway, and take back roads the rest of the way home.

I arrive in my parking lot and park in my assigned space. I can't move because I'm still so shaken up. There isn't a soul in the parking lot, and it makes me feel vulnerable. *What if she knows where I live? She could be here waiting for me.*

I need to calm down. My phone rings. It's Myles. I pick up the phone, breathless from all the excitement, and launch into him. "Your crazy fiancé just tried to run me off the road!"

"What?" he says in disbelief. "Are you serious?"

"Yes. Tell her to stay away from me, Myles," I scream, "or I'm going to the police."

My emotions take over. I'm screaming and carrying on. All Myles can say is, "Baby, I'm so sorry for this. I'm so sorry, baby."

I scream through my tears, "Myles, if you don't want me, let me go! Please just let me go! I can't do this!" My voice is trembling. I hang up the phone, and it drops to the floor of the car. My head falls to the steering wheel, and I sob uncontrollably for several minutes.

My phone rings again. I collect myself and pick it up off the floor of the car. I press speaker by mistake and hear Myles saying, "I promise you, Kennedy,

I'm going to make it better." I turn off the phone while he's still talking. I don't even care that my window is busted out. Hopefully my car won't get vandalized while it's parked in the private lot.

When I get upstairs, I call Lola.

"Hey, Kennedy," she says, and I start to cry again.

"What's wrong, baby?" she asks, sounding worried. "Are you okay?"

"I'm not okay, Lola," I say in a soft voice. "Turns out Trina is a bit of a psycho."

"What?" Lola asks. "Do you want me to come over?"

"No, Lola. I need to be alone right now. I just wanted to hear your voice."

"Kennedy, please let me come over," she pleads. "We don't have to talk. I can just be there, just in case."

"Lola, I promise I'll call you tomorrow," I say. "I'll tell you everything in the morning. I'm just filled with so many questions about Myles."

"Okay, girl. You know I got your back like a jacket, right?"

"Yes, I know." I manage a little laugh.

"Kennedy, has anyone told you they love and care about you today? Well, I do."

"I love you too, Lola. I'll call you tomorrow. Bye."

I go straight to my room and snatch the sheets off the bed. I throw them in the kitchen garbage can. I can't smell his cologne tonight. I don't even bother to put on clean sheets.

I should have stayed with Murphy, but I'm infected by Myles's love. I tried not to love him, tried to stay detached, but it didn't work. I grab the sleeping pills my mom left here from the medicine cabinet and down a couple. I grab a blanket from the closet, crawl onto the bed, and sleep on the bare mattress. Before I drift into intoxicated sleep, I pray, "God, please send me a sign if you think I should fight for this relationship."

My sleep is disturbed by a loud knock. I look at my clock. It's 2:37pm, the middle of the next afternoon. "Who is it?" No answer from the other side of the door. I repeat, "Who is it?"

"It's me, Myles."

I look up at the ceiling and whisper, "Okay God, I'm going to let you lead the way." I say angrily through the closed door, "What do you want, Myles?"

"I want to come clean, Kennedy."

I sigh and open the door to let him in, shaking my head in disbelief. I walk over to the kitchen and begin making coffee. The sleeping pills are still in my system. I think about kicking him out and going back to sleep, but realize I want to hear what he has to say. I'm curious as to how he's going to get himself out of this one. He closes the front door and trails behind me to the kitchen.

"Okay, what do you want to tell me, Myles?" I ask flatly.

"Kennedy, you sound so cold."

"This isn't about me, Myles, it's about you. Don't change the subject."

"You can't stop this, Kennedy."

"Can't stop what, Myles?"

"You can't stop what we have," he explains. "What we have going between us is too strong."

"I didn't stop it, Myles. You stopped it. Now stop stalling and just tell me why you're here."

He pauses. "Okay. I dated Trina years ago—before I met you."

"So now you know her?" I roll my eyes.

"Yes, I know her," he admits sheepishly.

"Why would you lie if the relationship happened a long time ago?"

"Because I knew she wanted something more than what we actually had. I wanted to erase her. I took her to dinner a few times. That's it. I swear that's as far as it ever went. She wanted more. I told her it would never happen. Then I hear she's telling people we're engaged, so I cut off our friendship completely."

Before he can continue explaining, there's a knock at the door. I feel irritated. I walk to the front door, but I'm hesitant to open it. "Who is it?" I yell.

A pause, then, "Trina."

"Who?" I ask again, thinking I must be hearing things.

"It's Trina."

I can't freaking believe it. I walk back into the kitchen. "Myles, Trina is at the door."

His mouth falls open. "What?"

I'm more annoyed than ever. "You need to go work that out, before I start tossin' tables and flippin' chairs." Myles looks flushed. And nervous. His facial features are twitching. As he's walking toward the door, I pick up the phone and call Lola.

"Hey, Kennedy," she answers, sounding relieved to hear from me. "Are you feeling any better?"

"Girl, you are not going to believe this," I say. "That girl Trina is at my front door."

"You've got to be kidding me! How did she get into your building?"

"I wish I knew. Probably snuck in behind another tenant."

"Are you sure it's her?"

"Yes, Lola!" I scream. "That psycho just showed up at my door."

"Well, where is she now?" Lola asks.

"In the entryway, talking to Myles."

"I'm calling the girls, and we're coming over."

"Lola, I can handle this," I assure her.

"Are you crazy, Kennedy? She crossed the line by coming to your house."

"Lola, if I need y'all, I promise I'll call." The situation with Sky and Fuji taught me a valuable lesson: only get Lola involved if you absolutely have to—for her own good, and yours.

"Kennedy, if you don't call me in twenty minutes," Lola threatens, "I'm calling the girls and we're coming over. Do you hear me?"

"I hear you, girl. Bye."

Myles left my front door slightly open. He's standing on the other side of it. I'm able to hear their conversation—or argument, I should say. Why did this relationship have to get so complicated? I just don't get it. I play by the rules, but it seems like the rules are designed to keep me down. My thoughts are interrupted when I hear him ask, "What the hell are you doing here, Trina?"

"I'm here for you, Myles."

"What? Are you serious?"

"Yes, I'm serious. I'm as serious as cancer."

"Trina, you and I have not been in a relationship in over seven years," Myles reminds her. "What is wrong with you? You need some help."

"We may have not been in a relationship, but we have been out on dates, Myles."

"Trina, we have dinner together occasionally," Myles says, "as friends. Get over it. I'm in a relationship with someone else. Now get out of here, or I'm calling the cops."

"I'll go, Myles, if you come with me." Trina sounds desperate.

That's my cue to open the door. "Excuse me," I say to her. "You're pathetic and should be embarrassed."

"I'm not talking to you, so stay out of it!" she shouts.

"You crazy!"

"You haven't seen crazy yet," she threatens.

"You tried to run me off the road!"

"Okay, now I'm calling the cops," Myles says. He grabs his phone from his pocket and dials 911. "Yes, I'd like to report a woman trespassing. I've asked her to leave and she refuses. Can you send someone over, please?"

"Really, Myles?" Trina sounds genuinely hurt as he gives the dispatcher my address.

"Yes, really," I answer for him. She reaches over his shoulder and tries to take a swing at me, but instead she hits Myles in the face. Myles grabs her and pushes her hard enough to knock her down. "Take your ass inside, Kennedy," he says.

"What?" I ask, taken aback.

"Kennedy, I will deal with this. Now go back inside."

I'm actually a little turned on by his demands. "Okay."

Five minutes later, he comes back into the condo and heads to the bathroom. He mentions that Trina has taken the elevator back down to the lobby. I see flashing police lights down on the street from my kitchen window. I run downstairs to meet the police. I see Trina sitting on the steps in front of my building.

As I step outside the main door, the officer is approaching Trina and saying, "We got a call there's been a disturbance here. Do you know anything about it?"

"No," she lies. "I've been sitting out here for about an hour, and I haven't seen or heard anything. Maybe kids are just playing on the phone."

"Do you live in the building, miss?"

"Yes, I live here with my husband, Myles."

She really is *crazy.*

I step forward. "Officer, *my* boyfriend, Myles, is the one who called you. This woman is trespassing. She doesn't live here. I do. I can go and get my ID if you like."

"That won't be necessary," Trina relents. "I'm leaving."

I hear Myles behind me, "No, I want her arrested," he announces. "Not only did she trespass, but she tried to run my girlfriend off the road last night."

"Is this true?" the officer asks me.

"Yes, she tried to kill me," I answer.

"Would you like to press charges?"

"Yes, actually I would."

Trina looks scared to death. I actually feel sorry for her.

The officer says, "Well, you'll have to come down to the station and give a statement."

I pull Myles aside. "Honey, I don't want this," I say, changing my mind. "I'm not going to press charges."

"Why, Kennedy?"

"A lot has happened in a very small space of time. I feel overwhelmed. I just don't want this." I walk to the officer, who now has Trina in handcuffs. While I've been talking to Myles, the officer has placed her under arrest.

"Can you just let her off with a warning?" I ask the officer.

"Ma'am, you can do whatever you wish. It's up to you," he explains. "But trying to run someone off the road is a serious crime. I urge you to think carefully about what you want to do."

I say to the officer respectfully, "Just make sure she knows this is a warning and that next time she won't get off so easy."

"Will do, ma'am," he says, and unlocks the cuffs.

I don't stick around long enough to hear his lecture. Myles and I go upstairs. I call Lola and tell her she doesn't needs to come over. Good thing I did; she was already in her car, ready to go.

Soon after I get off the phone, Myles says, "Let's talk."

I sit down at the kitchen table. "I'm listening, Myles."

He looks into my eyes and says, "I'm ready."

"Ready for what?" I ask, smiling.

"I'm ready to settle down," he announces. "I'm not talking marriage... yet. But I'm ready to make a commitment." I look at him, stunned. "I realize after almost losing you last night, there is nothing out there for me anymore. You're everything I want in a woman, Kennedy." I feel my heart melting. "You're smart, responsible, and beautiful. You're a sharp businesswoman; your company went from eight to twenty-three employees, like, overnight," he says, eyes wide and smiling. "I have never been more proud of you, never been more proud to be with you."

I'm overwhelmed and trying to process everything he's just told me. Then he says, "Why don't we start by moving in together?" He quickly adds, "No pressure. Right now, I just want you to be my lady—no more being just friends with benefits." He pauses. "I want more."

Tears are welling up in my eyes. "Myles, I'm scared to trust you," I confess.

"I promise you, Kennedy, from this day forward, I will never hurt you again."

I pause and take a deep breath. "Okay, let's do it. We'll take it one day at a time and see what happens."

He smiles. "Fair enough."

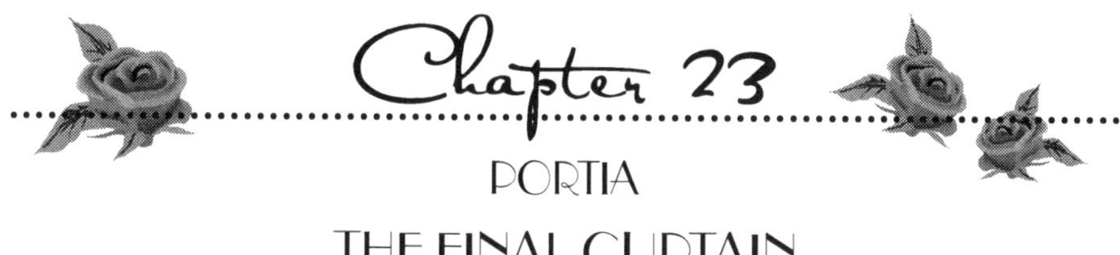

Chapter 23

PORTIA

THE FINAL CURTAIN

Dylan has been acting odd the last few days. I've been trying to comfort him, but I can't get him to open up to me about what's going on for him. He's completely shut down, and I don't know why. We usually have such an affectionate and loving relationship. My son can barely stand being around us when we're in public because we're always touching each other or holding hands. We always greet each other with a kiss or a hug, no matter if we're inside or outside.

My favorite time with Dylan is when we're in the kitchen, cooking together. We like to play music and dance around while we slice green peppers and onions and grill streaks.

But lately he's has been literally pushing me away when I try to show him any affection, never allowing me to get close. I'm starting to feel really scared. I'm even wondering if Diamond was right. Maybe there's another woman in Dylan's life.

We're in the bedroom. Things are so quiet between us that I feel myself becoming desperate. I attempt to open up a dialog with him. "Honey, will you please talk to me?"

"About what?" he snaps.

"Honey, it's clear that something is wrong. You've been pushing me away, and I want to know why. Whatever it is, we can fix it. But we can't fix it if you won't tell me what's going on with you."

"There's nothing to be fixed, Portia," he says coldly. "So just leave me alone."

I'm stunned by his demeanor. He's not himself, and it scares me. "Do you hear yourself?" I ask him. "You're shutting me out." I pause. "Sweetheart, are you planning to leave me?"

Dylan stands up and walks to the bedroom door. He slams it behind him on his way out.

Tears are welling up in my eyes for the third time today. I pick up the phone and call Kennedy. "Hi, girl," I manage to choke out when she answers.

"Portia, is that you?" she asks, sounding concerned.

"Yes, it's me."

"What's wrong, honey?"

"I wish I could tell you, but I don't have a clue. Dylan's been treating me like crap for days. I feel like I'm losing him, Kennedy, and I don't even know why."

"Portia, honey, try to calm down," she says. "Have you tried asking Dylan what's wrong?"

"Of course I have, and he won't answer my questions," I say dejectedly. "He's walking around here angry all the time and won't tell me anything. I'm getting really scared."

"Scared of what, exactly?" Kennedy asks.

I sigh. "I had a conversation with Diamond a while back. She kept trying to tell me that Dylan's been cheating on me."

"She actually told you Dylan's been seeing other women?" Kennedy says disbelievingly.

"Well, she didn't come straight out and say it like that. But she insinuated as much. The conversation came out of left field, Kennedy. Or so I thought at the time. I didn't know what to make of it, but now, the way Dylan is acting…I can't help but think maybe she was right."

"Do you want me to give her a call?"

"Please. Call me back and let me know what she says."

After we hang up, I sit in a daze, listening to the raindrops hitting the window. Tears are welling up in my eyes and beginning to spill down my cheeks. My heart aches at the thought of my husband leaving me. I say a silent prayer: *God, whatever is happening, I need your help to fix it. I can't lose my husband.* My prayer is interrupted when the phone rings. It's Kennedy calling me back.

"Hello," I say as I pick up the phone.

"Hey girl, I just spoke with Diamond," she says. "She doesn't have one lick of evidence that Dylan's been cheating on you. She was just voicing her general opinion on men, that's all." She sounds aggravated with our friend. "Portia, anyone with eyes can see that Dylan loves you more than life itself. There could be any number of reasons he's behaving strangely. It doesn't always have to be another woman." Kennedy pauses and draws a long breath. "When he's ready, he'll talk. Just give him the space he needs right now. It will work out, I'm sure of it."

"You're probably right, Kennedy," I say, not quite believing it. "When he's ready, he'll come to me. Thank you, girl. I feel better now," I assure her. "I love you."

"I love you, too. If you need anything at all, call. I'm only a speed dial away. Oh, and tell Dante I said hi. He's home from school, right?"

"Yes, he's here, and he can tell something's wrong. He asked me if we're getting a divorce."

"What did you tell him?"

"I just told him that we're not getting a divorce, that we're not fighting, and then offered an excuse on Dylan's behalf about being overwhelmed at work right now. He seemed to accept it."

"Hey, has anyone told you they love and care about you today? Well, I do, baby."

"Thank you for saying that, Kennedy. I really needed to hear that—because I don't feel particularly loved by my man right now. I love you, too. Goodbye."

"Goodbye, girl."

~~~

It's late in the evening, and I know sleeping will be useless. I'm just too upset. I decide to finish up some laundry. I go into our bedroom to put some clothes away. Dylan, who's been lying on the bed, staring at the ceiling, sits up when he sees me. "This came for you," he says, then launches an envelope in my direction. It lands on the floor. I pick it up and open it. The letter is typed on pink stationary.

> Dylan, you are a complete jackass. Your wife, Portia, has been cheating on you. Her entire family knows this man and welcomes him into their homes. Her girlfriends know, too.
~~~

You went and purchased a mansion for her. I heard you furnished the entire home for her. Well, she is enjoying it with another man while you're at work. That's right, idiot, he's been sleeping in your bed.

Even your son knows about this man. But you are so blinded by love that you don't even pay attention to the obvious. Everybody is laughing at you behind your back because it's happening in front of your face and you can't even see it. You work so hard for your perfect little family, and all for nothing. I couldn't stand her making a fool of you any longer, so I decided to let your dumb ass in on what's been happening.

Sometimes I think you can't be that naive. If this letter doesn't open your eyes then you are a fool.

Respectfully,
Someone who cares

I'm shocked. The letter drops from my hand to the bed. I'm completely disgusted that someone could do something like this. I look at my husband. "Dylan, you don't believe this bullshit, do you?" I ask.

"Why shouldn't I believe it?" he spits. "Why would someone lie for no reason?"

"Well, it's obvious, isn't it? This person is clearly jealous of what we have. Honey, look at me. This is garbage. I swear to you it's not true."

"Well, I don't believe you, Portia," he says.

I can't believe what I'm hearing. Dylan gets up from the bed and starts to leave the room.

"Where are you going, Dylan? You can't just get up and walk out on me. We need to talk about this!" My voice is shrill, desperate. I stand in front of the bedroom door to block him from leaving. "Dylan, stop," I command. "I'm not going to lose you over something that's not even true." Dylan grabs my right shoulder with his left hand, flings me out of the way, and storms out of the room.

My son, Dante, hears the commotion and comes running. "Dad, what did you do to Mom?" he asks.

"Shut up, traitor," he says to Dante.

"Traitor?" Dante echoes. "Dad, what are you talking about?" He looks so upset. My heart goes out to him. But Dylan offers no explanation to his son and walks out of the house. Dante runs to my side. "What's happening, Mom?" he asks, sounding even more distressed. I'm too emotional to speak. I point to the letter on the bed. After reading it, he looks at me, silent.

"Dante, it's not true," I say emphatically. "It's all lies."

"Who would do something so cruel?" he asks.

"I don't know." This is all I can offer him. "I don't have any idea why someone would do this to me. Oh my God, Dante, what am I going to do?" I ask, starting to feel desperate. I feel my life spinning out of control. "I can't lose your father." I look at Dante. "What am I going to do?" I repeat.

"Mom, calm down. We'll figure this out. We'll give Dad some time to cool down, and then we'll figure it out…together." He shakes his head. "I can't believe he hit you."

"He didn't hit me, baby," I say. "He shoved me away from the door. I was trying to block him from leaving. Your dad would never hit me."

"If he touches you again, Mom, I'm going to hit him," Dante threatens.

"No, no, no, Dante, you need to respect your father," I scold. "I don't want to hear you say that ever again. Your dad is a good man, and a great dad. Do you hear me? Your dad is a good husband."

He nods. "Yes, Mom, I hear you."

"Now, go to your room, sweetheart. I'll see you in the morning. I just need to be by myself right now." I want to call the girls to vent, but it's two in the morning, and I don't want to wake them. I decide to call Diamond and confide in her; she's always up at this hour. She picks up on the third ring.

"Hey, Diamond."

"What's up, Portia?" she says. "It's late for you."

"You're not going to believe this, but someone wrote an anonymous letter to Dylan, filled with lies about me cheating on him."

"What?"

"Here, let me read it to you." I read the entire letter to Diamond. The words are still so hurtful. By the time I'm through, I feel like I'm beginning to hyperventilate. I'm surprised when Diamond acts like she doesn't really care.

"Huh," she responds. "Okay, girl, I'll call you in the morning."

"What do you mean you'll call me in the morning?" I ask in disbelief. "Didn't you hear what I just read to you? My life is falling apart, and you couldn't care less."

"I'm sorry, Portia," she says, sounding annoyed. "Look, it's just that I took a sleeping pill and I can barely keep my eyes open right now. I promise I'll call you first thing in the morning." After we hang up, I hear the front door open. It's Dylan.

I stand up and wait for him to come to the bedroom. It's time to confront this head on. The light in the room is dim, but maybe that's better. I look a mess for all the crying and lack of sleep.

After what seems like forever, Dylan finally enters our bedroom. He's walking toward me quickly, and I see an object in his hand. Before I can identify it, he smacks me across the face with it, and I drop to the floor. Everything goes black.

When I come to, I'm lying on top of our bed. Dylan is pointing a gun at me. I realize I must have been out for a while, because outside, it's starting to get light.

"Dylan, what's wrong with you?" I ask, desperate for some kind of reasonable explanation. "Why would you hit me…with a gun, of all things?"

I get up off the bed and immediately hold my hands to my head. It's aching from the blow. My foot brushes against something. It's Dante. He's lying on the floor next to our bed, out cold. I assume he must have heard what was going on and came in to protect me. I bend down and attempt to shake him awake. "Dante, baby, get up," I say to him. "I'm just fine." But Dante doesn't move.

I look up at Dylan. "What's wrong with our baby?" I ask fearfully. "Why isn't he getting up?"

"I killed your son," Dylan says coldly.

I must have heard him wrong. I repeat the question. "What's wrong with our baby, Dylan?"

I see a flash of emotion in Dylan's eyes. He starts to cry and says, "Why did you make me do this, Portia?"

Reality is sinking in. I'm crying now, punching him in the chest and screaming, "What have you done to our baby?" Everything feels out of control. The room is spinning, and I can't make it stop. How can the man who blew the breath of life into my soul be the same person to take it away? The pain is overwhelming. I begin to pick up items from around the room and hurl them rapid-fire toward Dylan. He dodges the flying objects, grabs hold of me, and manages to tie me to a chair. When he's through, he pulls out the phone cords and closes all of the curtains and blinds.

"Dylan, are you insane?" I ask. "What have you done to our family?" I begin to cry again.

"No!" He points his finger at me accusingly. "What have *you* done to our family?"

"I told you, Dylan, the letter is *not* true!" I'm sobbing uncontrollably. "Why would you kill our son?"

"Because he knew about this other man, and I'm his father." His logic is so twisted. I can't believe this is my loving husband. "He allowed his mother to be a whore and make me look like a fool!"

"Dylan, who *are* you?" I ask, desperate to talk to my husband instead of this monster. "Why would you believe someone who doesn't even have the guts to sign their own name over your wife, someone you love and trust? You killed our son for nothing!" I scream.

Dylan rips off a piece of duct tape and places it over my mouth. "I don't want to hear your voice anymore," he says coldly. "You disgust me." He walks out of the room.

I hear the front door open and slam. I struggle to free myself from the chair before he returns. Finally, I manage to untie myself and rush to the dresser. I grab a pen and a paper and write:

> Please call the police. I'm being held hostage by my husband, Dylan. He has already murdered our son, Dante.

I'm hurriedly completing the letter by adding our address when I hear Dylan unlock the front door and begin ascending the stairs. I run across the bedroom, crumple the letter in my hand, open the window, and throw it as far as I can.

I'm afraid to turn around. I don't want to see my son lying on the floor, dead. I gasp when I hear Dylan enter the room. *How did he make it up the stairs so quickly?* I feel paralyzed. I sense him walking up behind me. When he reaches me, he grabs my shoulder and turns me around to face him. He's holding the gun in his right hand. "Portia, how could you do this to me?" he asks. "I love you."

I don't answer. I just stare in disbelief. My perfect life has disappeared, and I haven't begun to wrap my mind around the tragic events that have taken place.

Out of the blue, Dylan hugs me tightly with his left arm and lets out a loud, piercing cry. My arms are dangling loose at my sides because I can't hug him back—can't feel a thing. I hear Dylan say, "Please God, forgive me." Then I hear a deafening *crack*.

I try to cry out, but the sound is taken away before I can make it. I look at Dylan as he lowers me to the floor and holds me in his arms. I feel peaceful, the ache in my heart diminishing, the pain in my soul lifting. I have no worries. I know I'm dying, but I've never felt more alive. I'm no longer associated with my body. It's not like I'm looking down from above—more like I'm just another person in the room.

I'm at the entrance to a dark tunnel. I can't see a thing, but I'm not afraid. I step into the tunnel and walk forward. I see a dim light ahead that quickly becomes brighter and brighter until it reaches an unearthly brilliance, but somehow doesn't hurt my eyes. It feels like…perfect love. At the end of the tunnel, there is someone or something waiting—a spirit to guide and protect me. It has no physical body. It's more like something I can sense, rather than see. The touch of the spirit is a glorious feeling. I don't want the feeling to end. For within it are my son and my husband.

~~~

KENNEDY

"Diamond, I had to call you back," I say angrily. "You need to mind your own business."

"My mind *is* my business," she replies stubbornly.

"Seriously, Diamond, why would you purposely plant in Portia's head that Dylan is cheating on her?"

"I just told her not to be surprised if he is," she answers, not grasping the gravity of the situation. "Portia is so blinded by Dylan's money. She's ignoring the signs. I'm her friend. I'm just looking out for her."

"Diamond, if that's your idea of looking out for a friend," I snap, "you have a lot to learn about friendship. So do me a favor and get a life. And stay the hell out Portia's business…before I get Lola on your ass again!" I hang up before she can respond.

I have a bad feeling. I haven't heard from Portia, and I'm getting worried. Then again, maybe the lovebirds have patched things up and that's why she's not answering. Maybe no news is good news.

Myles always tells me that I have a low tolerance for boredom. He seems to think that when my life gets too quiet, I find a way to ignite action. But it isn't really true. I'm just extremely devoted to my friends. He says even superheroes need a day off. I suppose he's right.
~~~

I can't believe I just agreed with him. It's official: Myles has the key to my heart. And now he has the key to my condo.

Chapter 24

DIAMOND

MEANWHILE, BACK IN NEW YORK

Portia called me somewhere around two in the morning. I can't say exactly what time it was. She called to tell me that Dylan received the letter. What she doesn't know is that I wrote it. How ironic that of all of her friends, Portia called to confide in *me*.

I thought I would hear about the letter from Kennedy. When Portia called and read the letter to me, I couldn't get off the phone fast enough. I wanted to call Renee and let her know that the letter had been received and that it was having the desired effect. I made up some excuse about having taken a sleeping pill. My goal wasn't to destroy Portia's relationship forever, just to help her become more independent. I want her to be on her own for a while, get some idea of what it's like to struggle in life. And when my brilliant plan succeeds, I'll accept most of the credit. (Renee will get a smidge of credit for typing the letter.)

Someday, when Portia gets on her feet for real, I'll tell her the truth. They both should know that nothing is perfect—not even their relationship. No one should take that sort of thing for granted, and the best lessons are taught through experience. And that's why I'm here. Portia will be grateful once she makes it on her own, and she'll have me to thank for it.

If Dylan doesn't leave her after reading the letter, I'll set him up—hire a woman he can't possibly resist sleeping with. Then I'll pay her extra to show up at their house to confront Dylan in Portia's presence.

I've been trying to call Portia all day, but she hasn't been answering my calls. Maybe she's mad because I blew her off. I spoke to Kennedy, though, and she managed to convince Portia that Dylan isn't cheating on her. Kennedy is upset with me. She called me back later, cursed me out, and had the nerve to hang up on me. Kennedy needs to let Portia fight her own battles.

When Kennedy spoke with Portia, Portia hadn't learned about the letter yet. I know if I'm found out by the girls, they'll try to kill me. They'll think I'm being cruel because I'm jealous. But that's not the case. The problem is, people just don't get me. I'm not jealous; I just have a heart that's bigger than life. Writing that letter to Dylan isn't going to kill Portia, it's going to make her strong.

This is my moment, and I'm going to enjoy it. Portia can thank me later. Renee said that if they ever find out I wrote that letter, they'll realize that Diamonds are *not* always a girl's best friend. We laughed so hard we cried.

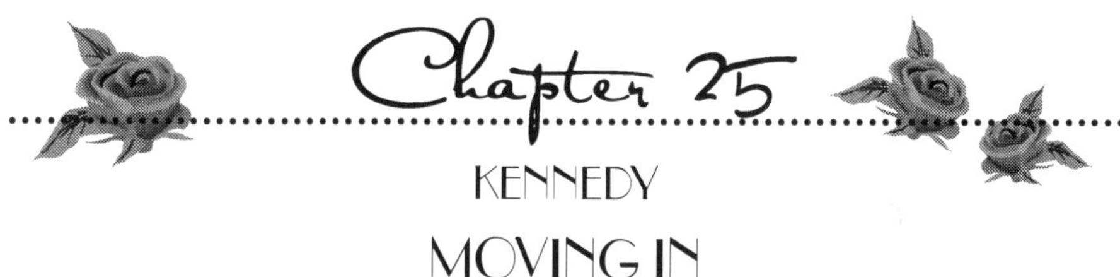

Chapter 25

KENNEDY

MOVING IN

It's been a week since the Trina episode. Myles wants to talk more about us moving in together. Presently, he's in my living room on bended knee with a diamond-and-platinum ring in his hand. He's not asking me to marry him. He's asking me to be his lady. The diamond screams, *I'm taken*.

I put his face in my hands and kiss him passionately. He grabs my hand, and we walk to the bedroom together. He picks me up before we step through the bedroom door and carries me to the bed. My back touches the mattress ever so gently as he lays me down. He kisses my forehead and then my nose. It feels like this is our first time. Our relationship has matured, and our connection feels deeper than ever before.

I feel an explosion of fireworks coming from within. Myles doesn't need a script to learn my body. He shows me this through his lovemaking. He begins at the nape of my neck with little kisses which give me goose bumps. Every time he makes contact with my skin, I melt a little more. His fingers wander down into my panties. The moisture flows with the help of his expert fingertips. His touch has me anxiously anticipating his next move. His mouth is warm and wet as he sucks each of my fingers.

He slowly makes his way down to my feet. He moves his tongue in and out between each my toes, then he works his tongue slowly up my legs to my buttocks. I lift my leg up and over his head so that his lips and tongue can make contact with my bald kitty. I feel the twirl of his tongue working the grooves on either side of my clit. Then he flicks his tongue over the top of my clit repeatedly until my body shakes with electricity. The fire between us is raging as his tongue wanders its way to my nipples, which are as hard as his cock.

I want to please him by taking him into my mouth, but he's left me weak. My strength is gone from the multiple rapid-fire orgasms he's given me. Our sex has reached a whole new level of passion. I can tell by the thickness of his penis that he's excited by having given me such intense pleasure. When he enters my vagina, I can feel his penis grow harder inside me. I can feel the love, but I can barely feel my legs that I wrap around his neck. My body is lost in the moment. Even touching him feels different now. He starts to hump me with steady control. I squeeze his penis with my vagina, then again.

"Ooh, baby," he exclaims.

"Yes, baby," I say quietly. I'm on the verge of climaxing...again. There is no better orgasm than the one that happens when his penis is going in and out of me. I feel my juices flow, and my body twitches with excitement.

Myles knows I'm about come to a climax and utters affectionately, "Don't you dare cum. I'm not done making love to you yet."

I try to hold it, try to extend the pleasure, but I have to let go. Something about the way he says the words, the way they roll off of his tongue. It's like he's fucking me with his words.

I release uncontrollably. The orgasm is incredibly intense and emotional. It actually brings tears to my eyes. "Sorry, baby, I just couldn't hold back."

He humps me with even more intensity than before. He is so lost in the moment that he doesn't even notice to wipe the saliva that has escaped his mouth and is rolling down his chin. *Damn—even his breath smells good.* His back is trembling in my hands. He rests his head on my neck and thrusts deep and fast with short, jerky vibrations. For the next twenty seconds, the world is completely quiet. Then he kisses my lips and says, "I love you."

I squeeze him tightly in my arms, his body still on top of mine, and hold onto him, sobbing. "Kennedy, why are you crying?" he asks, concerned. "This is the part where you're supposed to say, 'I love you, too.'"

I pull my head away from the crook of his neck and look into his eyes. "I love you, too," I say, and smile through tears. I lift my head up and begin to laugh. "This is the real deal, people!" I shout loud enough for the neighbors to hear. I look back at Myles.

Myles laughs and kisses my lips, still wet with tears. He is holding me so tightly that our two bodies feel like one. Into my ear, he whispers quietly, "I am never leaving you—you hear me?" I answer by looking into his eyes while running my fingers through the gorgeous curls on his head.

I've rehearsed this scene in my mind a million times, and now it's really happening. I literally crave this man. The way he is lying on top of me, covering my chest with his own. The scent of his cologne. The way he looks in his jeans and his Timberland boots. I crave the swagger in his walk and the attitude he projects when he's standing still. I have been craving for him to love me. He's been craving for me to love him, and I didn't even know it. But tonight, I got the memo. *I know what love is now.* My heart feels so peaceful. I have never felt more secure. I've already given him my body, and now I am letting him into my soul. I look up at the ceiling and mouth the words, *I love you, Myles.*

Myles rolls off of me and onto his back. He turns his head to look at me and says, "I want to thank your mother and father for having you."

I stare into his brown eyes and smile mischievously. "Want to do it again?"

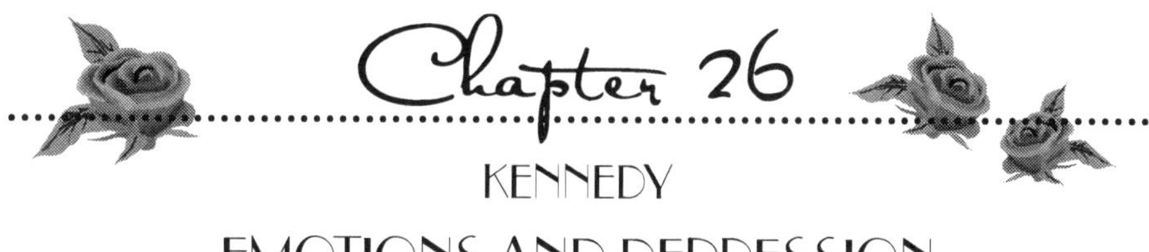

Chapter 26

KENNEDY

EMOTIONS AND DEPRESSION

I wake up in a cold sweat from another bad dream. Myles isn't here. He went home yesterday to pack the rest of his things. The only person I can think to call this late is Portia. She doesn't have to get up early because she doesn't work. It's nice for me because she's usually available to work at my office when I need extra help.

Portia isn't answering her phone. She must be asleep. I turn over in my bed and face the wall. I'm restless, but after a while, I manage to drift back to sleep.

I'm on a bus with Dylan. We're on our way to a festival downtown. Portia and the girls are meeting us there. The festival only happens once a year, and there are so many out-of-towners here for the celebration. We approach our stop. I'm anxious to get off the bus.

A tall man with a black leather jacket is standing behind me when I exit the bus. His baseball cap is pulled so low that I can barely see his eyes. The mysterious way he's wearing his cap makes the hair on the back of my neck stand on end. He follows us off the bus, and block after block, he continues to walk directly behind me. I feel like he's drilling a hole in my back with his constant stare. Dylan doesn't notice the man.

Rain falls from the sunny skies. It seems to come from nowhere. The man is still following. I pick up my pace. I can hear his heavy shoes behind me. He quickens his step as well. Dylan takes off running in the other direction, away from where we're supposed to meet the girls. I run toward the shelter of a sales booth selling handmade bags several feet away.

As I'm running, the tall man keeps pace behind me. I stop and turn to face him. He pulls out a gun and starts shooting at me. One bullet hits my right shoulder, and another hits my right leg. I fall from the hit in my leg. Helpless, I look to see if he is still coming for me, but I don't see him anymore. I need to get to the shelter quick. I drag my body forward with my left arm. The ground rips at my stomach as I inch forward. My shirt is thin, and I'm not wearing a coat. There's a woman sitting on the counter of the sales booth. She's wearing a red cowboy hat with matching boots. Her denim skirt stops mid-thigh. I can't see her face because there's a man standing between us, blocking my view.

I'm trying to get someone's attention because I'm hurt. But no one sees me. I hear someone call my name. I turn my head to the right. It's Diamond, and she's holding a baby. She sets the baby in a nearby chair, which is upholstered in green and white checks. After setting the baby down, she comes to my aid. As she approaches me, I see blood on her shirt. I turn my eyes back to the baby, but the baby is no longer a baby, it's a doll.

A woman distracts me from looking at the doll by helping me up off the ground. I know it's the same woman who was sitting on the booth's counter, because I recognize her clothing. Once we're at eye level with each other, I see that the woman is Portia. She screams, then points at the man with the gun. He's the same man who was standing in front of her while she sat on the table. It's also the same man from the bus who's been following me. He comes toward me with the gun, stepping over the dead bodies of a family he's murdered. He's apologizing to me, telling me the bullets weren't meant for me, that I just got caught in his path.

I want to run but I can't. The man kisses Portia on the cheek and then vanishes into thin air when he sees Dylan coming. "Oh my God, Kennedy, hide me!" Portia screams in a panic. "Dylan thinks I'm seeing that man, but we're just friends. You have to hide me! Later, I'll go and talk to him. I'll make him understand that it's not true."

"Hide behind the counter," I tell her. If I can just make it to Dylan before he reaches the booth, everything will be fine.

Diamond pulls me in the other direction. She's preventing me from getting to Dylan. "Diamond, get off of me!" I yell. "We can't let Dylan see Portia behind the counter." But Diamond won't let go of me. Her grip is too strong for me to break away. I try to overpower her, but I seem to have lost all of my strength…

~~~
~~~

The struggle to free myself from Diamond awakens me from another awful dream. I'm not physic, but something is wrong—I can feel it. The dream was so real.

It's eight o'clock in the morning. I'm tired from a night of fitful sleep. I walk to the kitchen and put on a pot of coffee. While I'm pouring and looking out my kitchen window, I see the paper boy down on the street, riding his bike away from the building. "Perfect," I say to myself. "Just in time for my morning cup of coffee."

Myles is supposed to be here already. He promised to join me for coffee this morning. I pick up the phone and dial Lola. "Hey, girl, have you heard from Portia?" I ask her.

"No, why do you ask?" Lola replies.

"I don't know. I keep calling her, but she doesn't answer."

"And..."

"And...I don't know, Lola. Something just doesn't feel right."

"You sure it's not just your mothering instinct taking over?" Lola chides.

"Girl, I had a hell of a bad dream last night," I confide.

"Girl, you've been having bad dreams for months now," she reminds me.

"This one was about death."

"So what are you trying to say? You think something is wrong with Portia?"

"Well, I don't think she's dead. But yes, I think something is wrong."

"Well, girl, drink your coffee and call me in a bit," she suggests. "I'm still tired. I need a few more winks. We'll figure it out, one way or another."

I hang up the phone and call Myles. "Baby, where are you?" I ask when he answers.

"I'm home, about to head over there right now."

"Hurry up," I tell him. "I started the coffee already."

"I'm on my way."

Coffee in hand, I walk to the door, open it, and pick up the newspaper lying on the welcome mat. I stand in the open doorway and read the headline: *Family of Three Found Dead.* I'm immediately reminded of my dream. *Death.* I feel an instant connection with the headline—almost like an electrical jolt. I scroll the page, eager to learn more, and immediately zero in on the victims' names...

The bodies of Dylan, Portia, and Dante Waters were found early this morning in their home, dead of an apparent murder-suicide. Dylan Waters allegedly shot his son and his wife before turning the gun on himself.

The police were alerted by a neighbor who found a handwritten note on her front lawn which was allegedly written by Portia Waters. The note explained that Mrs. Waters was being held hostage by her husband and needed help.

More facts on this case as they become available.

My coffee cup crashes to the tile floor of my entry way and shatters. I want to scream but my mouth is so dry, I can barely make a sound. When I'm finally able to release my pain, my neighbors come running, alarmed by my screams. But I can't hear a thing.

I run down the hall, into the open elevator, and ride it down to the lobby. Once out the front door of the building, I take off running in the direction of Portia's house. I'm running in the middle of the street. I feel like I'm in a dream—only it's not a dream. Myles is blowing the horn from his car, trying to stop me from running in front of him. Seeing him jolts me from my trance. I drop in front of his car, and I hear the tires screech. My neighbors, who followed me from my condo door, rush to assist me before Myles can even get out of the car. Myles forces his way through the crowd to get to me. "Myles!" I scream. I realize the newspaper is still in my hand. I hold it up for him to see.

He shakes his head. "Yes, I know, baby, I know," he says. "I heard it on the news on the way over here. I've already called the girls. They'll be here soon."

I grab the pocket of his blue button-down shirt and pull him toward me. It begins to tear in my grip. "You have to take me to Portia's house! I want to be with her in case she feels alone. She's my best friend."

I hear Lola's voice. "Honey, the girls and I just left Portia's house," she says, jumping out of Payton's car and walking toward me. "It's total chaos. The police won't let anyone near the house." Tears are streaming down her face.

"No, Lola, no!" I scream. "There has to be a mistake! Lola, please wake me up from this dream. I don't want to be here anymore!"

"I wish this were a dream, baby," she consoles me. "I really, really do."

The girls surround me, and we hold each other. We're all in unbearable pain. People in cars are starting to honk their horns, anxious for us to get out of the street. Myles helps us onto the sidewalk, allowing two cars to continue up the road. Payton looks at Myles and screams, "Why did this happen?" In an effort to comfort her, Myles pulls Payton close and hugs her. "I just want to go to sleep, Myles," she says. "I don't want to feel anything right now. Portia, her husband, her son—an entire family, gone in an instant. How can this be happening?" She pounds her fist on Myles's back, and he absorbs her pain.

"How are we supposed to live without them?" Brooke asks. She shakes her head in disbelief. "Why would he do this? Dylan *loved* his family."

"More than life itself," Sky adds.

"This just doesn't make any sense," Tasha offers. The neighbors are standing around, looking helpless and sympathetic, as Myles leads us back up into my building. I can hear them talking amongst themselves, trying to make sense of what they've seen and heard.

"Who's going to call her family?" Payton asks.

"My God, I didn't even think about that," I say, my thoughts still whirling.

"I'm sure the police already contacted them," Myles answers. They're usually not allowed to print victims' names unless the next of kin have been notified.

When we get back into my condo, Sky sits down at the table and begins to speak as if in a daze. "This wasn't supposed to happen to Portia," she says. "Portia and Dylan were so happy and in love. He's never been abusive. I just don't understand it." She looks around. "Can someone make me understand why my life has been spared from the hands of my husband, and her life has been taken by the hands of hers? This should have been me, not Portia. Why did he kill her?" Sky stands up. "Let's go down to the police precinct and see if we can get some answers."

When we walk through the doors of the police station, there are five cops standing behind the front desk. The officer closest to the entry door asks, "Can I help you?"

"Who can I speak to about this," I say, handing him the front section of this morning's newspaper.

"Are you family?" he asks.

"Yes, she was our sister," I say, speaking for the group.

"May I see some ID, please?" One by one, he checks each of our driver's licenses, and nods. "Okay, all I can tell you is that they are dead from single, close-range gunshot wounds," he explains. "Unlike the other two, Mr. Waters's wound looks to be self-inflicted. I can't speak as to motive, and I can't divulge any more facts from the case because it's still an open investigation. I'm very sorry for your loss. Is there anything else I can help you with?"

"Just please find out why this happened," I say respectfully.

"I promise you, ma'am, we'll do our best." He gives me a small, sympathetic smile. "I do have one question for you," he says.

"What is it?" I ask.

"Do you know of anyone who may have had an issue with Mr. and/or Mrs. Waters?"

"No, everyone adores them," I answer. "None of this makes any sense. They loved each dearly, and I can't for the life of me think of anyone or anything that could come between them."

"They sound like they were a very loving and well-respected couple," the officer says. He pauses for a moment. "So let me ask you this, is there anyone you can think of who might have been jealous of their relationship?" I shake my head. He hands each of us his card. "Please, call anytime," he says, then motions for us to lean in closer. "I shouldn't be telling you this," he says quietly. "There was a letter found at the scene next to where the bodies were found. It was addressed to Mr. Waters, and it alleged that Mrs. Waters was having an affair, but no one was named. The letter wasn't signed."

As we're leaving the station, I can't help but rethink the officer's last question. "Diamond," I say quietly. Lola hears me.

"Diamond would never go that far," offers Lola, but she doesn't look convinced by her own words.

Back at my condo, Tasha heads straight to the bathroom while the rest of us head to the kitchen. We can hear Tasha's muffled cries from where we're sitting. I walk to the bathroom. "Tasha, baby, open the door, please," I plead. "We're right here, baby."

"Tasha, honey," Lola says through her own tears, "open the door. I need you right now."

"Tasha, sweetie," Sky chimes in, "we have to support each other through this.

We only have each other right now. It's going to be hard on all of us."

"Let me try," Brook offers, her ear against the bathroom door. "Tasha, honey, I need you to open the door right now."

A pause, then Tasha opens the door and walks into our open arms. "This just isn't fair," she cries. "Why would God take her from us? She was a good person. Why? Why?" she keeps asking. She's squeezing me so tight I can barely breathe.

"I don't know why, Tasha," I say, "but we'll get to the bottom of this... together. I promise."

"We need to find out who wrote that letter," Lola says. "Who would do something so evil?"

"Jealousy is the root of all evil, in my opinion," Payton says. "It has to be someone who was jealous of what Portia had with Dylan."

"Yeah, but who?" I ask. "Who would be that desperate and obsessed with their relationship? I mean, I know Diamond was jealous, but she wouldn't do anything that cruel, would she?"

"No, Diamond loves Portia," Payton insists.

Outside the circle we've created around Tasha stands Myles. He's trying to hide that he's wiping tears from his eyes. I reach for his hand from the huddle. I realize he loved Portia, Dylan, and Dante, too. It was their family that inspired Myles to become the man he is now. "I promise you, girls," he says, "that I will work just as hard as the rest of you to find the answers to our questions. Dylan, Portia, and Dante were like family to me, too. Whoever did this probably didn't intend for them to die, but this is what happens when you don't mind your own business—the unthinkable." He sighs. "I hope the person who did this feels guilty as hell."

"If I ever find out who did this to my friend," Lola threatens, "I will catch another case—because I'm going to murder whoever's responsible."

"You don't mean that, Lola," I say to her.

"Right now, Kennedy, in my mind I mean what I say," Lola says, standing her ground. "I've killed a lot of people in my mind before. I can't be punished for my thoughts."

"You scared me for a minute there, girl," I say to her, and smile weakly.

"I'm angry, Kennedy, not crazy," Lola says, and smiles back.

"Let's just concentrate on getting through our loss before making threats," I suggest. "We have to remember the good times with our best friend. We shared a sisterly bond with her, and that bond can never be replaced."

I grab the girls' hands and lead them into the living room. I put in the DVD that Dylan recorded the day he brought Portia to the new house. Although all of us have a copy, I'm the only one of us who's actually watched it. They're surprised to see that Portia left a message for us at the beginning of the video. I pour some wine and hand a glass to each of the girls, because I know there's a toast at the end of Portia's speech.

The video plays...

"Kennedy, thank you so much for overseeing the decorating of my new home," Portia begins. "I would also like to thank you for keeping all of us together through the years.

"Lola, thank you for the framed pictures you contributed to my home.

"Tasha, Payton, Sky, and Brooke: Thank you for the paint on the walls, the glasses in the cubbies, and the wine in the cellar.

"To all my girls, Sky, Tasha, Payton, Lola, Brooke, and Kennedy: You are my sisters, and I love you guys for helping my husband with this amazing surprise—y'all know how much I love surprises. And Payton, I am particularly delighted that you were able to keep this a secret, because we all know you can't hold water," Portia jokes.

"This house is a home because of you guys. *Mi casa es su casa.*"

Portia is standing in the foyer next to the staircase, holding a glass of wine which she raises to the camera…

"Cheers," she says, and drinks to us.

Losing Portia feels like the end of the world—a senseless death that could have been prevented. Emotions are running high and going in all different directions at once—deep love for our friend, missing her terribly, hating the person who caused this tragedy. If only that letter hadn't been written!

I don't know how we'll get through this, but somehow we will. I remember her laugh and smile on the video. Her smile will help me heal. I sense that I will always carry pain in my heart, and I pray that living with that pain will get easier. I miss her deeply, but I am blessed by my friends. We are lucky to have each other. I thank God every day for bringing these beautiful women into my life.

I look around the room at my friends as they stare at the television screen. I realize that these women are my family, created not by blood, but by love. Our family will never be complete again because Portia is gone.

I pause the video, look at my friends, and say, "Has anyone told you they love and care about you today? Well, I do."

~~~

Four days after the tragedy, we're back in my living room with Portia's parents. They want to include us in planning her funeral.

Myles has gone down to the lobby to check my mail. When he returns, he tosses the mail, and it lands on the coffee table in front of me. A particular envelope stands out. It's addressed simply to KENNEDY in large, uppercase, bold letters, followed by my address. There is no return address.
~~~

I open the envelope and find a single piece of notepad paper. It reads:

Diamonds are not always a girl's best friend.

Beneath that, it reads:

This is your first clue.

29603796R00133

Made in the USA
Lexington, KY
01 February 2014